The edge of us

VERONICA LARSEN

© 2017 by Veronica Larsen

Editing by Lea Burn, Burn Before Reading
Published by Veronica Larsen
Cover design and interior formatting by Goudy Designs
Publication Date: August 1st, 2017

For Andrea,
One of the most whole-hearted women I've ever met.

ONE

MILA

THE SPOTLIGHT OVERHEAD SHOWERS me with prickling awareness. I'm exposed on this stage, in this backless gown, with every nuance of my expression open to the silent scrutiny of the faces peering up at me.

The audience is filled with women I admire, trailblazers who are fearless in the pursuit of their ambitions. Women who never worry about ruffling feathers. Politicians, actresses, media gurus, and entrepreneurs. Their applause dies out in scattered spurts. All that's left are faint murmurs and the rustling of fabric against seats.

I clutch the award tighter, stealing a glance at the stainless-steel cutout of an abstract female figure. Bold words are engraved on the front.

Mila Zelenko
Female Entrepreneur of the Year

Adrenaline courses through me, and the trapped breath I release into the microphone echoes around the room.

"Thank you so much for this," I say, my voice blaring from the surrounding speakers. "I am honored to be standing here in front of such awe-inspiring women."

I cannot control the breathless way the words leave my lips. I pause to glance down at my notes on the podium, willing myself toward calm. This may be the most important speech I've ever given in my career. When I wrote it, I was objective and careful in the message I wanted the words to convey. But I'd underestimated the effect this day would have on me. A day marking an anniversary I want nothing more than to forget.

I search the crowd for the only person who could anchor me in this moment. Someone who's been there for me through everything. The faces in the crowd blur together as I scan them, and I can't tell if he's among them.

I swallow, and begin again.

"When I was a little girl, I'd sneak down the stairs of our dingy little house in Long Island to spy on my mother's Tarot card readings. By day, she worked at a hair salon, but by night, she'd have visits from all sorts of people seeking her wisdom. One man came to see my mother every Sunday, without fail. He dressed in a sharp black suit and looked too important to be sitting on our tacky, plastic-covered furniture."

I pause to offer a tentative smile to Tobias Kreisler, sitting in the audience. I hadn't expected him to be here to witness this speech. But the man who's unwittingly been my mentor in many ways offers me a small nod of encouragement to tell the story he knows well.

"I'll never forget the intensity of those sessions and how this man hung on to my mother's every word as she explained his fate in her thick Ukrainian accent. I didn't know who he was. I didn't realize he was the most successful real estate tycoon in the country. So there he was—arguably the richest man in the city— asking my mother a stunning question: 'What should I do?' He'd wait with bated breath to be dealt advice from a woman who hadn't even finished primary school. It would be years before I understood the impact these moments had on me."

I swallow, fighting away the unrelated memory flashing before my eyes. Me in my wedding gown, storming over to my mother and snatching her beloved Tarot cards from her hands as my bridal party watched in silence. I'd been hurt at her insistence to taint the most important day of my life with ominous warnings.

"My mother, though by all appearances an uneducated immigrant, possessed one of the sharpest intellects of anyone I've ever known," I continue. "She had a gift. Not of card reading, but of reading people, of understanding their motivations and of seeing connections in their lives and relationships they themselves couldn't."

The way she did when she predicted there would be no wedding. She was right, of course. She was always right and I sometimes hated her for it.

I push past the smallest of knots forming in my throat and continue speaking.

"You see, my mother had much to offer the world, but she understood that without money, a title, or education, her words would be dismissed, her voice muted and overridden. And so, the Tarot cards became her proxy. They became the way through which she could assert herself. Not only did people come from all over to seek her wisdom, they marveled at it. As a child, I saw my mother's confidence in her own abilities, her fearlessness in showing them to the world. The unapologetic way she expressed her views and opinions, and the power she manifested when those opinions emboldened the actions of powerful people. It drove a need in me to do important work, to turn my thoughts into actions, and actions into change. But despite graduating top of my class from one of the most prestigious business programs in the country, I found myself underestimated at every turn. As a young woman, I was taken less seriously than my male counterparts. And though I was, by the estimation of my superiors, both sharper and better prepared than many of my peers, I was repeatedly passed up for promotions and overlooked for opportunities. Until the day I'd finally had enough. I realized that, like my mother, I too would need a proxy in order to be taken seriously. I decided the proxy would be a title, Chief Executive Officer. A title I would give to myself if no one else would—"

The audience cuts me off, erupting in cheers. A smile creeps onto my face as the nerves finally melt away. All that's left is the electrical current running through the room. The thread of the experience I've shared. The buzz of excitement brings on a sort of high, giving me the ability to take in the details of the crowd.

I begin speaking again over the remnants of applause.

"I founded The Zelenko Agency, a PR and consulting firm,

which—" movement near the back row of tables catches my eye "—would grow into a formidable force in—"

The figure's body language registers in my brain before any features do.

"A firm that would go on to become a force in…"

The words fumble from my lips again, but the rest of my speech slips from my head. I glance down at my notes but cannot decipher what's written there.

"A force in…"

My pulse pounds in my ears, picking up speed, and the award slips just enough to knock against the microphone bar, which emits an earsplitting squeal. My mouth remains open but words fail to come out. A low murmur builds as the crowd realizes something is wrong. They look from each other to me, to their surroundings, trying to figure out what my eyes are fixed on.

The entire room blurs at the edges and the only thing that comes into focus is the man leaning on the frame of the wide entrance archway. Black dress shirt, sleeves rolled up to reveal tattoos etched along both forearms. His lips are turned downward, but an air of confidence and trouble swirls around him like a vortex. The sight of him hits me square in the chest.

Cole Van Buren.

I haven't seen him in eight years, since the day he turned my life upside down and left me broken and humiliated. And now he's back, crashing into my world just as cruelly as he abandoned it.

TWO

MILA

Three weeks earlier...

TO SAY I DON'T like surprises would be a massive
understatement. I hate surprises. And yet, I've sought out a
career where they are an inevitable part of my day. I've learned
to compensate by making sure my mornings are the perfect
symphony of routine, a small reprieve before I dive into the
chaos of crisis management.

The town car picks me up at seven sharp, and drops me off
in front of the striking Seagram Building in Midtown
Manhattan. I smooth down my suit and step under the shadow
of the skyscraper. At the plaza just outside of the building, I buy
a cup of coffee and drown out the hectic sounds of the city with
the up-tempo beat of music in my ears. My playlist is filled with
rap and hip-hop tracks. If the people around me heard they
might be mortified at the profanities spewing in my ears. The
rapid-fire threats and proclamations of greatness. But to me, it's
like an aural shot of adrenaline as I walk through a sea of
corporate sharks.

I take my first sips of coffee as I ride the elevator up to the twenty-fifth floor. The newspaper I read on the commute to work is folded inside out in one of my hands. And when I glance down to adjust my footing, a bold headline in the entertainment section catches my attention. I couldn't care less about celebrity gossip, but this is a name I recognize outside of the tabloids.

Pulling my earbuds from my ear, I rush to read the article. But before I can take in the words, I stare at the picture under the headline. The gorgeous blonde walks alone along a NYC street. She stands tall but her gaze is cast downward, her face illuminated by the paparazzi cameras. One of her hands is up by her head, as though she was just about to tuck her hair behind her ear. The camera's flash reflects off the dazzling engagement ring on her finger.

"*Shit,*" I mutter under my breath. One of the people waiting in the elevator shoots me a look.

I skim the short article then tuck the paper under my arm, frowning. The pages now seem heavier than they were before.

I make it just two steps out of the elevator before the office doors spring open. Two men rush out into the hall, carrying a large shard of thick glass. I recognize them as part of the cleaning crew, but the tense concentration on their faces makes any question of what they are doing die in my throat. Their urgency suggests the glass is heavier than it appears and might slip from their grasp at any moment. I edge sideways and out of the way, holding up the contents of my hands to avoid blocking their trajectory.

Much of our office furniture is made of glass, part of the

aesthetic, part of the brand, and so it's difficult to guess where that particular piece came from.

The men set the shard down inside the elevator to catch their breaths. One of them wipes at his brow and grumbles something to the other as the doors close.

Locked in place from their sudden opening, the office doors remain parted wide. Four of my employees are huddled behind the front desk, visible from where I stand at the landing. I brace myself for bad news before striding toward them. The carpet muffles the clicks of my heels and my staff is so engrossed in their conversation that not one of them notices my approach until I set my newspaper and cup of coffee down on the desk in front of them.

Janet, my assistant, notices me first and straightens. She clears her throat pointedly, but not before I hear Andrew's name slip from someone's lips. Everyone goes silent at once, guilty faces meeting my eyes only briefly, before they sputter out nonsense about work and walk off to their respective spaces.

Janet raises her eyebrows at me in apology. Her gaze darts toward Andrew's office, from which another member of the cleaning crew exits with an industrial vacuum cleaner and a black plastic bag. I wait until he passes through the front doors and out to the hall.

"Is everyone okay?"

Janet's mouth does an awkward twitch of silent words as she tries to find a way to tell me.

"Is anyone hurt?"

"No. Everyone's fine. No one else was here when it happened. Just me."

"And what exactly happened?"

Janet bites her lip. "I...I'm not sure. I just heard a crash from Andrew's office. I didn't even know he was in there. I rushed over. He's fine, but...I don't know what happened. He told me to call the cleaning crew and wouldn't say anything else."

"Thanks, Janet. Push my meetings back an hour, will you? Andrew's too."

She scribbles down notes. "Will do."

"And, Janet? Direct the gossip to the staff break-room next time. It's hard to sell the concept of a judgment-free zone when there's a judgment party at the front desk."

"Of course," she says, giving me a small, apologetic smile.

I grab the newspaper and coffee from the desk and head to Andrew's office. At his doorway, I find him standing in front of the windows staring out into the city, the way he does when he's strategizing.

The room looks half empty. His desk chair seems out of place with no other furniture around it and the carpet has lines from where it was just vacuumed. The contents of his desk are stacked in a neat pile against the far wall. His laptop, his notebooks, the stupid silver panda cup he keeps his pens in.

His glass desk is missing.

"Well, that explains the broken glass," I say from behind my cup of coffee then take a sip.

He stiffens for a split second before relaxing again, but

doesn't turn to face me.

"Good morning, Mila."

His baritone voice seems relaxed and unassuming. I keep mine the same as I respond.

"I don't know about that. Seems like you're off to a rough start." I wait, but he offers nothing. "Drew, are you going to tell me what happened, or are you going to make me guess?"

He knows when I call him Drew, I'm not asking as his boss but as his friend. I've known Andrew a long time. Long enough to know it takes a hell of a lot for him to lose his temper. Not to mention, it would take a hell of a lot of deliberate force to break one of our desks.

The newspaper is a brick under my arm now. The second I saw that headline, I knew I should be the one to break the news to him before it caught him off-guard. But judging from the current state of his office, it already has.

I let silence fill the space between us until he has no choice but to acknowledge it. He turns from the window to face me. To anyone else, his tall, imposing figure would be intimidating in his navy suit. Perfect posture, hands in his pockets, dark hair smoothed back. Unreadable to most, but I can see everything he's trying to hide.

"The desk was an accident."

"An accident?" I ask. "You double-clicked your mouse so hard the glass cracked beneath it?"

"I should lay off the gym for a while."

I stare at him, deadpan. He arches a dark brow at me in a

clear attempt at playfulness, but the expression in his blue eyes is too guarded to pull it off.

Two interns walk past the door rather slowly and peer into the room at us. There's too much intrigue surrounding Andrew in the office. I'm still not sure how to quell it. The dynamic we had before him of transparency and comfortable chemistry was disrupted by the deliberate aloof energy he gives off to everyone else. I thought he'd shake things up for the better. Comfort is stagnation, and stagnation is death in business. But now I worry the preoccupation with him might be more distracting than anything else.

I shut the door and step farther into the room.

"You want to know my guess on what's really going on with you?"

"Well, Mila, you're the expert at reading people. Go ahead, tell me about my feelings."

He's bluffing, of course. Every part of his body language is poised in careful contradiction. He doesn't want me in his head.

There's only one way to get him to drop the act and admit what's really going on. I hate to do it, but nothing but the blunt approach works with Andrew. Taking the newspaper from under my arm, I shake it open and find the article I read on the elevator ride. I walk over to him and hand him the page.

"This. This is my guess."

He stares at the image of the blonde woman for several long seconds before dragging his eyes back to me.

"You really think I care about some gossip column? Let's

get back to the desk. Look, I'll pay for it — "

"Forget the damn desk," I snap. "The same morning the news breaks of Amber's engagement I come in to find your desk in pieces. Are you really trying to tell me the two aren't related?"

Tension works up his sharp jawline and his blue eyes grow cold as they search mine with small traces of surprise.

He thinks I don't know how he feels just because he's never admitted it. But I know.

The silent resentment radiating from him worries me because it's all directed inward. He hates himself for what happened between him and Amber. He's tried banishing his ex's name from his vocabulary much in the way I've banished mine. Just to try to move on.

"She has nothing to do with it. This news…" His mouth remains parted as he takes in the sight of Amber's photograph one more time. "I couldn't care less about this. She and I are ancient history."

He's so convincing I almost believe him. But then there's the way he crumples the page up in his hands and stalks over to where his desk used to be. Walking away from me, adding space between us to keep me at bay. To keep himself at bay.

No way in hell I'm letting him push me away now.

I've been indebted to him from the night we met. The night I downed liquid courage and resolved to have a one-night stand wearing my bridal lingerie. I was broken and wanted revenge on the ex who'd left me stranded at the altar weeks before. I thought I'd found the perfect, handsome, dark-haired stranger to screw.

Instead, I ended up sobbing half-naked on Andrew's shoulder for almost two hours. He was just a stranger, with no context for what I'd been through, but he didn't ask questions. He sensed my desperation, my embarrassment, my pain, and he held me in the dark.

The morning after the failed one-night stand, I rushed out of Andrew's apartment, mortified and sure I'd never hear from him again. Instead, we went on to become friends. I watched him meet and fall in love with Amber. I watched them fall apart. And now, I'm watching him pretend the news of her engagement doesn't pick at his wounds.

"You need to go home," I say.

"Is that a suggestion or…?"

"It's not a suggestion. I'll handle your clients, but right now? You're a bull." I throw my hands up at his near-empty office, only a set of side tables and a couple of chairs remain. "This is a china shop. I happen to like my glass furniture."

"It won't happen again."

"I know it won't. I know this isn't you. That's why you need to go cool off…" I pause, fighting the guilt of juggling the needs of the company with the needs of my friend. Andrew is as good at reading people as I am, and it's always a standoff between us when one of us tries to hide something from the other. "Let's get together tonight and talk over dinner. You can let all your caveman feelings out with words instead of smashing things."

"I don't have feelings, you know that."

We lock eyes, a staring game we play too often. I don't care about winning today. I walk over and set a hand on the side of his face. He tenses for a second then averts his gaze, jaw flexing under my fingers. This kind of tenderness makes him uncomfortable, but that's exactly why he needs it.

"Your hands are freezing," he says, trying to mask his reaction.

"Be serious for a second," I say, lowering my voice until he meets my eyes. "You stopped me from spiraling once. And now you're stuck with me. I won't let you push me away. You know that, right?"

He lets out a breath, his shoulders sagging a fraction.

"I know, Mila, but that's not what's happening here." He brings his hand over mine and gives it a light squeeze before removing it from his face. "And for the record, I'm no hero. I was trying to get into your pants."

I laugh and his lips twitch upward for the first time all morning. And just when I think the moment has passed, he pulls me into a hug. One of his rare hugs. A truce. I hug him back and his strong arms squeeze me for a few seconds too long. A silent admission. Maybe even a subconscious one. To what's really going on inside his mind, to the things he can't admit to himself. The genuine moment loosens up something in me, too. The smallest trace of a realization. That sometimes the past can resurface, wrap around us and consume us in all the ways it did before.

THREE

ANDREW

I KNEW IT WAS only a matter of time before Mila figured out how to get me alone to talk. I've managed to escape her attempts at a heart-to-heart discussion all week. A work emergency made us cancel our dinner plans Monday night. On Wednesday, Mila tried again, but we ran into friends on our way to dinner. I invited them to join us, even as Mila glared at me in disapproval.

I thought her urgency to get me to open up would fade with each passing day. But here we are on Saturday night, taking a cab to the restaurant of her choosing.

Only, that's not where we're going at all.

Mila's distracted, her fingers moving across the screen of her phone as she drafts emails to put out a small fire at work. She hasn't yet realized we're headed in the wrong direction. The look of concentration on her face is too entertaining to disrupt. When she finally peers up from her phone, she hesitates at the street signs we pass.

"We're going to the harbor?"

"I know how you like surprises," I say.

Mila narrows her eyes at me, her face framed by strands of jet-black hair. She grabs her purse from under her seat, slips her phone into it, and takes out a tube of lipstick and a compact mirror.

Passing headlights illuminate her face as she glides the red color across her lips. Her hand remains steady even as she mutters something that sounds a lot like, *tonight was supposed to be low key.*

"Low key? Is that why you wore that dress?"

"Is that your way of telling me I look nice?"

"You look more than nice."

She snaps the cap back on to her lipstick and throws it and the mirror back into her small, black purse. Her lips now match her form-fitting red dress. The sleeves are long, the neckline modest, but the hemline is much higher than anything she'd wear at work.

The driver pulls to a stop and Mila continues her dissent even as I process my card payment on the display.

"I know what you're doing, Drew."

I allow the feigned expression on my face to convey my innocence.

"Did I mention you look pretty tonight?"

"And you...need to work on your deflecting skills. You're bringing me somewhere crowded and loud so you don't have to talk about your glass cage of emotions."

"Let's go," I say, enjoying the combativeness in her eyes. "Quit stalling because you know you're going to twist an ankle in those shoes."

"These are practically flats," she shoots back.

She leans over to adjust her shoe and my gaze follows down a pair of legs impossibly long for someone so short. Mila's stunning in heels, but I like to give her shit about her shoes because I'm amused by her insistence to appear taller than she is.

The cabbie watches us in the rearview mirror, waiting for us to get out of his car.

"Remember the time I bought you a pair of ballerina flats and suggested you keep them in your purse?" I ask Mila.

She lets the sound of her seatbelt unlocking be the response, before adding, "Watch yourself. I'm getting hungry and stabby."

I get out of the cab and come around to her side to find her standing, poised and ready for the long walk up the brick pedestrian road of South Street Seaport, past shops and stores, to reach the pier at the harbor.

"Bet those ballerina flats sound really good right about now," I tease.

"Shut up."

She takes off, drawing up every millimeter of her small frame and walking effortlessly down the uneven road. She doesn't glance down at her steps, yet her feet land between the cracks at a steady rhythm. I imagine she's putting all her effort into not falling on her face, but outwardly she appears more comfortable than someone walking barefoot on a yoga mat.

Her confidence is a magnet and it draws the attention of every hot-blooded male we pass. I adjust my pace to walk alongside her. At six foot two, my natural strides are three of hers. I'm like a bodyguard, towering over her and daring one of those assholes to try their luck.

We reach the pier and find the bar and grill I frequent with the guys; the loudest place I could think of that's not filled with kids. I walk off toward the front door, but Mila comes to a stop and stands with her hands on her hips. An argument brews in her hazel eyes when they move up to take in the crowded open deck on the second floor of the restaurant.

"*Come on*," I taunt, waving her over. "Those shoes can carry you another few feet. You can make it."

I pull open the front door and noise pours out onto the sidewalk. Inside, televisions blare a boxing match and patrons jeer at the screens, their drinks spilling onto the bar. Mila isn't a fan of crowded places or loud bars, but she should've known better than to think I'd reserve a table at some quiet little spot to talk about my feelings.

She marches past me and into the bar without argument. When the hostess greets us, Mila asks to be seated near the back of the restaurant, where the sounds from the bar aren't as intrusive. As we walk in, one of the boxers on screen brings around a monster of a right hook that connects with his opponent's temple and sends the poor guy toppling over. The screams of excitement from the bar reach an earsplitting level.

"This is everything I hate about the world," Mila yells up at me.

"You'll be fine," I shout back.

We are led to a small table in the very back, set in front of a wall of exposed bricks with fake vines growing in the pattern of an arch.

"How quaint," Mila says, taking the seat that brings her back to the wall. "From this spot you can barely tell everyone's here to cheer on two men as they beat each other's faces to a pulp."

I move my chair from the spot across from her and slide down to sit beside her.

"You're crowding me," she says.

"Get over it."

Our server is an older woman with strawberry blonde hair. She takes our drink orders then hovers as Mila and I argue over appetizers.

"Are you sure I should only order one?" I ask.

"Yes, I'm fine."

"Don't say you're fine and then pick at my appetizers because you're too hungry to wait for your food."

"Quit telling me how to live my life." Mila looks up to the server and the woman smiles. "Can you believe this guy?"

She takes the rest of our order, then with a knowing gleam in her eyes, asks, "How long have you two been together?"

My mouth snaps open to correct her assumption, but Mila beats me to an answer.

"Eight long years with this grouch."

The woman gives us a small laugh, but when she reaches for our menus, she notices our bare ring fingers and blurts out, "Oh, I thought you were married."

"Sometimes I think so, too," Mila says.

The server's brows pull together, but she holds the menus to her chest and asks one last time if there's anything else we need. Her words fade away as I notice the spinner ring on her pinky finger. It's a ring with a second plate on top that spins over the first. She uses the ring finger of the opposite hand to twirl it as she speaks. A nervous habit. She turns to go and I'm left staring at the spot where she stood for several long seconds, remembering a similar ring I gave to someone once. A long time ago.

When I bring my attention back around to Mila, she's watching me in silence. Her cunning eyes trace every nuance of my face, catching every micro expression.

"Stop," I say, leaning back in my chair.

"What?"

"Stop trying to get in my head."

"I thought I was being subtle," she says.

"Then you should work on the way your eyes move like little gears across every inch of me. No wonder people are scared of you. It's fucking unnerving."

"Fuck off. I didn't mean to. But just so you know, you do it to me all the time."

We promised each other to leave work in the office. The analysis of body language, the leading of conversation. These are all tactics we use on our clients, to predict the blind spots and gauge our strategy to give them what they need from us.

"I'm going to save you the trouble," I say. "We're not going to talk about my ex's engagement."

"But I've been looking forward to seeing inside your soul all day."

"And here I thought you just wanted to enjoy a nice dinner with me. Did you think we'd braid each other's hair and talk about our feelings? It's not my style."

"Bonding makes friendships stronger."

"Let it go already," I warn.

Our eyes lock for several seconds as she seems to debate how final my words are. Her lips pull inward and she looks past me toward the bar, where the boxing match now yields sounds of pained anticipation from the drunken spectators.

"I'll just have to carry my dreams of finally witnessing your feelings to my grave," she says. "An unsatisfied death. For the record, you were an open book the night we met. Do you remember?"

That night, I talked to distract her from her own pain. She'd fallen asleep in my arms as I told her things I'd never told anyone before. We went from being complete strangers to knowing way too much about each other, all in one night.

"God, are you kidding?" I laugh. "It was the most confusing night of my life. I was ready to list out my social security number, whatever I could say just to keep you from soaking my sheets—and not in a good way. There I was, thinking I was about to get laid…"

"Okay, no," she says, shaking her head. "Time to abort this conversation."

It's too late. She brought it up and I love to see the way she flushes at the memory of our almost hookup. Not much gets to Mila, I have to take what I can get. She adjusts her dress, pulling down the hem that has somehow inched even farther up her toned thighs.

Just as I open my mouth to continue, the server shows up with our drinks, and I spare Mila the embarrassment because she'd make me pay for it at work.

"I thought telling a chick she looked hot in her underwear was a compliment not —"

"A trigger for hysterical crying?"

I pick up my beer and take a long sip, shaking my head. "You were a mess."

"I was a mess," she agrees.

The sounds of the bar sweep in to fill the lull. Mila stares at her drink, a cocktail, and tilts her head a fraction in realization. Her fingers curl around the glass, lifting it from the table, but she hesitates before taking a drink.

She sets the glass down and says, "I don't think I actually ever thanked you for that night."

"Thank me? Thank me for what? I didn't do anything. I just sat there trying to hide my boner while patting your head from an awkward angle."

"You didn't judge me."

"Oh, I judged you."

Ignoring me, she continues, "I don't know, I think meeting you was just what I needed at that exact time in my life. I thought you'd be a one-night stand but…eight years later and we've fucked everyone in Manhattan but each other."

I lift my glass. "To irony."

"To irony."

Our glasses clink together and we both take a drink. I chuckle and she joins me for a few seconds. We fall silent at the same time, gazes locked.

There's a flicker of something in her eyes and I wonder if she's thinking what I'm thinking. This is the first time in a long time we've both been unattached. I was single when we first met, but she'd been all messed up over her ex. Then I met Amber and thought I'd found The One. Mila's never been concerned about finding The One, darting in and out of relationships for years. I've done my share of dating around since my breakup with Amber. All the while, Mila and I have gravitated around each other. I can't deny I'm drawn to her. She can't deny we've been spending more and more time together since she hired me.

Mila breaks contact first. She drops her attention to the napkin she places on her lap for something to do with her hands.

"Drew?"

"Yeah?"

She lifts her gaze and her expression dings me before her lips part with the words.

"Can we be serious for a minute?"

"Absolutely not."

"I'm worried about you," she says anyway. "I'm worried that you just bottle everything up. I'm…I'm worried that you don't talk to anyone."

"I don't know if you've noticed, but you're good about forcing me to talk to you." I duck my head to bring our eyes level. "I promise you, Mila. I'm fine."

My answer doesn't satisfy her, it's clear by the frown tugging at her lips. Mila thinks she knows things about me I don't.

"You can't blame me for being worried. Your reaction on Monday...was extreme."

"I know."

My jaw ticks before I can stop it and she reads the answer on my face. Mila knows the reason behind my reaction. There's no way for me to spin it. One second I got an email with the link to the article. The next second the desk was cracked in half and my steel chair lay in the center of it. It's never happened to me before, for so much to come out at once. After all these years, Amber can still bring out the worst in me.

"Are you over her?"

"Are you over him?"

Mila freezes, mouth half-open. She wasn't expecting me to volley the question right back and it hits her hard. The noises around us, the screaming and laughing, chairs scraping and glasses clinking, all of it highlights the cruelty of our discussion.

Why? Why are we talking about this in the first place?

"Okay." She sits back, her nostrils flaring on a sharp intake of breath. "You want to know the truth?"

"*Mila*, we don't have to go there. I was only trying to make a point—"

"I still think about him."

That shuts me up.

She swallows hard and goes on, "I do all the time. Eight years later. And the truth, Drew? It's not because I'm not over him, it's because I'm not over what happened. It still hurts I could be so stupid. It hurts I didn't see a single red flag. I grew up with everyone telling me how bright I was and how far I'd go, but when it came to Cole, everyone looked at me like I was the biggest idiot on the planet. I thought I could see things no one else could, I thought I knew him better...I..." She shuts her eyes then lets out a hollow laugh. "I was just a stupid little girl caught up in a cliché with the tattooed bad boy."

At the mention of tattoos, I eye the sleeves of her dress. I was there when she got her ink, but she's been careful to keep her arms covered in public since. It's not that she's ashamed of her tattoos, she's just protective of their meaning. The words on her arm are the equivalent of her heart on her sleeve and she couldn't bear to let anyone see.

"Did I ever tell you what happened on the morning of my wedding?" she asks.

She knows she hasn't. I don't want her to talk about him, not when it makes her eyes grow glassy with an anger I've never witnessed from her. The bitterness changes her features, morphing her sharp beauty to an even sharper, but menacing point.

"The morning of my wedding was like a goddamn funeral.

Every single person in my bridal party thought I was making a mistake. I could see it in their eyes, in their weak enthusiasm. Even my mother's Tarot cards predicted it would be a disaster. All I wanted was to prove them wrong. But...well, you know how that went."

Our food comes and we eat in silence. I'm glad for the noises of the restaurant masking the buzzing of thoughts between us.

I lift my drink to my lips, then gesture with the glass, extending a finger toward the bar's entrance. "What would you do if Cole walked through those doors right now and said he wanted you back?"

"I'd tell him to eat his fucking heart out. I might kick him in the throat for good measure."

"No offense, but there's no way you're getting your leg high enough in that dress."

"You've always underestimated me."

"Touché." I lift my glass and add, "Fuck him. Fuck Cole Van Buren—"

I say it loud enough people sitting nearby glance in our direction. Mila's eyes grow wide and an embarrassed smile splits her face.

She hates making a scene.

She has no idea how much attention she commands even when she's silent.

"Andrew, come on. Cut it out."

I lower the glass a fraction at the way her expression

wanes.

Hearing his name stings her. I'm not a fan of the guy, either. There was a time the youngest Van Buren's impulsivity and recklessness had been documented in the tabloids. It was a source of entertainment for his father's competitors. I followed the stories with more interest than I'd care to admit.

"What's with the face?" Mila asks.

"I still can't believe you almost married a Van Buren."

"Yes, I know. They're the definition of loaded, but this girl's got her own money, thank you."

I lean back in my seat for a moment as I consider saying something else, something I've never told her before. It's a conversation that should've happened a long time ago. But now? There's no point in bringing it up.

I sit up again and push my plate back. "Come on, let's get out of here."

I pay our tab, after a short argument where I remind Mila I owe her a desk and she laughs in my face and points out we are nowhere near even for that. We head toward the front doors, but I steer her to the bar.

"We need to finish our toast," I tell her.

I order us a round of shots and Mila doesn't seem amused by the crowd that swallows us in all directions. I understand now why she insists on wearing high heels, she'd be lost if it weren't for those damn things.

Someone nearly spills their drink on her while trying to talk to her but backs away at the sparks flying from her eyes.

I clear my throat to bring her attention to the shot glass I hold out in front of me.

"*Fuck you, Cole Van Buren.*" My shout thunders between us but is drowned out by the surrounding crowd. Only a few people glance our way.

Mila shakes her head.

"Come on," I urge, keeping the glass in the air. "You know you want to."

She bites her lip and glances around, then shrugs and lifts her drink up to meet mine.

"*Fuck you, Cole Van Buren. Fucking motherfucker,*" she shouts.

We clink glasses then throw back our shots. Mila laughs and some of her drink spills down her chin. I lean in and wipe it away with my thumb. She tenses and her smile wanes a fraction at my touch, but her eyes aren't on me. They are on the large windows facing the street. Her expression drains over several seconds as though she's seen a ghost. I check over my shoulder but whatever she saw is gone.

"Mila, what's wrong?"

She points to the windows, then blinks and shakes her head.

"Sorry, I think I'm hallucinating. For a second there I thought…" She trails off, shaking her head some more. "Never mind. Should we call a cab now? Or do you plan to continue tricking me into talking about my feelings?"

"Hang on. You thought you saw Cole? Out there?" I eye what's visible of the sidewalk from the bar windows.

"No, it wasn't him. Last I heard, Cole was living in Chicago." She straightens. Tucking her purse under her arm, she adds, "That was years ago. Anyway, it doesn't matter. Even if he were in the city, he'd know better than to come anywhere near me."

FOUR

MILA

THE ENVELOPE IS SOLID black and draws my attention long before Janet sets it down on my desk. I stare at it for a few seconds before picking it up to read my name. It's addressed in the careful white lettering of someone with messy handwriting trying to make an impression.

Janet is halfway to the door when I set down the phone, ending the call I'd been on.

"Hey, Janet, who sent this?" I ask, turning over the envelope. There is no return address, no logo, or branding.

"Not sure." Janet clutches her tablet to her chest. "I didn't open it because it looked personal to me."

She waits for a follow-up question, but my attention is back on the envelope. I yank open a desk drawer and find my letter opener. Slipping the blade through the seal of the envelope, I rip it open until the seams separate to reveal a thin, electric blue card inside. I'm unsettled by it. The color brings me back to a time I held a different invitation in my hand. It was a deeper, more sophisticated blue, with a glow to it much like this one.

It'd been a cold, rainy day in Manhattan, and I shivered slightly as I got out of bed and wrapped a blanket around myself.

I found Cole hunched over the dining room table, which was littered with stacks of cardstock and envelopes.

"You," I started, sitting down beside him, "are seriously insane."

He didn't look up, a pensive expression on his face as he expertly wielded the calligraphy pen to form the words:

We request the honor of your presence for the wedding of
Mila Zelenko & Cole Van Buren

Cole didn't answer me until the final loop of the last letter was completed. Then his green eyes flitted up to mine, a small smile twitching at his lips.

"Good morning, beautiful."

He set down the pen and leaned in to kiss me with the type of sweetness he never showed in bed. Not that I could complain. Cole was intense in everything he did. His kisses were the type of tender that would melt me. His lovemaking was the type of passionate that set me on fire.

He sat back in his chair and I picked up one of the finished cards to examine his work.

"Your lettering is gorgeous. I didn't realize you knew calligraphy."

"I don't. I'm just copying a font I found online."

I snort. "You do know we can pay someone to do this, right?"

"No need, I've got maybe seventy left."

Sighing at his stubbornness, I reached over to weave my fingers through the hairs at the nape of his neck, and watched him go back to work on the invitations.

I'll never forget how content I felt that morning. As though the whole world lay at my feet. My heart was full, my mind relaxed. All of my desires fulfilled.

For a brief moment in time, I had it all.

But none of it was real.

The click of the door closing behind Janet snaps my instincts into place. Still, there's a vague sensation of Cole in this piece of mail, the way it draws attention to itself.

It's a stretch.

He's never written me, he's never so much as texted.

Still, the thought sends a flurry of hope and anger through my stomach.

Just last weekend, I said his name aloud for the first time in a long time. Andrew somehow recognized how much I needed that moment—maybe because he can picture his own ex in a bar somewhere, lifting a glass and sending *him* to hell. If I were as superstitious as my mother, I would think the angry toast had summoned my ex right back into my life.

Cursing Cole's name was childish, but I'll be damned if it didn't feel amazing. It was cathartic to express my frustration at the part of him still lodged in me. I need to get him out. Out of my head, out of my skin. Even the simple act of saying his name made a vision of him materialize before my eyes. I thought I saw him walking along the street outside the bar. It was one of those moments I have occasionally, where I'm sure I see his face in a crowd and time lurches to an excruciating stop, only to realize it was just a mirage.

Oh, to live in a desert of resentment. And to be its queen.

My fingers are unsteady as they fumble to retrieve the card from within the envelope. When I read the printed text, there's no denying the sinking disappointment, slight though it may be.

It's just a random solicitation, an invitation to a gallery opening in Brooklyn. I toss the card onto my desk and it lands on top of a stack of notes. What had I expected? A handwritten apology letter? A page for each year he's left me with no answer and unable to truly move on?

"Mila?" Janet calls through the speaker of my phone, snapping me out of my thoughts. "Mr. Kreisler is here. He wants to know if you have a few minutes."

Frowning at the announcement, I rush to tuck the invitation back inside the envelope and slide it into one of my desk drawers. The act should shove the damn thing from my thoughts, but a nagging feeling remains. Something about it still doesn't sit right with me.

The unsettling feeling joins a fresh concern over the impromptu meeting. Clients don't drop by unannounced to inform me everything is going well.

Then again, Tobias Kreisler is not just any client.

"Yes, of course," I tell Janet. "Send him in."

The door to my office opens and Tobias Kreisler ambles in, older and thinner than the last time I saw him. I get to my feet and round my desk to meet him. There are bags under his eyes and his body language is distracted and tense. The man who grew a modest inheritance into one of the largest fortunes in the country now moves as though his entire net worth sits in pennies on his shoulders.

I've known him since I was a little girl, from when he would visit my mother for Tarot card readings. As he and my mother grew close, he developed an interest in helping my family. It was on his recommendation that I was awarded scholarships to one of the best prep schools in the city. He seemed indebted to my mother for her sage advice. And though I've always sensed his affinity toward me, there's been a subtle distance between us from the moment my mother passed away.

"Good morning, Tobias," I say, shaking his large hand.

He clasps his other hand over our handshake, a subtle symbol of power I'm accustomed to from him.

"Good to see you, Mila."

His greeting is typical but his tone muted. I gesture for him to take a seat and move around to take my own. A genuine smile forms on his face, and he lifts his hands in a gesture of surprise.

"Congratulations on the nomination," he says. "Female entrepreneur of the year. Your mother would be proud."

"Thank you," I say, bowing my head.

"I only wish she were around to see you receiving it."

"So do I."

He goes on to ask me questions about the awards ceremony, questions that only serve to highlight the fact he didn't drop in for a last-minute meeting to discuss my nomination.

It's too easy to tell when someone is hiding or avoiding

something, the tricky part is figuring out what that something is. There are ways to read between the lines, listening to not just what someone says but what they don't say. To put their body language in context of their words, to piece together true intentions. But most of the time, the quickest way to a direct answer is to ask a direct question.

"What really brings you here today? I don't think you came all this way just to congratulate me."

Tobias steeples his fingertips and brings them to his lips as he stares past me at the wall-to-wall windows. There's a long-standing weariness to his face, deep lines and coarse skin hinting at the years of drugs and partying that destroyed his reputation and shrouded his company name long after he'd straightened out his life. My mother's advice helped him turn it all around in just a few years.

"I'm going to come out and say it, Mila. I received a grim diagnosis from my doctors a few days ago. They say I should begin to settle my affairs."

I glance at my hands and swallow, resisting the urge to apologize for his circumstance. Tobias Kreisler is not a sentimental man. He does not appreciate being pitied, but he has to notice the sting in my eyes when they meet his. I keep my tone steady when I respond.

"How can I help?"

"Legally, everything's taken care of. My son is set to inherit my fortune and take over the business. And that..." He rests a hand on his chin and taps a finger to his lips. "That is the problem."

"You don't believe your son is ready?"

"It's not a matter of ready," Tobias says. "I was once in a similar position, coming into a large sum of money unexpectedly. Granted, it was only a fraction of what he stands to inherit, and yet it almost crushed me simply by showing me who I really was."

I resolve to keep my responses short, sensing all Tobias needs is a sounding board. He has a Trust and Estates Attorney to work out the details of his will. But he's here because he has something else in mind.

"Tell me, Mila. What do you make of Grant?"

Grant's the type of guy who thinks the world belongs to those who can afford anything it has to offer. I know him well. In fact, I've known Grant for as long as I've known Cole. I met them both on the very same day.

It'd been such a bizarre day.

Tobias had invited me over for a New Year's Eve party. It'd been the first time he'd invited me to his estate in all the years I knew him, and I was confused why the invitation did not include my mother. But when I arrived, his intentions became clear. There was an awkward excitement in his eyes when he introduced me to his son.

"Grant, this is Mila. The one I've been telling you about."

"Right, yeah. Hey there," Grant said, shaking my hand. But his greeting was distracted, his attention fixed on another party guest.

An older woman in a skin-tight black dress stood just outside of the living room. She was breathtaking, oozing sex appeal, and stared at Grant like he was something she could eat.

I remember a pang of envy at the way Grant eyed the woman with such tantalizing, carnal intent. Not because I wanted Grant, but because no one had ever looked at me that way. Ever. Then again, I was wearing a cardigan over a sweater dress precisely because I hated drawing attention to myself. I didn't know then that my femininity could be one of the sharpest weapons at my disposal, one I should've wielded with pride.

Not wanting to force Grant into small talk, I quickly excused myself to the restroom, allowing him the room to pursue the focus of his desire. I never made it to the restroom. I grabbed a drink from a server passing by and sulked at how out of place I felt surrounded by these beautiful, powerful people. Manhattan's elite.

"You look like you want to be here less than I do."

The gravelly voice came from behind me, low and strangely appealing even before I saw whom it belonged to. When I turned to face him, I gave a small start.

"*Oh*."

I wanted to slap myself for my reaction, at the breathy way I'd spoken the word.

My eyes widened at the sight of the most gorgeous man I'd ever seen. His bone structure was stunning and masculine, and his lips were full and inviting. *But those eyes*. Dark brows framed a pair of intense emerald eyes I struggled to stare into, but couldn't look away from. The expression in them made my stomach tie into enticing knots.

He was the kind of guy who made you blink and stutter if you weren't prepared to see him appear in front of you.

"I'm Cole." He reached out a hand for me to shake. "Cole Van Buren. I don't think we've met."

The name was familiar, but I wasn't in a state to immediately work out why. I was too busy piecing together exactly why he'd left me flustered. It couldn't have been his face alone—everyone at the damn party had a perfect face. No, it was something about the way he carried himself…

"Uh, Mila. Mila Zelenko."

I shook his hand, feeling stupid for mentioning my last name—like it would mean anything to anyone here. All the while, my gaze moved down his body. He wore a black t-shirt and faded blue jeans, while everyone else dressed in formal attire. And yet he managed to fit right in, giving off the impression it was everyone else who was ridiculously overdressed.

Tattoos ran up both of his toned arms. The sight thrilled me. I'd never met anyone with full sleeves of ink. But then, I'd been pretty sheltered most of my life. By my overbearing mother, but also by my own fear of making mistakes. Everything about Cole screamed he was exactly what I'd been sheltered *from*. It didn't matter. Nothing could work against his insane allure.

"Mila," he repeated, and I liked how my name rolled off his tongue. "That's a beautiful name for a beautiful woman."

"Thank you." I blushed.

Was he flirting with me or just being polite?

Someone cackled with laughter and Cole looked over at the small group of people standing right next to us. He edged closer to me, bowing his head so I could hear him speak without him needing to raise his voice.

"Are you here with someone?"

"Oh, uh, Tobias invited me. He's a family friend. But, honestly, I think he wanted to set me up with his son…" I glanced over my shoulder and caught sight of Grant sweet-talking the woman he'd been staring at. When I looked back at Cole, he was staring at *me*.

"You don't want to date Grant."

"I don't?"

"We've been friends my whole life and I love him like a brother. But he's not the kind of guy you date."

"Oh? And you're…what?"

Mischief gleamed in Cole's gaze.

"I'm a guy who knows how to treat a woman right."

I wanted to roll my eyes, but God, the way he said those words only made me want to call his bluff…

I blink several times, breaking out of the memory. It only lasted a few seconds, but it was long enough for Tobias to misinterpret my pause as hesitation.

"You can just say it, Mila," Tobias blurts out.

Taking a deep breath, I look down and consider my response to his question.

What do you make of Grant?

"He…has a lot of growing up to do," I say, "but he's not a bad person."

"No one ever means to be a bad person, Mila, but that's beside the point. This type of fortune, this level of influence, it can…"

He trails off, not wanting to finish the sentence. But I already know what he's thinking. Money is often villainized for the way some people seem to change under its influence. But all money does is give a person the freedom to reveal their true colors.

Grant's always had all the money he could want, but his father has held the purse strings, leveraging the unspoken threat of cutting him off. Tobias is afraid Grant is who he unwittingly raised him to be.

I press my lips together, allowing the silence to nudge Tobias to continue.

"Grant is detached from reality and that's largely my fault. I've been too preoccupied to worry about the person he's becoming. And now I'm afraid he's too self-serving to carry on the Kreisler legacy I've worked so hard to build."

I set my elbows on the desk and cross my arms. Tobias is a smart man. He knows there are a number of ways he could ensure his son doesn't spiral out of control. But he's here because he's not interested in adding conditions to the inheritance. This isn't an issue of tying up loose ends after he's gone. It's an issue of finding the trust in his son so he can…

I push back the thought, and listen as Tobias admits his aversion to adding conditions to the inheritance and the lasting message it would send to Grant about his lack of confidence in him.

I watch a man I've known for much of my life fighting against his love for his only son just to find an objective stance.

The people we love are our blind spots. Our biggest problems often orbit them, just outside of our realm of acknowledgment. Sometimes all we need is perspective.

What my clients want, most of all, is to have the burden of their toughest decisions lifted.

No one's immune to this desperate wish. Because from the time we are kids, we're guided by rules and constant feedback. Then we enter adulthood and there are no marks, no averages, no real way to gauge whether we are moving in the right direction. In the end, all Tobias wants is to be relieved from the crippling fear of making the wrong choice. He wants reassurance of the plot he's already devised in his head. Tobias Kreisler has always seen life as a chessboard and situations like this as an opportunity for a moral test.

"If your concern is the money's impact on your son, then there's only one way for you to know its true effect while you're still with us. Because if this situation were an experiment, money's the one factor you're entirely in control of."

Tobias raises his gaze from the ground while lowering his hand from his face. I can see the way my words fit into the plan brewing behind his eyes.

"Absolutely," he says. "You only know a man's true character when you give him all the money in the world, or take it all away."

It's a myth money and power change people. They can only highlight traits a person already has. The same goes for misfortune. It shows you who you really are.

Tobias rises to his feet, a sudden lightness to his movements. I get up from my own chair and reach over the desk to shake his hand.

"Thank you, Mila. This is exactly what I needed."

"Does your son know? About your health?"

"No, of course not."

I nod, my lips tilting down. I don't say what we both know. He needs to tell Grant.

Tobias turns away and heads toward the door.

"If you need anything," I say, and he pauses, but doesn't look back. "Please, let me know."

Tobias raises a hand in thanks and disappears through the door.

Alone in my office, I sink back into my chair and take a moment to let the dread spread through me. I don't expect it to lift anytime soon.

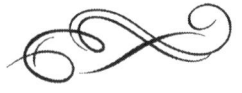

FIVE

MILA

THE MORNING BRINGS ANOTHER, less eventful meeting, but the entire time the news Tobias delivered to me hangs overhead. Sometime around noon, I take advantage of a lull and try to clear my head.

The view from my office offers little trace of the sky. Instead, asymmetrical blocks of glass and steel appear stacked on top of each other. The skyscrapers surrounding this building cradle it, and from this angle they look close enough to touch.

It's a view I prefer to a higher vantage point where the city becomes a vague sea of lights. Being boxed in by the city breathes energy and life into me. I suspect I'd be claustrophobic in a field of grass.

A knock on my door claims my attention.

"Hey, did you get the...?" Andrew's question falls away. "What's wrong with you?"

I shake my head then sit back in my chair, not knowing where to start.

"Tobias Kreisler came in this morning to talk about settling his affairs. He's dying."

"Damn."

Andrew reaches my desk and stands there, watching me.

"Tobias is a good man. He bailed my mother out of some tough times."

"I'm sorry."

"His son doesn't know yet. Is it weird I've got this...I don't know, this guilt that I know before him?"

"Nothing you can do about that."

"I know. I think it would be easier if Grant was a stranger."

Andrew frowns. "Did something happen between you two?"

"No, of course not. Grant was Cole's best man. And for a while, he was the only one who knew where Cole was. Not that he had the decency to tell me."

I let out a tired breath. The memory is as exhausting to think about as it was to live.

"That's it." Andrew slices his hand through the air, a serious expression on his face. "New rule. We don't talk about your ex at work. It drains the life force out of you."

"Alright. I mean, you don't make the rules around here. But, sure."

His eyes lower to the envelope. It's in my hands and I don't remember pulling it out of the drawer. How long have I been holding it?

"What's that?"

"This? Uh, it's an invite to an event. But, there's only... one." I look up at Andrew. "There's only one," I say again, finally narrowing in on the nagging feeling when I first opened it.

"That's weird, right?"

"People mail in event tickets all the time."

"Yeah, but half a dozen. Two at a minimum. Never one."

"Maybe someone's cheap. Or they want you to go alone."

"Well, it's the weekend of the awards gala, so I don't think I'll make it. Besides, I don't even know who sent it."

"I'll take it," Andrew says with a shrug. He picks up the invitation, but when his eyes narrow in on the words printed on the card, he adds, "An art gallery opening? Yeah, no. You can have this back."

He sets it on my desk with careful deliberation.

"What am I supposed to do with this?"

"Throw it out."

"But it's so pretty." I lift the card between my fingers, the color so vibrant it hums in the air. "You know how I feel about cardstock."

"I forgot who I was talking to. You hoard greeting cards out of guilt."

He comes around to sit on the inside edge of my desk as he speaks.

"Get off my desk and get back to work," I say, tucking the invitation back into the envelope.

"I'm just saying, boss, I wouldn't catch feelings over that. Looks like a mass mail-out to me."

He reaches over me to open one of my drawers and grabs a Starburst from my secret stash. I catch traces of an unfamiliar, alluring scent.

"That's a new cologne," I say.

"Is that your way of telling me I smell nice?" He throws the piece of candy in his mouth, seeming pleased that I noticed.

His warm and delicious scent settles in, and as he chews, the movement of his jaw brings my attention to how much sharper his features seem today. It's like suddenly, all his most attractive qualities, his jawline, his eyes, his lips, are fighting for my attention.

It takes me a few seconds to realize what's different about him.

"And you got a different haircut?" I tilt my head. "What's going on, Drew? Is there a new woman I don't know about? Who are you trying to impress?"

"Maybe I'm trying to impress you."

I'm not prepared for the way warmth swirls in the pit of my stomach at this. I've trained myself not to look at Andrew that way, simply because I've been emotionally unavailable most of the time I've known him. The rest of the time, one or both of us have been tied up in short-lived relationships. But it's been three months since the last time I heard him mentioning seeing anyone and that was around the time a disastrous blind date stole my appetite for dating around. We've been spending a lot more time together since we've both been single.

I blink at my own reaction, the way I stall. My senses have become bewitched by a scent I've had no time to grow immune toward.

"You can impress me by going back to work," I say, waving

him away.

"Alright, alright." Andrew gets to his feet and straightens his suit jacket, a small grin curling his lips. "I'll leave you, then. Ms. Female Entrepreneur of the Year."

Inwardly, I cringe. It's such a bizarre proclamation to hear.

"I was hoping you hadn't gotten the memo."

"The whole city got the memo. It was in the paper."

"Ah," I say. "I guess I'm a big deal, then."

He half-turns to leave but hesitates.

I wait, staring up at him as a suggestion forms in his eyes before leaving his lips.

"How about I take you out for drinks tonight," he says, "to celebrate?"

I'm caught up in the quick flash of excitement in his expression, as though the invitation carries an implication of things it never has before. Am I imagining this? Am I seeing what I want to see? Am I hoping for things I shouldn't?

I'm being ridiculous.

I look down at my desk and snap myself into focus.

"I'll pass. I've got other plans for the night. Plans that involve me, myself, and I."

"You're so boring, Mila."

"Yeah, I'll go sob about it over a pile of money."

"Alright, then…"

He gives me a lingering look before walking out of the door and into the hall. I watch after him for a few seconds, tapping a finger on the envelope now sitting on my desk. Taking a long breath, I snatch up the invitation up and toss it into the trash bin. It lands on top of a hill of crumpled up memos. Such a waste of gorgeous cardstock.

As if on cue, Janet comes over the phone speaker again to tell me Camille Roberts is on the line. I freeze when I hear the name. It can't be a coincidence, can it?

I tell Janet to put her through and sit back in my chair.

Camille's raspy voice comes over the speaker and fills my office.

"Hey, stranger."

Nostalgia washes over me yet again today. I think back to Camille helping me into my wedding gown. And the pep talk she gave me afterward.

She'd gone looking for me when I disappeared to check my makeup in the bathroom for what must've been a suspiciously long time. No one else had noticed. They were too busy whispering amongst themselves.

Camille knocked on the bathroom door and I straightened where I stood in front of the sink, my gown spread out around me. The door was unlocked and she pushed it open slowly until I was in full view of her.

"Don't say it," I pleaded, taking a deep breath to calm myself. "God, if one more person says it."

She hesitated before entering, careful not to step on my dress.

"No one's said a thing, Mila."

"Yeah, but they're all thinking it. I'm about to walk out to a sea of people who think I'm an idiot for marrying Cole."

Camille moved closer and set her hand over mine.

"Fuck them." Her fingers squeezed mine until I met her eyes. "Seriously, Mila. Fuck them. It's not their decision. It's yours. Let people think whatever they want. Their perceptions can't touch your reality unless you let them. You know Cole. You know he's crazy about you. I've never seen him like this, he's finally ready to settle down. And I know for a fact he wants a life with you more than he's wanted anything."

I swallowed hard, emotional from the disappointments and excitements of the day.

"Also," Camille added, "you wouldn't be such a ball of stress if you'd just smoked that blunt with me earlier."

I snorted, then full on laughed. She smiled wide, satisfied at my reaction.

Of all my interactions on that day, hers was the only one not weighed down by silent disapproval. Camille was the only person who thought Cole and I were good together.

But of course she did. Back then, she and I believed a lot of things that weren't true.

I sit at my desk, clutching the phone tighter and waiting for my old friend to speak.

"I'm betting you can guess why I'm calling," she says.

I swivel my chair side to side, resisting the urge to jump to conclusions as I try to remember what I could've forgotten. Last time we talked, she'd invited me to the opening of her bakery in Brooklyn. But that was last summer.

"The invitation, Mila. I'm pretty sure you got it."

First, tightness forms in my chest, followed by an instant wash of relief.

"*Oh,*" I sigh, "it was you. I couldn't figure out why someone would send just one and not even bother to add a return address."

"It's obvious, isn't it? He wants you to go alone, but he knows you won't, so he made sure I got one, too."

The tightness rears back, closing around my throat.

"What do you mean *he*? Who are you talking about?"

"Mila, the invitation is from Cole. This is the opening of his exhibit."

SIX

MILA

SIRENS WAIL SOMEWHERE IN the distance and the sound joins in with the honks from the cars crawling through mid-town. Even at noon, the plaza in front of my building is cast in shadow. Two large fountains frame the walkway down to where Camille waits for me.

She stands on the last step before the sidewalk, her golden hair drawing my attention because it somehow picks up sunlight lost to the rest of her surroundings. Behind her the sidewalk is packed with pedestrians, many dressed in business attire.

Even from a distance, I can tell she's much thinner than the last time I saw her, but when her features pull into sharper focus, I blanch at how much she's changed. Not noticing my reaction, Camille opens her arms to greet me and I move between them to give her a hug. She's wearing flats to my five-inch heels and yet still manages to be slightly taller than me.

"It's been forever," she says.

"I know," I say. "It's so good to see you."

I return her smile but continue to scan her face in disbelief. I can't get used to how different she is from the image I hold of her in my brain. I always remember her as the Camille I met almost a decade ago, the girl who welcomed me into her family from the moment I started dating her brother. Her hair was lighter then, her eyeliner darker, but her skin bright and glowing. But today she seems exhausted. Her shoulders have lost their squared confidence, her eyes have grown more intense, yet less sharp.

"Thanks for meeting me," I say, so distracted I forget for a moment just why I asked her here.

"Well, this is the first lunch break I've taken all month. I'll let that speak to how much I missed you."

I smile, then say, "Come on, I know you don't have long."

I set a hand on her forearm to lead her forward, and we walk down the rest of the steps of the plaza, and onto the sidewalk to fall in step with the foot traffic. We pass street vendors and a couple of food trucks with their colorful signs. Cars honk along the street at our side, a man argues into his cellphone, and a construction site jackhammer rattles the pavement somewhere behind us.

We make small talk along the way, catching up in the awkward way friends who haven't talked in a long while do. Without time to offer context for what's happened over the past few months, we stick to vague impressions of events. She tells me her bakery is doing well and I apologize for not coming by again after the grand opening. Camille dominates the conversation for several minutes, seeming to ignore the elephant in the room. There's more than one elephant. There's the reason we've come out in the first place, and then there's the way her energetic mood is at odds with her tired appearance. Unable to pin down the mixed signals, I ask her if she's doing all right, if she's feeling well. She assures me she's doing great, just running a million miles an hour for work.

About a block from where we agreed to have lunch, Camille falls silent. We reach the crosswalk and come to a stop in front of a flurry of cars passing along the road. I press the button for the walk signal and turn to face her. The question burning my throat comes out.

"Why didn't you tell me he was back in the city?"

Camille looks over my shoulder and the corner of her mouth tilts down for the first time. "I'm sorry," she says. "I didn't say anything because he asked me not to."

The words slice through to the reality of our friendship. She might have been my closest friend, she might've been my maid of honor, but the wedding never happened and she and I grew apart. In the end, what she and I had built could fade with time, but she would always be Cole's half-sister. Meeting with her was my idea, but I realize now it's exactly what Cole wanted to happen. If Cole is suddenly interested in reaching out to me, it makes sense he'd use the only person he could to get to me. Camille is the last real thread connecting us.

The light changes and Camille takes off. Halfway across the road, she stops and notices I'm not beside her. By then, I've managed to pull myself together and take the last few steps over to meet her. We reach the other sidewalk and stroll by a few storefronts in silence, coming to a stop in front of the restaurant.

She pulls the door open, but I catch it before she can open it all the way.

"I don't want anything we talk about to get back to Cole," I say.

Her brows pull in. "*Of course.*"

"I want your word, Camille."

"You have it. You have my word."

It's not that I'm any less hesitant, but the boundaries needed to be drawn before we could go any further. I release the door and follow her inside. A hostess greets us and leads us to the only open table by the window.

I sit across from Camille, setting my purse down on my lap, and take in our surroundings.

"Mila," Camille says, drawing my attention to the way she fiddles with her charm bracelet, then up to where worry etches across her face, "I know you're upset I didn't tell you, but honestly, you made it clear Cole was a topic we didn't discuss."

A server sets a tall glass of water on the table in front of me. I take it, lifting it to my lips, and force the liquid down my throat, which insists on clamping up every time I hear his name.

"How long has he been back?"

My stomach hurts. I'm not sure I could eat if I wanted to.

"I'm not sure. This isn't his first time back, but he never stays with me," she says.

Her tone is tart and I catch subtle traces of suppressed resentment. Camille had been barely two when her mother, already pregnant with Cole, married into the Van Buren name.

Growing up, she'd never considered herself a Van Buren. Not just because she didn't bear the name, but because she'd always felt like a castaway child from a previous life her mother wanted to forget.

Here she is now, a castaway from a life I'd like to forget, too. I cut everyone else off, I untangled myself from anyone from that time in my life, but I've never been able to fully disconnect from Camille. She's remained one of the last strongholds from that era.

She goes on, "You know it's true. You couldn't say his name for months. I honestly thought the only way we would remain friends was if I pretended he never existed. But he's my brother, Mila. Every once in a while I'd get the stray email, and without fail he'd eventually ask me if I'd heard from you. He'd ask what you were up to."

"So all this time," I say, "you've been keeping tabs on me for him?"

My eyes lower to her hands, which move from fiddling with her bracelet to twisting the napkin on the table.

"It wasn't like that."

"Tell me what it was like then."

I lift the glass to my lips again, this time taking only a small gulp of water. I'm careful to keep my words unemotional. It's the only way I can make it through this conversation.

"I knew you wouldn't like him poking around, so I never told him anything he couldn't find out on his own. I swear."

"You could've just not told him anything at all."

"God, this is exactly what I didn't want." Camille lets out a breath then brings her twitching fingertips to her temples. "I never wanted to get in the middle of you two."

It's such a cowardly move of Cole to leverage his sister to keep tabs on me. He knew my number and never called. He walked out on me without a single explanation and yet thinks he's entitled to check in on my life?

Fuck Cole Van Buren.

Fuck his entitled face straight to the pits of hell.

"What does he want from me?" I snap.

"All he wants is for you to see the exhibit."

"Well that's too damn bad because I'm not going."

Disappointment floods Camille's face. She goes quiet, but her mouth moves in tiny twists as though she's chewing over her next words.

"You should think about it. Really, you should consider going. You inspired his art."

"Look," I say, "I'm glad he's finally doing something with his life instead of wasting his talents. But I don't owe him anything, Camille. In fact, I owe him exactly nothing."

"Yeah...I know."

"What would be the point of me going? Does he want me to be happy for him? To be proud of him?" The questions fly from my lips in quick succession before I take a breath and settle myself down. "I inspired his art? Big deal, he inspired my tattoos. Look, I'm glad he got his life together, but I managed to get mine together a long time ago and I have zero interest in being pulled backward."

Camille appears to be trapped in an impossible situation. And she is. The truth is, nothing good could've come of her telling me Cole had been asking about me. A part of me is glad she didn't.

I sigh. "I'm not upset with you, Camille. I'm sorry for how I'm coming across, you don't deserve it."

"It's fine, Mila. If I were you, I'd react the same way."

I reach into my purse and pull out the invitation. I took it from the trash bin on my way out of the office, not knowing what I was planning to do with it.

I set it on the table.

"Tell him I said congratulations. And tell him I said to not reach out to me again. I'm serious."

Camille's green eyes take in the envelope, but she doesn't try to reach for it.

"Just hang on to it, Mila. You might change your mind."

"No, I won't." I slide the envelope across the table.

Her mouth opens then closes again, as she shakes her head. For the first time, I see it.

She knows more than she said.

"What are you not telling me?"

She shuts her eyes for several seconds then takes a breath.

"Maybe you're right. Maybe you shouldn't go," she says. "I used to think you two balanced each other out, but sometimes I wonder if all you do is consume each other and everything that comes between you. You know, Mila, when everything happened, I lost my best friend. You realize that, right? You wanted nothing to do with me anymore."

"That's not true," I say, but the sting in my eyes proves it's a pointless lie.

Now I'm the one rubbing my temples, taking a deep breath that rakes against a hollowness I spend most of my days pretending doesn't exist.

"I didn't mean to upset you," she says, genuine regret in her eyes. "You know I care about you. Always have."

I nod, my heart aching along with my stomach. I let Cole take my best friend from me. I let my aversion to him push space between her and me. Maybe one day we can find a way back to how things used to be. But right now? All the emotions from the day are a stew of discomfort inside me.

"I'm sorry," I say, getting to my feet. "Camille, I'm feeling sick to my stomach. I really should get going."

"I get it. It's a lot to take in." She glances at her watch. "Honestly, I'm better off just grabbing a sandwich at a stand and heading back to the office."

She rises to her feet and I join her, walking around the table to give her a hug. She squeezes me tight.

"Can we talk some other time?" she asks, and there's an eagerness in her gaze that breaks my heart a little. "About anything other than my stupid brother?"

"You've got it," I say with a tight laugh.

I watch my old friend walk away then I sit back down and stare at the invitation she left behind.

SEVEN

MILA

THERE WERE NO SIGNS. The day before the wedding, Cole and I woke up tangled in each other. He hovered over me, his arms cocooning me in place. He had the most satisfied smile on his face as he watched me with those clear green eyes. He stroked my hair back out of my face and away from my bare shoulders with a soft brush of his fingertips. He'd been anything but gentle when we'd made love the night before, but that morning he trailed kisses across my collarbone with such tenderness they made my heart throb. Even then, loving him was so intense, it was almost painful. Pain so good, I thought I could never get enough. And when those hands ran up my back and curled, I arched my body to let him in all over again. He moved over me, serving me with hard, passionate thrusts that rendered me delirious.

"Tomorrow," he said by my ear, "you'll be mine forever."

The words were too sweet to be erotic, but the tremble of his coarse voice sent shivers through every inch of me and brought me shaking into climax.

Afterward, I had wrapped my legs around him when he tried to pull away. He laughed and kissed me and suggested we could just stay in bed. But we couldn't. We had a long day ahead of us, preparing for the vows we would never say.

I spent years replaying our last encounter over and over again in my head. How were there no signs of what was to come? There were none, not a single one, and I'm starting to think this is why I've had such a hard time letting go of the anger. Cole's groomsmen told me he was putting on his suit one second, the next he was stepping out of the room for a few minutes. He never returned. I waited in a massive gown for my cue to walk down the aisle, but it never came.

At first, I was worried, convinced something horrible had happened to him. Nothing else made sense. Cole wanted to marry me. I knew that to be true more than I knew anything else. But the truth came later that night, as a phone call came in from Grant Kreisler to tell me he'd found him.

I asked to speak to him, but he said it wasn't a good idea. I battled relief and anger, demanding answers no one would give me. Days passed, then weeks. Grant wouldn't return my calls and Cole's phone went straight to voicemail. The anger grew steady as all questions from friends and family were routed to me. It was hard to accept the truth. That nothing had happened to Cole but a change of heart and the cowardice to show his face.

He left me scattered and now every time I think of him it's a knife to my gut. How the hell does Cole think he can come into town after all these years and summon me?

He's out of his damn mind.

My breathing is still heavy when I return to the office from my lunch date with Camille. Janet starts to give me a message but reads my expression and allows her words to fade away. I close the door behind me, the tightness behind my eyes growing into a mild headache.

I plop down behind my desk and bring my laptop to life with a few taps of the keyboard. I go to check my emails but somehow end up with a browser window open.

My fingers fly across the keyboard until the words *Cole Van Buren* appear across the search bar. I tap the surface of my keyboard a few times without pushing down. I know I shouldn't, but if I've already gone this far, I might as well. I hit enter and the results begin to load, then the space beneath the search bar goes blank and a message appears: *keyword blocked*.

I laugh, relieved and annoyed. I forgot about the software I installed years ago. That's how long it's been since I tried to search for Cole. There was a time, in the beginning, when I would search for his name obsessively. I'd try to piece together what he was up to, whom he was with, and why…why he wasn't with me. It was pathetic. I hated that version of myself and I'm not going back.

The next few hours stretch out to infinity, with each human encounter I have requiring a controlled tone and leaving my facial muscles sore from holding a neutral expression. It's been years since I've experienced anger this fresh.

All this time I thought the wounds had been sealed, but they were just scabs ready to be picked.

I leave half an hour earlier than usual, packing up and

slipping my laptop into my bag with the intention of bringing work home. On my way out, I stop by Andrew's office and catch him on the phone. He pauses mid-speech when he notices me standing at the door. I offer him a tight smile, and gesture for him to continue. He picks up his conversation but tilts his head at me in a silent question. My smile wanes. I'm afraid he can read me better than his nonchalant expression lets on.

I jerk my head toward the door, signaling I'm heading out. I'm not sure why I felt the need to stop by his office, but seeing him makes my anger ebb away a fraction.

He mimics eating his phone receiver then points to his watch. I take a breath and the familiar hollowness in me confirms I'm not up for company. I shake my head and give him a small wave. He turns from me and responds to the caller as though he'd been listening all along.

I walk away with an unsatisfied feeling I can't pin down because it has nothing to do with the day's events. What's happened today is a flurry at the forefront of my mind. But, no. This feeling peeks out from somewhere in my subconscious. It's like having something at the tip of your tongue but losing it again.

The sensation follows me all the way home.

I peel off my shoes as soon as I walk through my door and step down to my natural height. That's the first unwelcoming shift in vantage point. The second comes when I tread across the cold tile of the entryway, past the collection of paintings and sketches hanging along the wall. My movements echo throughout and I stop to consider the vastness of the space around me. The rooms in my house have more art on the walls than furniture on the ground. Nothing's changed from yesterday or the day before, but I somehow notice it more than ever today.

There's a third unpleasant shift in vantage point, which comes after I settle down in my living room with freshly delivered Chinese food in front of me. The current image of myself snaps into focus. I've removed my suit jacket, but I'm still wearing my work shirt and pants, button undone, bra unclasped. I'm shoveling Chinese food into my mouth like it's going to help me not feel feelings anymore.

I'm moping and it needs to stop.

Andrew's face flashes in my mind, the disappointment there when I shook my head at his offer to get dinner. Just like that, I nail down the discontent that followed me home from the office. I've had a nagging feeling about Andrew lately. His recent increase in outing invitations hints at his aversion to being alone. He's the quintessential extrovert, craving constant social interaction, and I'm sure now more than ever he's avoiding being alone with his thoughts. I don't care what he says, hearing an old flame is engaged is always a mindfuck. I stare at the phone for several seconds before I make the call. Andrew answers on the second ring.

"Hey, Drew. Can I come over?"

EIGHT

MILA

THERE'S SOMETHING JARRING ABOUT catching someone in casual clothes when you're used to seeing them in business attire. Whenever I think of Andrew, I picture him wearing a suit. Even the times we've gone out, he's dressed in crisp button-down shirts. But when his apartment door opens, Andrew is in a sleeveless t-shirt, running shorts, and sneakers.

I blink a few times at the disorienting sight.

"Hey," he says. "Come in."

His face is flushed and his hair slightly disheveled. He catches me eyeing his appearance and runs a hand through his hair to smooth it back.

I hold up the bag in my hand. "I come bearing half-eaten Chinese food."

"You really shouldn't have."

He takes the bag from me and walks ahead into the kitchen to set it on the counter. When he peers inside, he chuckles.

"You weren't kidding, you really did bring half-eaten Chinese food."

"It came in before I called and I was starving."

"I already ate."

"Ah. Well...I'm going to need to take that back, then."

"Nope." He grins. "It's going away, I'm saving it for later."

He ties up the bag again and turns to his fridge.

Music plays at a low volume from the living room, where a set of free weights sits in the center of the carpet. Andrew moved into this apartment a few months ago. The last time I saw this place, there was no furniture and all of his belongings were in boxes stacked along the walls.

The place is put together now. Most of the furniture is dark wood or black, and the accents are gray or light blue. A large, sophisticated painting of the Brooklyn Bridge hangs over his tan leather couch. On either side, drapes frame large windows overlooking another building right across the way. I make no attempt to be subtle in my analysis of the space and do a full circle to take it in.

"I'm impressed," I say. "The place looks great."

I take off my shoes and sink my feet into the plush carpet. Andrew responds from behind the open refrigerator door.

"Wish I could say it was me. My sister decorated it. I wrote her a check and she took care of everything."

I lean against the countertop behind him as he talks.

"Ah, well, for a minute there, I thought you had good taste."

"Never. I have awful taste."

He shuts the fridge door and gives a small start when he turns to look at me. The space is small but I didn't anticipate him being so close. He lifts his arms to keep from colliding with me, stopping inches short. There's a protein drink in his hand and he holds it overhead like an offering.

"*Jesus*," he says, stepping back. "I keep forgetting how short you are. I thought a squirrel had gotten in from the balcony."

I cross my arms and glare up at him. "Why are we even friends?"

"Sometimes I ask myself the same thing. Only thing I can come up with is you like looking at my pretty face."

He shakes up the protein drink, his arm flexing in the process, and proceeds to chug the drink down in front of me. He's not lying. I hate how he can't manage to be unattractive even when he tries. My gaze moves up his arms, across his chest, and down the front of his shirt.

His head cocks to the side.

"What?"

"Do you do competitive jar opening on your time off? You work at an office. What do you do with these things?"

I poke at his biceps with my finger and find them to be as hard as they look. The action does nothing to minimize their appeal.

"Make yourself at home," he says. "I've got to hop in the shower real quick. I'll be back in a few minutes."

It's a simple statement, but I catch my gaze before it starts to move over his body again. Not that it matters, because I'm now picturing him naked. I wish he'd just put on a suit, or a shirt with sleeves. Seeing this much of his skin messes with me. There are some logical issues with having a friend who I am, at times, attracted to. It's hard to forget he and I would've had sex once, had I not collapsed in a heap of tears.

"Alright, I'll just...be out here." I clear my throat, scratching at the back of my neck.

Andrew disappears into his bedroom. A few minutes later, the muffled sounds of the shower trickle from under his door.

I pour myself a glass of water. I'm warm all over and can't understand why. My hormones have been on a bizarre ride today. From sadness to shock to anger to...whatever the hell this is.

I know exactly what it is.

This is the first time in a very long time that I've been alone with Andrew in private. We're around each other all the time, but when we hang out outside of work, it's always out in public and almost always in a group.

Being here tonight feels different. Intimate.

I swallow back the contents of the glass and set it down in the sink. With Andrew in the shower, I walk around his apartment, taking in the details of the decor. I wonder how many women he's brought home. It's an odd thought, but just because his last relationship ended months ago doesn't mean he hasn't had female company. I'm sure he spares me the nitty gritty details of his sex life.

Still, we've both been single for months and if he's made a move, I've missed it.

I've wondered before if I'm even Andrew's type. After all, I chose him to sleep with and, well, I did come on a bit strong. It's rare I catch his eyes wandering, and moments where a silent suggestion settles between us, like the slightest hint of an opportunity, are even more rare. Those times I get the overwhelming sense the ball is in my court and has been since the night I slammed on the brakes.

And…I don't know why I'm thinking of this tonight.

I slide open the glass door of Andrew's balcony. It overlooks the courtyard nestled between this building and the next one over. It's a mild spring evening, and the distant sounds of traffic come in waves and lulls, almost soothing, until someone yells out on the street below and a dog starts barking.

"There's no furniture out there."

Andrew's voice comes from behind me. I turn to find him coming out of his room. His hair is still damp but smoothed back, giving his appearance a rejuvenated look. His white t-shirt hugs his chest.

"You want a drink?" he asks, heading over to the kitchen.

"I'll have whatever you're having."

There's a clinking of glasses and the rush of liquid as he fills them. He walks to me, a glass of amber liquid in each hand. He hands both of them to me then grabs a couple of pillows and a throw blanket off the couch. I step out onto the balcony and hang back as he lays the blanket down and props pillows against the outside of the doors for us to lean on. Andrew takes his drink from my hand and sits on the blanket.

"Are we sitting on the floor like animals?" I ask.

He peers up at me, his brows rising over his clear blue eyes to form lines on his forehead, but his attempt at a serious glare brings an unexpected flutter to my stomach.

"My house, my rules."

"Alright, settle down," I say, suppressing a small smile.

I lower myself down next to him and fold my legs into a comfortable position. The bars of the balcony railing now splice the view.

"I feel like I'm in jail," I joke, cradling my drink in my hands.

"A man was stabbed out here last month."

"On your balcony?"

"No, out on the sidewalk."

"Oh," I say. "But...just one man, right?"

He laughs with the glass halfway to his mouth. The sight shifts the weight that's been sitting on my chest all day. Andrew will crack the smallest of chuckles at my jokes every once in a while, but very rarely is he forced to admit he thinks I'm funny.

"What made you decide to come over?"

I open my mouth to answer then close it again until I bring the drink to my lips and take a sip. I could tell him I sensed he didn't want to be alone, but he'd just deny it.

"What is this stuff?"

"Dominican rum."

"I wouldn't have pegged you for a rum guy."

"I would hope you never peg me at all."

I snort.

"You haven't answered my question about why you decided

to come over."

I sigh, then shrug.

"It's been a really rough day, and being around you just makes it all suck a little less—don't get a big head about it."

"Too late." He pauses to take a drink and when he speaks again, his tone grows somber. "Man, you're really taking Kreisler's news pretty hard."

Of course, that wasn't the only news that rattled me today, but there are things I can't bring myself to talk about either. I change the subject because Andrew's expression grows more and more curious.

I bait him into arguments to distract him.

Our glasses get refilled, and we do what we do best—argue about things that don't matter and make bets we'll never follow up on. The night comes to life around us, the creaking of bugs, distant voices, and even fainter sirens.

Why? Why can't I bring myself to tell Andrew about Cole's invitation? Is it because I'm afraid of what he might say? Am I worried he'd agree with me, or worse, agree with Camille?

A question slips from my thoughts and out of my lips.

"What would you do if Amber came looking for you?"

Andrew's demeanor changes in an instant. His arm is stiff as it raises the glass to his lips. He takes a large drink but is slow to swallow it, unconcerned I'm waiting for his answer.

"I told you," he says. "I don't want to talk about her. And she wouldn't come looking for me. You know that. You know what I did."

We grow quiet for several seconds and for the first time, an uncomfortable silence creeps between us, making me aware of every nuance of the night around us.

In the flash of an instant, I see it. I see Andrew through Amber's perspective. It's jarring. And yet, even knowing what he did, even understanding why she could never forgive him, I can't wrap my head around the Andrew I know, with his big heart and sometimes charming personality, being the bad guy.

With Cole, I was kept in the dark in such a cruel way. But Amber has always had all the answers, known all the reasons, seen the whole picture.

Is that why she's been able to move on?

I let pain solidify into hatred until I could convince myself I didn't want answers anymore. It never mattered, though, because I didn't have a choice but to remain in the dark.

I look over at Andrew, who's still tense from the mention of his ex. Why haven't we moved on—Andrew and I? Why have we allowed relationship after relationship to slip through our hands?

I drink some more and breathe in deeply, seeking relief, but the night air goes down like sandpaper.

"I'm sorry I brought her up," I say. "I wasn't thinking."

"It's fine."

"No, I hate seeing how angry you get with yourself."

"I know. Me too."

A realization settles over me, elusive like a feather, teasing at the corners of my mind. We take a drink in unison.

"Drew? Can the rum ask a lame question—but not about exes?"

He eyes me in a careful way he never has before. I can feel the intensity in my own stare, my head abuzz with questions. It can't be the drink that's plunging my thoughts into a fog.

He sighs. "Fine."

"If we met today, do you think we'd be friends?"

Andrew stares at me for a moment, then scratches his brow and laughs. "No, I don't think we would."

I sit up, taking offense. "No?"

"Let's be honest, Mila, if we met today—and I'm talking right now at this point in our lives—we would've fucked once, maybe twice, and never seen each other again."

My mouth falls open. I shake my head and let out a low whistle, which comes out broken because I can't actually whistle.

"*Andrew Pearson.* You'd hit it and quit it? You're stone cold."

"Me?" Andrew's hand flies to his chest and now he's the one who's offended. "No, I say that because of you. You're the one who doesn't keep a guy around if there's even the smallest chance of something real."

I tilt my head, my brows furrowing. These words are even harder to process.

"Sorry, what? The guys who didn't stick around weren't worth my time. Am I supposed to settle?"

"No, that's not what I meant."

I think back to what he said, my head fuzzy from the rum.

"*Wait*, you're saying I'm commitment phobic? Fine, but

then, what are you? Why haven't you been able to keep a serious relationship either?"

Setting his drink down, he leans back, biceps flexing as he crosses his arms behind his head.

"I don't see a reason to."

"Why can't that be my excuse too? Hmm? Oh, that's right, because my vagina can't possibly see the point in sex unless it's with a man who can agree to take care of me."

"I don't make the rules."

I snatch the pillow from behind my back and hold it up over my head. "Do you want to die? Because I will smother you to death right now for that sexist bullshit."

He brings his hands around to hover at his sides, ready to react.

"You're adorable when you're angry, Mila. I think you actually grow a few inches when steam comes out of your head."

"You're dead."

I draw up to my knees and swing the pillow with all my strength, but he's too quick. He grabs it from my hand and flings it aside. I flail around trying to reach it, but he wraps an arm around my middle, trapping me on top of him. At first I'm too busy struggling to notice my real predicament but once he loosens his hold, our laughter dies away in unison.

Andrew's pulled me right onto his lap, our faces inches apart. My breath catches for a second and he seems caught in a trance, his eyes softening as he takes in my features.

Him eyeing me this way, it feels good, fills me with a

giddiness beyond the reach of the alcohol. Like the first taste of something you never realized you craved.

He moves his hand from where it had landed on my leg down to his side. Maybe it's the alcohol or the insane pounding of my heart, but I take his hand in mine and put it back on my thigh. He glances down at it, but doesn't say anything.

"Drew?"

"Yeah?"

Something lights up behind his eyes. Our entire friendship has walked a tightrope, hinging on a silent understanding, so confusing I've never been brave enough to question it. Until now.

"How come we've never…?"

"How come we've never what?" he asks.

I swallow at the sound of his voice. It's different from the one he normally uses with me. Lower, feral at the edges. Every second I'm on his lap heat pools between my thighs, suffocating my thoughts.

"How come we've never…done anything?"

Andrew's gaze slides down to my lips. He wets his own. And I can't come up with a reason for why our faces shouldn't be this close.

"You know why," he says, "you were there. I didn't want to be that guy, trying to get with you when you were vulnerable."

He tucks my hair behind my ear then softly grazes the side of my face with his knuckles.

"What about now?"

He breathes out a small breath, so slight I'd miss it if my face wasn't right in front of his, and says, "You tell me."

Neither of us moves and gravity works to pull our faces closer, millimeter by millimeter. I turn my face from his. The spell that held our lips a breath apart breaks, but I'm still tingling all over even when I slide off Andrew's lap and get to my feet. He doesn't look up at me. His shoulders sag a fraction, and he scrubs a hand across his face.

It's the rum. It's the rum. It's the rum.

But I don't care. My body moves as though controlled by an instinct I've kept caged for years. I come down over him, setting a knee down on either side of him. His wide eyes stare up at me, hovering overhead. I take his face into my hands. His mouth parts on an intake of air when I press my lips to his and kiss him.

Our mouths move with a wicked slowness, both succulent and agonizing. Each caress of his tongue sends a pulse through me. My hair falls over one side of our faces and his hands rub up my legs, settling at my hips. And with each second, the kiss rages deeper until I'm unable to catch my breath.

I pull back, enough for our lips to graze and our foreheads to touch. His breath brushes against my lips, awakening a desire to have his mouth on mine again.

He kisses me first this time. And it builds into a frenzy in seconds until I'm throbbing all over. I'm still kneeling over him, too aware of the space between my lower body and his. I start to sink down onto his lap, but his hands tighten over my hips, holding them where they are.

"Wait. I don't want to fuck this up."

At first, I don't understand what he means, but when I ignore his warning and bring my body flush with his, I understand. Somehow, this, more than the kiss, changes everything. There's no denying how turned on he is, rock hard and pushing back against me in just the right spot. The effect is immediate, a sudden shiver runs up my spine, and I suck in a breath against his lips right before he speaks again.

"We're in trouble now."

NINE

ANDREW

I HADN'T FELT THE rum until the moment she crashed down on me. I'm buried under an avalanche of need eight years tall. I never expected this to happen. How could I ever imagine she'd climb over me like this? So bold. So fucking sexy.

Her forearms rest on my shoulders, her hands in my hair. My dick is rigid in my pants and she drags her weight up and down my lap like she enjoys discovering the outline through my pants.

And fuck if it doesn't feel good as hell.

"Should I stop?" she asks against my mouth.

"Abso-*fucking*-lutely not."

My hands ache to tear off her clothes and run down her bare skin. If she were any other woman I'd get impatient. I'd want her naked already, flat on her back with her legs around my neck. I'd want her screaming nice and loud for the whole damn neighborhood to hear.

But this is Mila. How many times have I seen her walking in front of me with that tight little ass and imagined what it would be like to bury myself inside of her? No way I'm rushing a second of this. A part of me thinks this might be all in my head.

The moment seems fragile, wrapped in a bubble of lust and on the cusp of breaking at any moment.

If this is all I'll ever get of her, I need to enjoy the hell out of it. I take her mouth with mine and savor the taste of rum on her tongue. I'm already drunk off her. She grinds on me like a fucking dream, mindless and delicious, like she's got an itch she's been dying to scratch. She does it again and again, until we've forgotten our kiss and enjoy just the pressure her body places on my cock. I'm losing my mind here, so hard I might burst through my pants.

"*Oh*," she breathes out, so low I'm not sure she meant for me to hear.

I steal a glance at her beautiful face, eyes closed, lips parted just enough for the faintest moans to drift from them. She's really into it, she's got to be so fucking wet.

Don't ask. Don't ask.

"Do you know what would feel even better?" my dick asks.

My fingers slip under the hem of her shirt, grazing the skin of her stomach as I reach the front of her pants. She lets out a sudden breath and freezes. I shut my eyes. I've just tipped the house of cards. The delicate set of elusive circumstances that somehow led us to this moment.

"Wait," she says, her voice small. "What are we doing?"

"This…" I close my hands over her ass and urge her even closer, holding her tight against the tent in my pants. "We're doing what feels good. And *fuck, Mila*. This feels so good."

She buries her face in my neck and the movement brings

her hair by my cheek. The scent of her shampoo washes over me. Sweet, subtle, intoxicating. I breathe it in. She goes still, too still.

"Mila?"

"Oh my God," she says. "*Oh my God, what am I doing?*"

Her voice is muffled, but she sounds mortified.

"Mila, look at me."

She shakes her head, keeping her face hidden in my neck. I shut my eyes and hold her. The situation in my pants is now an awkward intrusion, and she's still sitting squarely on top of it. Damn it. I was slow, so careful not to ruin the moment, I allowed bullshit thoughts to slip into her head. If I'd done my job right she wouldn't be thinking about anything else but how good I felt inside her right now.

Seconds creep past, each one sobering me up, but I can't form coherent thoughts with her on top of me like this. I slide her off to sit beside me. She stares straight ahead.

"Drew, I'm so sorry."

"Don't apologize to me. I enjoyed that very much. We can pick it back up anytime, no problem."

She laughs, shakes her head, then rubs her face with her hands.

"No, it's just…everything today just fucked with my head."

"Did something else happen?"

She gets to her feet, still not looking at me. I stand up too, and turn to face her. Taking her chin in between loose fingers, I nudge her face upward until her eyes meet mine.

"Mila, don't go. Everything's fine. Look, what happened

just now, it doesn't have to be anything you don't want it to be."

"No, Drew," she says, frowning. "It was impulsive and reckless. It was a mistake, and I'm sorry."

She turns away, slides open the door, and walks back into the living room. I stare after her, like I'm seeing her for the first time since the moment we met. What we did just now? It wasn't a mistake. It was the realization of something so obvious, I don't know why it took this long to hit us in the face.

Mila and I, we make sense together.

We make so much fucking sense, and I'm going to prove it to her.

TEN

MILA

I ONLY HOPE THE weekend was enough time to flush away the awkwardness of the situation. Being around Andrew has always felt good in a way I can't describe, but climbing on top of him was like realizing I've had a ticket to a rocket that could shoot me right out of this world.

I'd been too comfortable with my surroundings to anticipate falling under a spell of longing. Our proximity dragged me into a haze and I couldn't stop long enough to think. It's been a while since I've been turned on like that. I led with secret urges and relished the confirmation Andrew felt the same. But now, the encounter is just another layer of mindfuck on top of everything I'm still trying to wrap my head around.

That kiss, it was the most incredible kiss I've had since—

"*Stop it,*" I scold myself, aloud.

But it's too late.

A different memory slams into me, materializing in my mind's eye too fast for me to push it away. It's from a long time ago, yet the details are as clear as if it'd been last night.

I stood in the middle of Tobias's New Year's Eve party, growing impossibly warm in my cardigan and sweater dress as I flirted with the most intriguing man I'd ever met. We talked and talked for what seemed like forever, and I was surprised at how much I enjoyed our conversation.

The party grew louder around us as the clock neared its final countdown to midnight.

Cole and I had inched so close, all I could smell were the delicious notes of his cologne, and all I could see were the intricate strands of colors in his eyes. I was out of my mind attracted to him, every millimeter of my body hyper aware of every millimeter of his. And when he leaned in to ask me a question, my response came a split second later.

"Do you want to go find some place quiet to—"

"*Yes.*"

He chuckled at my eagerness. And though I blushed, I really didn't care he'd noticed. There was something about this man's energy that emboldened me. It made me want to do things I would typically be too cautious to do. I'd always played it safe, always followed the rules. But that night, I wanted to finally have some fun.

For the first time in my life, I saw myself having a one-night stand. I'd only ever had sex with college guys. Boys. But Cole? He was a man.

And I could tell this man fucked as good as he looked.

We made our way through the house and out to the massive backyard. There were guests milling around there, too, but Cole knew the property well. He led me around the pool house and to a section of the backyard obscured by tall shrubs.

There was a beautiful wrought iron bench there, and a stone fountain. The lampposts on either side of us made the area glow amber in the dead of night.

The moon was lost behind clouds, just as I was lost to my own fog of need.

Cole and I stood facing each other, my hand still in his from when he walked me out here. The sounds from the party were muffled and distant.

"Now we can talk," he said.

"Talk? You brought me all the way here just to *talk*?"

He bit his lip in an unsuccessful attempt to hide a grin.

Fuck. He was so goddamn sexy.

I knew I was practically throwing myself at him. And he'd have no way of knowing it was so unlike me. It's just, I could picture myself pulling up my dress and climbing on top of him...

My breath caught in my chest when he set a hand at my waist. He eyed the buttons of my cardigan as though considering undoing them.

"I did bring you here to talk," he said. "Because I like the sound of your voice, and I hated it kept getting lost in obnoxious, drunken laughter."

His words were sweet, but my heart sank a few degrees.

What did I think? That this guy who could screw any woman he wanted would choose to screw me? I wasn't unattractive, but I also wasn't blind. I had nothing on the women at the party. Compared to them, I was just a short, plain, nobody. And yet this man looked at me...

The same way Grant looked at the woman he was desperate to be with.

And yet he brought me here just to *talk*.

Cole seemed to read my ridiculous disappointment in my body language, because he brought a finger under my chin and tilted it up to his.

"You think I don't want anything more? Because I do. Of course I do." He bit his lip again, almost as though trying and failing to bite back words. "Talking isn't the only thing on my mind when I look at you. There's a part of me that's picturing what it would be like to touch you. To peel up that dress and spread those thighs of yours and feel you around my fingers."

My pulse throbbed between my legs, and I had to squeeze them together at the growing burn. I wanted him so intensely and so desperately it felt reckless. And the recklessness was exhilarating.

"Yeah?" I nudged, my thoughts spinning.

"Trust me, beautiful. I've got solid proof of how much I want you. I'd show you, but…I did promise I knew how to treat a woman right."

No. Please show me.

No one had ever talked to me like that. No one had ever set me on fire with words.

And no one had ever looked at me the way he did that night.

Sounds from the party grew louder, people started counting down to the new year.

Ten.

Every bone in my body pleaded for him to treat me any other way but right.

Nine.

Because if him doing the things he described was wrong, then I sure as fuck didn't want to be right.

Eight.

I tried to say this, but the way he stared at my mouth rendered me speechless again.

Seven.

"I've got to be honest...," he went on, lowering his voice further as the countdown ticked on.

The cold crept up my dress and between my thighs, making me aware of just how wet I was.

Four.

"...your lips, Mila...they're making it damn hard for me to be a gentleman."

Three.

"Then don't be," I breathed out.

Two.

And that was all it took.

One.

He sunk a hand into the back of my hair and bowed his head toward my face. And right as he closed the gap between our lips, his fingers curled and tugged at my strands, sending the most delicious sting running down my spine. His mouth crashed over mine and commanded me like I'd belonged to him long before we met. And when his other hand tugged at my waist, drawing my body flush to his, I gasped. His hard-on was massive and pushed back against me, until I physically hurt from need.

I could barely hear the explosion of noise from the party when the clock rang in the new year. Cole and I were lost in each other. We kissed and kissed, forgetting the cold, forgetting the world. We kissed until snowflakes dropped down onto our faces, littering us and the grass around us in a thin sheet of white. And we continued to kiss until we could taste the snow melting against our heated skin. It wasn't until the snow picked up and became too thick to ignore that Cole finally pulled away.

"Goddamn," he'd whispered against my swollen mouth.

"*Goddamn it.*" I slam my dresser drawer shut, trying to drown out the memory.

I'm furious with myself for allowing it to take over.

Furious for the sensations it can still ignite inside me.

Stupid. Stupid. Stupid.

Why won't my damn subconscious file those fucking memories under *bullshit*?

My bad mood only lasts a few hours. By the time I get to work, my frustration and embarrassment have morphed into calm resolve. I'm determined to follow my typical routine, determined not to think of new kisses or old kisses, or anything in between.

I'm busy enough that this isn't hard at all.

Everything goes well until Andrew knocks on my door.

"Morning," he says, peering in. "Do you have a minute?"

"Sure." I stare down at my desk and move some folders out of the way, mostly for a chance to swallow and take in a subtle breath.

Slipping in, he closes the door behind him, and heads toward my desk. He looks like a different person in his suit, polished and professional. The sight makes the memory of what happened between us seem like a distant dream, except for the tightness creeping across my body as he approaches.

He's got a hand in his pocket, the other he brings up to drag across his lower face. Instead of coming up to the front of my desk, like I expect, he moves past it and around to where I sit. It's not unusual for him to sit on the inside edge of my desk when he comes by for chats. But this time my mouth goes dry.

A small smile grows on his face when our eyes connect.

"Hi," he says.

"Hi…"

I'm hesitant to say much else, not wanting to assume I know why he's come to see me.

"It's a miracle I made it today."

I tilt my head. "Why?"

"I had a rough weekend suffering from a near fatal case of chronic blue balls."

A laugh bursts from me before I can muster a serious face again. "Is that what you came to tell me? Because you asked me if I had a minute and now your minute is up."

"Come on, Mila. You've gotta give a guy longer than a minute to work with."

I start to speak, but he reaches for my hand and tugs me up and out of my seat. My empty chair slides back, hitting the other side of my desk. Andrew keeps my hand in his as he sits back on my desk. He guides me to stand between his parted legs.

"So," he says, lowering his voice, "about the other night…"

His hands settle at my hips, drawing me even closer, until our mouths are a breath apart and the air thick. My face betrays me by angling automatically toward his. My lips tingle in memory of our kiss.

"We can't do this right now," I say.

"I thought you made the rules around here." His hands inch down my sides.

"You want me to write a rule making it okay for you to come into my office to put your hands on me?"

"Is that too much to ask?"

"I can run it by HR, but I'm pretty sure they won't think it's appropriate."

"Fuck appropriate."

Andrew's hands close over my ass, squeezing tight and pulling me in until our mouths connect. His tongue teases me and before I know it, I'm leaning into his kiss. My body relaxes against his, even as sparks ignite between us.

Our kiss heats up too fast and soon the small brush fire is the size of the elephant in the room. Or, rather, the elephant in

Andrew's pants. I graze it by accident once. Then again on purpose.

There's no rum to blame this time.

A reckless little voice taunts, *just a little more. What harm could it do?*

Andrew's right hand moves around to the insides of my thighs as we kiss. His fingers work slowly to hike up my pencil skirt, inch by inch.

Just a little more.

"Do you know how many times I've thought about fucking you on this desk?"

His words are a stroke between my thighs, sending a thrill through me, my whole body reeling from the thought of letting him screw my brains out. I crave the kind of mind-numbing pleasure that could wipe away my thoughts. It's been a while since a man has been able to bring me to orgasm.

My hand gains a mind of its own, moving over his chest and down the front of his pants. He does not disappoint, feeling him in my hand makes my mouth water.

"Hey, Mila? There's a—" Janet's voice coming from the phone speakers startles me "—a woman here to see you, Camille Roberts?"

I push Andrew away and straighten, working fast to smooth out every part of my outfit. The room's suddenly a thousand degrees and I'm mortified at how obviously aroused Andrew is. I jab a finger toward his crotch, silently demanding he deal with it, but he lifts his hands in a shrug.

He can't exactly smooth away his erection.

"Mila?" Janet asks.

I rush to answer. "Yeah, uh, sorry. I'm just finishing up Andrew—*with* Andrew. A quick meeting but…uh, just give us a minute."

"Um, *okay…*" Janet clicks off the line.

I cover my mouth, staring wide-eyed at Andrew. That might as well have been a billboard advertising an event that I didn't get to enjoy to its completion. Holy crap. That might have been the dumbest thing I've ever almost done. Andrew and I are acting like stupid hormonal teenagers. We need to get a grip on ourselves before someone gets hurt.

Andrew seems amused by my desperation, but I'm relieved his erection is disappearing by the second.

Fucking snakes, that's what penises are.

He leans in to try to kiss me again, but I push him away.

"Damn it, Andrew," I hiss under my breath. "Get out of here."

"Come over tonight? You know, so we can talk?" I start pushing him toward the door, and he adds, "Or we can just rub our crotches together, whatever you'd like."

I snort even before I decide to be amused. "There's nothing to talk about. You and I are not doing this. We are not hooking up. It's not what we do."

"But—"

"*Out.*"

Once he steps out, I reach behind my desk again, clear my

throat, and let Janet know I'm ready for my visitor. It's not until Camille walks through the door that I'm hit with a realization of why she must be here.

I greet her with a hug.

"Is everything okay?" I ask. I wouldn't normally ask this, but she must know the expression plastered on her face.

"Look, I can't stay long. I just... I have something to tell you but I'm not supposed to. Cole asked me not to."

"Just say it," I mutter.

"The gallery opening. The art. It's all about why he left."

I blink like the words pelted me in the face.

"Okay..." I scratch between my brows. "Camille, you didn't have to come all this way to tell me this."

"No, I did. I need you to understand. The entire exhibit, it wasn't just inspired by you. It was made *for* you."

I press my lips together, refusing to allow the cluster of words to pour from them. Camille said she doesn't have long, and my time is short, too. There's only one question I want to ask.

"Why didn't he want me to know that?"

"He wanted you to take it in, one piece at a time, until the end." She taps a foot as she speaks, her body showing signs of impatience even while her voice remains calm. "You will understand if you go. And you should know, he won't be there. He just wants you to see the art and understand."

My eyes snap to hers. There's fire in my veins. Am I supposed to believe he's back now, after all these years, to offer me the answers I never got? No. That's bullshit. If Cole has something he wants to tell me, he can pick up the damn phone and tell me himself. He knows where to find me. He can march his butt right to my office and tell me to my face. But he's a coward. He sends an unsigned invitation and plots with our only mutual connection to get what he wants.

"Jesus, Camille. I don't give a fuck what he wants. You can go ahead and tell him that, since you've volunteered to be his little ambassador."

The words fly from my lips before I can stop them. Camille straightens the handle of her purse on her shoulder. Her fingers twitch.

Why is she so restless?

My stomach sinks. The pieces from when she and I met last week fall into place to reveal a bigger picture. *Holy crap.* Is Camille on drugs?

I look away from her sullen face and swallow, more uncomfortable than ever. The signs could point to other things. She could just be under stress, overworked. We're no longer close enough for me to ask, and my guess is she'd lie if I did.

"Cole didn't send me," she says. "Like I told you, he didn't want you to know this. But I thought you should know, in case you were looking for closure. Because, Mila? You obviously need closure."

Closure is a trap. It's the little voice of addiction telling you to go back, one more time. As if some word, some act, some gesture could somehow change the outcome.

"No," I say. "There's no such thing as closure. What happens, happens. You deal with the fallout and move on."

Camille eyes me for several long seconds. I know the accusation on the tip of her tongue.

But that's just it, Mila…you haven't moved on.

ELEVEN

ANDREW

I'M SURPRISED WHEN MILA stops by my office.

She's got her purse over her shoulder like she's heading out for lunch. My lips twitch, thinking she's changed her mind about what she said earlier. But the smile fades when I spy the far-off, distracted look in her eyes.

"Hey, I have a question for you," she says. "Have you had any contact with Tobias Kreisler recently?"

"No. Why?"

She shakes her head, scrolling through her cellphone.

"I've been trying to reach him all weekend. He won't respond to my calls or emails."

"You're worried something happened to him?"

"No, his assistant got back to me this morning. Says he's fine. I just…I guess I just thought…" She stares past me for a second, then blinks a few times.

She thought he'd let her into his life more now that he's sick. The man's warmer toward Mila than he is to anyone else, but that's not saying much. Though Mila would never admit it, she idolizes the man. She's never wielded his name for gain, but there's no doubt he's been a huge influence in her life. I have my suspicions Tobias and Mila's mother did a lot more than read cards together, but I've never said as much. If Mila hasn't figured that out, it's because she doesn't want to.

"Give him time," I say. "I'm sure he's still processing. People don't just rebound after having their world rocked like that, I don't care who they are."

She holds my gaze for a moment too long, like she's reading more into my words.

"Yeah, it's a lot," she says, that faraway gleam is still in her eyes. She seems to zone out for a few seconds, then says, "Do you want to grab some lunch with me? I'm still working on my speech for Sunday—you know, in case I win—and it just doesn't feel right. I want to get your thoughts."

"Of course, I'd love to help."

"Full disclaimer, I'll be ignoring you most of the time while I keep working on it."

"I've got some stuff to catch up on, too." I lift the tablet in my hands. "I'll choose lunch with you ignoring me over lunch without you any day."

Her eyes flick to the ceiling, but she smiles. After what happened this morning, I never expected her to seek me out. We talk about work all the way to the elevator. Two other people from our office hop onto the elevator before the doors close. Had we been alone, it would've been hard not to touch her.

Out on the street, Mila and I pass a construction site and head to the deli we frequent. She's been impossible to read after what happened Friday night. Her energy cluttered by things she won't talk about.

When we reach the deli, we grab seats by the window just as an older man in a blue tie stands up. She settles in, pulling a notebook out of her purse while I go off to order our food. We fall into a comfortable flow where neither of us seems to mind the long bouts of silence between us. She reads segments of her draft aloud a few times, and I give her my thoughts.

She seems relaxed and focused, and for a moment it seems nothing has changed between us. But everything has changed. For me, anyway. It was a wake-up call, what we did. I held myself at bay for years because I got laid often enough to not have sex cloud my judgment around Mila. I was smart enough to know the only way anything could happen between us was if and when she decided it would. We could've never bounced back from me crossing the line before she was ready. It had to be her.

Now that she has, it's like she's lit a match in me. I'm hungry for her, and at the rate I want to move, we'll blow past our chance at this being about anything other than fucking. We'll go from being friends, to being the friends who fuck. It's a recipe for disaster.

Her eyes rise to mine as I pull my drink's straw to my lips.

"Why are you looking at me like that?"

"I was thinking about what you said earlier."

"Wait—you were thinking? With your big brain instead of your little one?"

"First, both of my brains are big, thank you very much. And you were right. You and I, we can't just hook up."

She brings her pen to her mouth. "Go on…"

"Think about it, Mila. You and me, there's something here. It's so obvious. Maybe the reason we can't move on with other people is because we're supposed to move on with each other."

She stares at me for a long time, several expressions flashing across her face.

I go on before she can voice her objections.

"I want to show you this can be something real. I want to do it right. No mindless hooking up, no sneaking around the office trying to cop a feel—although, maybe yes to that."

"*Oh God.*" She cringes. "I thought we had a silent understanding to never discuss what happened this morning. I almost died of embarrassment."

"Mila, this isn't a thing we'll do in hiding. This is a thing we'll do for real."

"Are you asking or telling me?"

She cocks a defiant brow, waiting for my answer. The threat of her cunning tongue whipping back at me is one of my favorite parts of being around her.

She keeps me on my toes.

"I'm asking you out on a date, so I can prove to you we make so much sense together."

She pulls her bottom lip into her mouth, glancing down at the pages of her notebook. I slide a hand across the table and lay it over hers. Her gaze meets mine.

"I need to get this speech ready. The awards gala is Sunday night. The speeches get streamed online, shared hundreds of thousands of times. I need it to be…I need it to be real. And important."

"You're beating your head against every detail. You've got to let go a little. Real is messy. You can't manufacture real."

She drags a hand over the base of her neck, fingers splitting between the opening of her button-down blouse.

"You're right. I've got a dozen drafts. I've got to let go and pick one."

I grin wide. "So you'll come out with me?"

"Friday night. I've got a lot to do this week to prepare for the gala."

"Fri—But that's not for another four days."

"Yes, Andrew. That's typically the way the week works."

"Can we at least sneak in a little groping in your office until then?"

"No."

"Your conditions are unreasonable."

"I'm not done. When we do go out, I'll also need my feet massaged every five city blocks."

"Why don't you just wear sensible shoes like a reasonable person?"

"Why don't you quit making me walk fifty blocks anytime you take me on an outing. It's like you're a reincarnated medieval torturer."

"Date," I correct.

"Huh?"

"You said outing. This isn't an outing. I want to be clear,

Mila. This is a date. If you need more time to think about it—"

"No, of course not. I think a real date's in order. I mean, I did just feel up your dick this morning."

She looks so beautiful with that coy smile on her face. I resist the urge to lift from my seat and lean over to plant a kiss on her lips. Instead, I make a show out of straightening my suit sleeves.

"I don't like to brag, but...there's a lot to like."

"Oh, trust me," she brings her straw to her lips, "I'm quite aware."

TWELVE

MILA

ANDREW CALLS ME ON the way to my place and tells me to put on dancing shoes. After all these years, he still can't accept that I can walk a tightrope in stilettos. The cab drops us off in front of a lively restaurant. Patrons sit out on a balcony and Spanish music blares in the background. But walking in, I realize this place isn't just loud, it's alive.

All the sounds pulsing through the city are weaved into the ambiance, from the music to the hum of conversation to the glasses clinking and drinks pouring. Excited screaming and cackles of laughter. I typically shy away from loud places, but tonight, the sounds welcome me, pushing away all my thoughts, allowing me to enjoy the current moment in its purest form. I guess it's the perk extroverts enjoy naturally. The ability to put aside thoughts and feelings, to not be trapped inside their heads. The energy in the room elevates mine like a hit of adrenaline.

The walls are speckled in bright Caribbean hues and resemble the canvases of expressionist paintings. Andrew takes my hand and we follow our hostess between loud, crowded tables to sit at the edge of a dance floor. Our table is flush against a wall with a mural of people donning hats and playing music on a beach.

Andrew sits beside me, the way he always does when we are at a table for two. I'm starting to wonder if he's always opted for noisy places to justify our proximity.

The energy of the place is infectious, the music stirring my instincts to move. Several people are already on the dance floor, moving with exceptional rhythm. We watch them as we eat tapas and sip our drinks.

I lean into Andrew and ask, "Are you really going to dance with me, or are we just here to watch?"

I love dancing but as I've gotten older the opportunities to dance have dwindled down to private sessions in my living room.

"Why is it so hard to believe?" He leans in closer. "You don't think I can dance? I'll have you know, I'm pretty damn good."

I shrug and pick up the cocktail the server set down moments ago. Most men I know don't know how to move their bodies. The Hispanic men here, though, make it tough competition for Andrew.

He waits for my answer, his beautiful blue eyes narrowed and a playful smirk on his lips.

"You just don't look very coordinated," I say. "Look at your arms."

My gaze moves over the sleeves of his navy blue button-down shirt, which hug his large arms. Those firm, masculine curves are erotic in an almost confusing way. Biceps should not have so much power.

"What about my arms?"

"How do you even move them?" I mimic stiff, robotic arm movements.

"You've got jokes, Mila. How about I just show you?"

He gets to his feet and stands in front of me. For a moment, I just stare. He's so handsome. The color of his shirt makes his eyes glow in the dim lighting. His wide shoulders give me the urge to be between them and feel his arms wrap around me.

"Are you going to take off your shoes?" he asks.

"One more comment about my shoes and I'm going to stab you in the eye with them."

"Quit talking dirty to me, woman. You know I like it when you're angry."

He extends a hand and I take it, smiling despite myself. We head to the dance floor, squeezing past sets of couples that weave in and out of the way without disrupting their dance steps.

Andrew brings me out to the center of the dance floor, where we are cocooned between dozens of other dancers, moving at an intimidating pace around us. They don't pay us any mind, though, as we take our time positioning our bodies in front of each other.

He grabs one of my hands in his and settles his other at my waist. The very next thing I know, Andrew is moving to the music, guiding me along with him. My jaw drops as I struggle at first to match his pace.

"Holy crap, Drew. You really can salsa." Still not quite believing it, I add, "How did I not know this about you?"

"There's a lot you don't know about me, Mila."

He tugs me close then releases me for a spin, before reeling me back into him again. My head swirls in delightful bliss at the way my body moves at his command. The way he leads, the effortless yet masculine way he moves is sexy beyond belief.

"Clearly." I set a hand on his chest to steady myself and I find his muscles firm under my fingers. I enjoy them for only a second before he has my hand in his again.

"I grew up in the Bronx," he says, "I chased Latinas most of my life. Of course I can dance salsa."

He extends his arm. Holding out the hand clutching mine, he steps back while continuing to dance. His gaze travels down my body in a bold and unapologetic way I've never seen. And the look in his eyes when they slide back up to mine? It sends a rush through me.

"You're doing great," he says. "I can't believe how you dance in those heels. It's such a fucking turn on."

He spins me around and presses me to him, swaying for a few beats as his hand crawls over my stomach, before spinning me back to face him again.

"My heels turn you on? I thought you hated them."

"Are you fucking kidding? I only hated how much they turned me on."

He pulls me close again, and our bodies become as flush as our movements allow. His lips are by my ear.

"One day," he says, "I'm going to fuck you with your stilettos on."

His words hit me in the knees, weakening me. Lord, help me. That day could be right this second as far as my lady parts are concerned. He slows our movements down, despite the music being the same. He sets his forehead on mine and sways us nice and slow, his hands holding me tight.

How can this feel so new, so exciting, when we've known each other for so long? The Andrew in front of me is the same man I've known and yet, completely different. There's a look in his eyes now, a door that opened when I kissed him. Possibility lingers between us, anticipation for the things to come.

Strange how he's been in front of me and yet I feel like I've been missing him all this time. I didn't allow myself to see him clearly. To see us clearly. He's right. There's something here. We make so much fucking sense.

We forget the people surrounding us and dance like the floor belongs to us. We laugh and when I stumble, he catches me with ease. We enjoy a moment that stretches seamlessly to the next and is everything I want it to be. The songs blend together, and the steady flow of people around us grows and ebbs away in waves. Every time he spins me, he brings me back even closer and it stirs a flurry of butterflies in my stomach. For a time I cannot grasp, everything I've been carrying around for the past few weeks drifts far off into the distance. I know, with the clarity that comes from pure giddiness, this is what I want.

Andrew slows down our dancing again, bringing my hands up around his neck. His hands glide down my arms, eliciting shivers throughout my body. He sways us back and forth, ignoring the urgency of the song and creating our own. I'm glad because the soles of my feet are beginning to ache, but I'll drop dead before I complain to Andrew about my heels.

"I'm having a great time," I say.

"I am, too. I like to see you like this. Letting go and enjoying yourself."

"It's you. You bring this out of me. You make me…you make me happy."

"For a minute there, I thought you were going to say I make you horny."

I throw my head back and laugh, louder than necessary. Because loud laughter blends into the sounds around us and we've been laughing with ease all night at even the slightest amusement. And you know what? It feels damn good.

I've barely had anything to drink all night and I'm buzzed, feeling lighter than I have in months. It's not just my feet aching, it's my face, too.

Andrew takes my hand and leads me off the dance floor to the bar. I slide onto a stool and catch our reflection on the mirrored pane behind the shelf of alcohol.

"We look good together," Andrew says over my shoulder.

I bite my lip, resisting the urge to tell him I was just thinking the same thing.

He slips his hands around my middle and lowers his face to the crook of my neck. I stare at our reflection and a sudden worry clouds my happiness.

Every single man I've dated since Cole has faded with time.

I've got so much baggage to let go of before I can even think of getting into a real relationship.

Cole is a shadow, approaching from the horizon.

I've tried to push Camille's latest visit aside, but the offer of answers hangs over my head, tantalizing and elusive. Years and years have passed since Cole left, and the one thing I've been unable to shake is the desire to have the final piece of the puzzle. The one that will help everything click into place and finally set me free.

THIRTEEN

MILA

THE DECIDING IS THE hardest part. The torment is in the back and forth, the uncertainty, in the threat of coming to a decision I will regret long after it's made.

I've always believed myself to possess an acute intuition. My mother taught me how to narrow in on my gut feeling and how to translate it into simple truths. The skill helped me amass great success in my career, but when it comes to matters of the heart, my gut has failed me more times than I can count. The heart, it always fucks everything up. It disrupts intuition and warps sensibilities beyond recognition.

And since I can't rely on my gut, I gnaw over the choices, flipping between going to the exhibit and deciding against it. I spend the day alone, working on the speech I may or may not have to give tomorrow night. My gaze darts up to the clock every so often, the time on Cole's invitation lurching closer and closer.

When I think of Cole, my insides wrench tight, and I'm sure I will never set foot in the exhibit. When I think of Andrew, the knot in my chest loosens. I get flashes of laughter, the colors of the room spinning around me right before he catches me in his arms and the world steadies. He brings a rush of oxygen through my veins. He makes me feel like I can start fresh and break free of the binds that kept me from seeing what has been right in front of me all this time.

My ego offers up the lure of proving myself. It teases me with a glorious vision of walking into the exhibit and finding it all falls flat for me, nothing more than vague notions of things I used to feel and a man I used to love. It's a trap, but one I've yet to grow immune to. The urge to be the cool girl, the newer, better version of ourselves we all secretly wish to flaunt in front of anyone who's ever slighted us.

Back and forth my thoughts go until, right as the clock marks a quarter to seven in the evening, I get to my feet. I pull on a pair of dark jeans and a blouse, and call a car to pick me up.

I make the decision to go. I'm done with the questions, done having Cole-related things hanging over me. Camille said he wouldn't be there and I believe her. He ran from me and never looked back. I don't expect him to show his face now.

A sense of peace comes over me when I slide into the back of the car and tell my driver where I'm going. I'm heading straight to my demons because they only grow bigger if you let them chase you. I'm going, not because he wants me to, but because I'm ready to blast right through them.

I'm fucking over you, Cole Van Buren.

The drive is not long at all, but when the driver turns down an isolated road, I'm sure it's because he's gotten lost and needs to make a U-turn. But the car comes to a stop, and the driver's seatbelt clicks.

"This is it?" I ask, staring out the window. "Are you sure?"

"Yes, ma'am, this is the address."

He steps out of the car and rushes to open my door. I thank him, but my brows tense as I take in my surroundings. The road is sandwiched between two large buildings and ends at the entrance of what appears to be a massive warehouse.

"No, this is the wrong place," I say. "There's no one here."

The building is well lit, far better than any of the others around it. It looks as if someone put time into fixing up the exterior to give it more appeal than the surrounding buildings, which all reek of neglect. I suppose this could be the right place, but that doesn't explain why there's no one here. If this is an art gallery opening, where are all the people?

"Do you want me to wait?" the driver asks.

"Yes, please. I'm going to go see if anyone's there."

I step up to the steel door and my attention fixes on the small poster affixed to the door. It's the same design as the invitation. I hold my fist out to knock, but the metal rumbles against its frame as someone opens it.

An older man with tired eyes opens the door. He's dressed in a gray suit. Behind him, there's a small reception area with some lounge furniture and a television mounted on the wall. The design is modern and clean, but the room is also empty.

"I'm sorry," I say to the man. "I think I've missed the opening."

"What is your name?"

"Mila Zelen—"

He cuts me off before I can finish. "No, you're right on time. I'm Jeffrey, please come in."

I don't move. "Why is there no one else here?"

"Only one person is allowed into the exhibit." He pauses, glancing at my driver. "He can wait in the reception area if he'd like."

"How long will it take?" I ask.

The man shrugs. "As long as you want it to."

I glance back at my driver, who takes a few steps toward us as though wanting to ask questions. I know he'd stay if I asked him to, but I have no inclination to do so. I might not be Cole's biggest fan, but there's not a single bone in my body that believes he'd put me in danger. But perhaps he wasn't sure I'd come to this conclusion, which is why he wanted Camille to come with me, to ensure I wasn't put off by the isolated surroundings. I'm not afraid. I might be small, but I can handle myself.

"It's alright, Thomas," I say to my driver. "I'll call you when I finish."

He nods but waits for me to enter the building before getting into the car. Inside the reception area, there's soft music playing in the background. All of the walls are exposed brick, giving the place a charming vibe.

"Would you like some water?" Jeffrey asks. He moves with an awkward limp as he heads toward a pitcher sitting on a round table.

"No. Thank you."

My gaze travels along the walls, where hand sketched images are displayed in black frames. I recognize some of them. A sketch of a hand pressing onto a glass and its reflection pressing back. The one of the little boy walking in impossibly large boots. These were drawings Cole made in the time we were together. I stare past other sketches I've never seen before, one of a mansion made of matchsticks. Another of a grand sandcastle with a foundation the width of a toothpick. Cole was always incredibly talented in making lifelike sketches. I always knew he was meant to be an artist, but he never took it seriously. I guess he finally did.

"Ma'am," Jeffrey says, calling my attention. "When you're ready, the exhibit is a series of rooms where you start here — " he points to a door to my left " — and they will eventually bring you back here — " he indicates another door on the opposite end of the room. "But there are emergency exits that lead outside if you need to leave early."

I nod, waiting for my nerves to kick in. They don't. The decision was the hardest part. Now that I'm here, I'm just ready to get it over with. I march over to the first door and pull it open. I pause and glance back at Jeffrey before stepping into the room.

I'm plunged into blackness but not darkness. It's a strange sight. The black walls are almost indistinguishable from the black carpet. The immediate point of interest is the vague impression of a door at the far end of the long, narrow room. Standing here by the entrance, I start to get the sense I'm floating, but when I peer to the high ceiling overhead, lights and equipment reveal it to be an illusion. As if on cue, the stillness of the room is broken by the low mechanical hum of something turning on overhead. I stand and wait, but nothing else happens.

Is this it? This can't be it. My heart sinks, as I look around again for any semblance of art and find nothing. There's nothing on the walls, nothing on the ground. Absolutely nothing. I can't believe I fell for this. I run my tongue over my teeth and shake my head. This. This is nothing more than some pretentious attempt at a metaphor. What am I supposed to believe this black, empty room represents? His sad, sad heart?

Cry me a fucking river, Cole.

I take my first steps since entering the room, with the intention of turning back to the door behind me, but an explosion of color on the floor stops me.

Specks of paint appear by my feet. I step again and more colors appear. My eyes snap upward, wondering how a projector is sensing my movements. I take another step and other splashes of color scatter across the carpet.

I stand still, taking in the sight of the bright, floral hues of pinks, red, greens, and blues humming vibrantly against the black canvas.

I take more steps, but no matter where I move, the paint scatters in a widening pattern, creeping across the room toward the next door. The intent is obvious. He wants me to go through the door.

I was not expecting an immersive art show. I'm not sure if this makes dealing with it better or worse. And even as I'm sure I don't want to move forward, even as a voice inside of me tells me to turn around and go back home, my foot taps the ground to create more thin splashes of paint. There's an instinctual gratification in witnessing the previously black carpet become plastered with bright paint every time my foot touches it. The specks grow to brush strokes, slowly appearing closer and closer together. Soon, the seemingly random splatter begins to take form. As I move closer to the door, the figure of a person forms over the wall above it. I stare up in amazement as the likeness of a face and upper body materializes before my eyes.

By the time I stand in front of the door, a giant portrait of a woman is plastered over the wall. She's a giantess, sitting along the edge of the top frame of the door. Her skin is composed of thousands of little multicolored strokes that somehow come together to form a smooth and vibrant skin tone. Her eyes are tiny little strokes of greens weaved into flecks of brown. Her hair is browns and blacks with wisps of light that give it depth and sheen.

There's a serene, but deep expression on her face as she stares down at the door in front of me. Her shoulders are relaxed and poking out of a sweater. She seems at ease with her surroundings and unaware she is the subject of attention. And though she looks like no one in particular, she also looks like me. She *is* me.

The careful way she is painted, the way she is composed of all the random splashes of paint scattered about the room, give her the impression of disintegrating around me.

No.

Every speck of paint scattered across the room is angled toward her. It leads up to her, becomes her. She's not a woman scattered, she is a woman composed.

I tear my eyes from her and stare at the door. I reach for the handle then hesitate. A small displeasure at not being able to predict what lies ahead is overshadowed by the tantalizing curiosity dangling over my head.

I take a moment to assess my state, surprised to find I'm at peace. My curiosity is detached from any feelings I expected to experience. The painting of the woman is breathtaking in its detail. But it's just a painting. Whether or not she's meant to represent me doesn't matter.

I close my hand over the doorknob and slowly push it open. At first, I'm sure I've walked into a closet, and double back to catch the door before it shuts. But the glow of light from another room pours in around the edges of a second door. I head to it, and this door swings open to the second room.

I'm greeted by haze. Wisps of white fog float across the air, making it hard to distinguish the white walls of the room. Somewhere, gentle music plays. A slow piano tune, woeful and hopeless, resonating in my core with every chord. My instincts propel me forward to reach the door I spy just beyond. But more fog pours down from either side of me, filling the room and eating up my field of vision. The fog is odorless and clears my airways with ease, but I clasp a hand over my chest as I hurry forward. The more the fog fills the room, the more I'm overcome with the sensation of being unable to catch my breath. My hand stretches out, reaching for the door just feet away, but disappears before my eyes into the mist.

A soft, subtle fragrance reaches my nostrils. It's soothing at first, twisting slightly into a fresher scent before plunging into deep woodsy notes. The combination stirs inside of me, knocking against memories I've long forgotten.

A flash of Cole's smile materializes in my mind's eye like a pang to my stomach. It hurts to remember the way he looked at me. I shake the image away and rush forward, reaching the door and grasping around for the knob.

Yanking open the door, I plunge myself into the next room and suck in a breath of clean air. This space is small but clear compared to the previous room. My eyes take a few seconds to adjust. The walls and floors are both the same shade of a soothing, aquamarine blue. There's nothing in the room but unused space. The door to the next room is straight across, and I know I have to move toward it for the current exhibit to begin.

I can do this. I can finish this and know I did it, know I took the bait—not for him, but for myself. Because the last thing I want is more *what if*s knocking around in my brain. I don't care what lies ahead so long as it doesn't smell of Cole.

The moment I start to walk across the room, an image of the bottom of a pool is projected onto the floor from overhead. The lights mixed with the cool colors have a pleasing effect. Every step I take disrupts the patterns, sending ripples across in every direction. A low sound emits from the ceiling. It's more of a hum playing over other muffled noises somewhere overhead. Cold air sweeps into the room, and I wrap my arms around myself as I pick up the pace.

The projection is no longer the visual idea of walking along the bottom of a pool. It's now the very real panicky sensation that I've somehow fallen to the bottom. I look up to remind myself none of this is real, but all I find is bright light stinging my eyes. The music and the unsettling hum grows louder and louder until my ears are clogged.

The colors are no longer relaxing to me. I want out of here. It's becoming harder to breathe. I keep holding my breath, forgetting there is no water.

I clear the room and when I step into the next, my stomach drops. It's another fog room. Only this time, the fog is dark gray and menacing, wisps of it hanging in front of an endless hall. The hall stretches out before me, disappearing into a black abyss. It takes me a few moments to realize what I'm staring at is a giant mirror reflected back on itself. This room is actually the smallest one yet, but it's also the one I've been most desperate to leave. I've always hated the effect of mirrors reflecting on each other. It's eerie and unnatural. The mirror in front of me is angled to reflect another suspended overhead. The most unsettling part of it all is the way the angle prevents it from catching my reflection from where I stand. I resist the urge to step up to it as I walk past to reach the next door. I hope I'm nearing the end of this exhibit. How is this abstract art supposed to bring me answers?

I can't wrap my head around what any of this means.

The next area I walk into is the most beautiful room I've ever seen. The walls and the ceiling are made up of LCD panels, giving me a panoramic view of an ocean off in the distance. The ceiling depicts a starry night sky. But unlike all the other rooms, the path from one side to the next isn't clear of obstacles. Instead, bars run along the room in a back and forth pattern, like the lines to an amusement park ride.

The metal bar is colder than I expect when I run my hand down its length to begin crossing the room. I'm in no rush to set one foot in front of the other, awestruck by how crisp and realistic the ceiling is. At first I think nothing happens as I walk, but then I become aware of the changes. The ocean is creeping in from the horizon. Rhythmic waves crash in growing intervals, each reaching a little closer than the last. The sensation is of the water moving toward me, versus me moving toward the ocean.

The sight is mesmerizing, but being forced to zigzag between the metal bars is tedious. I weave up and down the room, back and forth, battling the urge to jump over the bars and clear the room faster. But that would be more exertion than necessary given the fact that I don't mind this room at all. The rumbling sounds of the ocean build, rising in volume as the ocean grows closer. By the time I'm halfway through the frustrating labyrinth of bars, I realize what's really happening.

The waves aren't just creeping in closer, they're growing larger and larger. The once beautiful sight becomes antagonizing as the waves roll toward me from every direction. A massive wave crashes just feet from the screen. The next wave swells up, a massive wall of water towering high overhead and growing even larger as it approaches. Soon the wave is taking up part of the ceiling too. It churns as though it might crash on me at any moment. The sight is so realistic, the sounds so intense, they cause panic to well up inside of me. I get the irrational feeling if I don't get to the door I'm going to be submerged underwater.

I half run the rest of the way, vaguely aware of the subtle sound of fast, urgent music playing. The music, it's manipulating my mood, driving up my panic. There's a giant knot of anger in my chest at Cole for orchestrating this.

Does he get off on making people experience panic and helplessness?

When I plunge into the next room, I sink back against the door as it closes behind me, squeezing my eyes shut and taking deep breaths.

This is it. I'm done. I can't do this anymore. There are no answers here. I open my eyes and the sight before me punches the breath out of my stomach. My hand comes up over my parted lips then down to my chest where a sharp pain grows with every passing second.

"How is this possible?" I whisper.

The room is an exact replica of a place I never wanted to return to. My eyes burn as they take in the hundreds of chairs lined up on either side of a long aisle. The marble floor littered with white rose petals, trailing a path down to the end. There sits a magnificent gazebo of white roses.

A memory flashes past my eyes of the first time I walked

into this room. Of course, none of the decorations were in place, but the opulence of the vast space took my breath away. I'd grabbed Cole's arm and he had leaned down to kiss me.

"What do you think?" he asked, smiling because he already knew the answer.

"*Yes, yes, yes.*" I was bouncing on my heels, giddy, and so happy I thought I'd float away. "Oh my God, Cole. This is perfect. This is it. This is our wedding venue."

The memory vanishes as brutally as it appeared.

There's no real logic to loving another person. No sane reason in surrendering your heart and mind to what cannot be seen or measured. To allow such a volatile force to reign over you. Love is neither patient nor kind, because love can't be tepid. It's unrelenting, all consuming, and unreasonable. Never in a million years would I have imagined myself falling as hard as I did for Cole.

The pain in my chest spreads across my body as I take jagged breaths, my gaze traveling up to the vaulted ceiling, across the massive chandelier casting the room in a soft amber glow. The sight would be romantic, beautiful even, if it weren't for the massive, menacing spiderweb stretched across the length of the room. All the while, the chandelier rattles softly as though something barely managed to escape alive.

FOURTEEN

ANDREW

I RACE DOWN THE streets, zipping through yellow lights seconds before they turn red. My hands tighten on the steering wheel as I try not to imagine the worst.

What the hell could've happened? Mila texted me earlier in the night telling me she went to the art show alone. I'd asked her if she wanted me to join her but her response did not come until an hour later when she called me hysterical.

"Drew, please. Come get me. Please. Hurry."

The call was minutes ago, but my heart's been jammed in my throat ever since. There was a man's voice in the background, urging her to calm down.

"Ma'am, ma'am, sit down."

And Mila screamed, *"Don't fucking touch me,"* and I just about jumped out of my skin. I yelled through the phone, demanding to speak to whoever was there with her as I threw on my jacket and raced to my front door.

The man must've heard me, because he picked up the phone and informed me in a professional and clipped tone that my friend was being belligerent and violent.

"You need to come get her before I call the police."

"*Who the fuck are you?*" I hissed into the phone.

But the line went dead.

I slam on my brakes at a red light, unable to clear it in time. The GPS system in my car tells me to turn left ahead, between two large industrial buildings, and the arrow marking the final destination sits in the center of a large city block.

The light turns green and I hit accelerate down the rest of the road, taking the turn with reckless speed. The street narrows between the buildings, forcing me to slow down to avoid clipping the cars parked on either side. I reach the end of the road, my car's headlights illuminating a woman sitting on the sidewalk with her head in her hands. A man in a suit stands over her, speaking into the phone.

I throw the car into park and run out to Mila. She looks up at me and sucks in a shaky breath.

"Drew."

There's makeup smeared around her eyes, her nose is red, and shiny wet streaks line her face. There are pieces of plastic in her hair and clinging to her clothes, as if she just shredded a wall of Saran Wrap.

"*Jesus.*"

I take my jacket off and pull it over her, then help her up to her feet. The man stands there staring at us with a detached expression. He's older, but tall, with a large middle, and a thinly shaved beard running along his jaw.

"What the hell happened to her?" I ask him.

He ends his call and slips his phone into his pocket. With a calmness I find infuriating, he crosses his arms and shrugs. "She lost it in there. I had to pull her out of a side exit, but not before she destroyed one of the exhibits."

"Are you hurt?" I ask Mila.

She lets out a laugh. I stare at her, realizing she's mentally checked out and in no state to offer an explanation. Her hands are wrapped around her middle and she looks smaller than ever in my jacket. Her gaze is on the ground, but darting around as though lost in thought.

"Come on," I say to her. "Let's get you in my car."

I glance over my shoulder at the guard or bouncer, or whatever the hell he is, as he heads inside the warehouse. Why the hell would Mila come to a place like this by herself?

Setting a hand on her back, I guide her across the street. She remains silent, but when I pull open the passenger door and rush to help her in, she shakes free of my grip.

"I've got it," she says.

I step back, pressing my lips into a thin line. I don't know what's gotten into her. She moves like her skin is crawling with things I can't see. Did someone hurt her?

I walk around the car and get into the driver's seat. I start the engine, but leave the car in park and turn to Mila. She's staring straight ahead, to the entrance of the warehouse building.

"What happened? Do I need to call the police, take you to a hospital?"

I ask the questions slowly and with as much composure as I can muster. Mila shakes her head after each one. Her lips turn down and she whispers something under her breath I can't hear.

"*What did you say?*"

She brings a hand up to her face and says, "He's a sadistic pig."

"*Who?*" I touch her shoulder, urging her to look at me, but she doesn't, she keeps her hand at her forehead, shielding her eyes from me. "Mila, talk to me. Who?"

"It was our ceremony venue, tangled up in a giant fucking spider web." Her words are low and angry. She sucks in a shaky breath and continues. "What—like I trapped him? Like he was so miserable and I was some insidious spider luring him to his death?"

"Mila, I don't know what you're talking about. You're not making any sense—"

"The whole thing, it was all about suffocating and…and drowning. And being trapped. Why? Why would he go through so much trouble to make sure I knew that was how I made him feel? How could he be so cruel?"

I reach across and take her cheek in my hand, nudging her face toward mine.

"*Mila,*" I say, staring into her eyes. "Who is *he?*"

"Cole."

The name bursts from her lips like a curse. I set my jaw and drop my hand from her face. His is the last name I want to hear.

"What does he have to do with this?"

The question is redundant, but a part of me hopes the name

left her lips in error. Even while knowing exactly where this is going, I hang on to an irrational hope I'm wrong.

"This was his exhibit, and it was all about me. He's back, Drew. He came back just to fuck with my head."

The way she's been acting, everything that's happened between us...all of the dots connect in rapid-fire succession until a clear picture forms in my head. I sit back and let out a humorless chuckle. For a brief moment, I consider unloading more questions on her, but manage to contain myself. Instead, I check my mirrors and pull the car out of the parking spot. The three-point turn on the narrow street gives me a much-needed reason to pour some of my frustration into the gearshift.

Mila's eyes are on me, probably because she's piecing together my thoughts. Reading me as always. If I'd been better at reading her, I would've known what this was all about early enough to stop it.

"You're upset I didn't tell you," she says, her voice low.

The rhythmic sounds of the road fill the silence. My fingers close tighter over the steering wheel, but I keep my breathing steady. I don't need to answer her question. All I need to do is get her home safe and gain the clarity I can't have when she's this close to me.

"I'm sorry," she says. "I just needed to sort it out on my own."

"The night you came over, the night we kissed...Did you know he was back?"

I can't *not* look at her now. My eyes are drawn to her face.

Her features are beautiful even when their canvas is a mess, even as guilt etches across her face.

It's all the answer I need.

"I thought so," I say.

"Drew—"

"Don't. Just don't, Mila." I drag a hand across my forehead, smoothing out the tension creeping down my face. "I'm such an idiot. I should've known all this has been about him. It's always been about him."

"That's not true…"

I shake my head, bringing my eyes back to the road and pressing the gas pedal. The car hums underneath me.

"We're not doing this right now."

"No, I need you to understand. I went there because I wanted to let it all go—"

"Right, because look at you, you're clearly over him."

"You have no idea what it was like in there," she snaps. Her tone is the loudest she's ever used with me, it cuts through the icy air.

"I'm not going to sit here and argue with you, Mila. It's obvious what's happening."

"Drew, look at me. I don't want to be with him, I promise you that. I want this. I want…I want to figure out what this is between us. I want *you*."

I can't lie, it feels good to hear her say that, but I pretend it doesn't. As much as I want to believe she means the words, I'd be an idiot to ignore what's right in front of my face. She's lying to herself. The night we met, this whole time I thought we were finally settling into something more, Cole has been on her brain. She might want to be with me, but she's still in love with him.

FIFTEEN

MILA

THAT NIGHT, I DREAM of fog twisting into ropes and slithering up my body like a snake. I struggle against my sheets, thrashing around until I wake, tired and hungover from the reality of the night before.

I lay still for a moment, thinking maybe the whole night was part of the dream, too. The exhibit, the hurt look in Andrew's eyes. But when I touch my fingers to my lips I remember the sting of Andrew's rejection. He dropped me off at my door. I whispered to him to come in, but he shook his head, jaw ticking the way it does when he's biting back words. Coldness seeped from his demeanor and left me feeling more alone than when I sat on the sidewalk.

I didn't know what to say, so I lifted to my tiptoes to plant a kiss on his lips, but he barely moved, hands by his sides. That was real. The clipped way he said good night stung more than the rejection, and every step he took without glancing back made me realize how hurt he was.

I shouldn't have gone to the exhibit. I knew the art might elicit a reaction from me, but I couldn't have imagined it would ensnare me the way it did. It wasn't art, it was a mindfuck. A cruel game I didn't know the rules to.

I did lose it.

I tore the spiderweb apart, screaming things I can't remember. Plastic flew in every direction until one of the doors in the room opened and the man who'd let me in ushered me back out onto the street.

I kept expecting Cole to step out from the shadows, but he didn't. I was left to process everything in front of a stranger who watched me like I was deranged. I left angrier and more confused than ever. If I had known taking a step inside that building would mess things up with Andrew, I would've set the invitation on fire the moment I received it.

I rub my face and use the back of my hand to shield my eyes, the brightness in my room too harsh. I blink a few times until a realization bolts me upright. *No, no, no.* Reaching around to my nightstand, I find my phone and check the time.

It's noon.

In a few hours, a hairstylist and makeup artist are coming over to help me get ready for the gala tonight. The gala where I might have to give a speech in front of hundreds of influential people. A speech...I still haven't finished.

The idea of it bears down on me, knotting up into a giant ball of nervous anticipation and dread. I do the only thing I know to do when I'm faced with something I'd much rather not deal with. I pull myself out of bed, throw my hair up, and fucking deal with it.

My eyes are half-closed as I head down the hall toward my

kitchen. I'm not just tired, I'm emotionally drained. Last night turned me upside down until everything I've been trying to keep buried tumbled out of me. Now I'm numb and raw all at once.

I brew a pot of strong coffee, and as I wait, I lean back on the countertop and stare at the phone in my hand. The screen is open to a message to Andrew. The last text I sent him last night when I let him know I was going to the art exhibit.

I tap the phone in my hand, trying to think of what to say to convince him last night wasn't about wanting Cole, but wanting to free myself. Whatever the words are, I need to say them aloud, to his face. He's just going to have to give me a chance to get them out.

[*Will you come to the gala tonight?*]

My finger hovers over the send button. Is it fair of me to ask? I know he's upset, but is he mad enough to miss the ceremony when he knows how much it means to me? And I know me wanting him there is selfish. It's about looking out to the crowd and seeing his face, knowing he's been by my side. The sight of him makes my crazy brain go still, his smiling eyes settling down my nerves.

He's good for me.

I bite my lip then press the send button before my pride has the chance to talk me out of it. We may not always get the things we want just because we ask for them, but there's no hope of us ever getting the things we want if we *don't* ask for them.

With a cup of black coffee in hand, I head back to my home office and settle in to finalize the speech. Maybe headaches lower standards, but there's a lot more to work with than I remembered seeing yesterday when I'd scribbled notes all over the margins. I thought I'd have to write another speech from scratch. I mean, none of the drafts are great on their own, but when I lay them out beside each other, there's a lot of usable content. The first one I wrote was too personal. I talked about my mother's death and the effect it had on my career. The second, I go into too much detail about the psychology behind my mother's Tarot card readings, and how I applied a lot of that knowledge and instinct into my own business. One of them revolves around the major life changes—including Cole—that shaped me as a person and businesswoman. A few others seem too technical in their descriptions of how I grew my company.

I end up piecing together a speech using elements from the best parts of each. I don't take a real breath until I've typed up and printed the final copy. It takes me three hours and by then, my headache has loosened into a general body ache. It seems to me I had dozens of dreams last night, and yet my body feels like it got no sleep at all.

By the time Jenny and Breanna come knocking, I've showered and washed my hair. They're loud and excited as they clear right past me with their rolling suitcases, chatting animatedly with each other. The energy of the room shifts from drab to fab in seconds flat. I smile despite my physical discomfort.

I've known the pair since high school and love any opportunity to throw their salon some business. They can take a raccoon and make it look like a swan. And that's fitting, seeing as I'm very much a raccoon today.

"Set up wherever you want," I say, from behind my second cup of coffee.

They barely hear me, already busy making themselves comfortable. I'm relieved to not have to deal with strangers today, to not feel obligated to make small talk.

Instead, I pace my kitchen as they set up and mutter the lines to my speech under my breath. Every so often, my eyes dart to my phone on the counter, but the screen display remains clear of message notifications.

Jenny calls me over.

"Honey, come sit down," she says, tapping the dining room chair she's dragged into my living room.

I walk over, my eyes still on the page in my hand as I continue mumbling my speech. Jenny and her sister have been so preoccupied with setting up they were not paying much attention to me. I felt comfortable practicing my speech, but now that I sit in the chair in front of them, their attention fixes squarely on me.

"*What the* —" Breanna's eyes widen as she takes in my face for the first time since coming in. "Mila, girl…what in the world happened to you?"

"It's waterproof eyeliner," I say. "It somehow smeared and I couldn't get it all the way off."

Breanna shares a look with Jenny, who fiddles with the row of torture tools she's lined up. A blow dryer, hair straightener, and curling iron, all plugged in and ready to go. I'll never understand the true purpose of using each one since they effectively cancel each other out.

"Tell us what happened."

"Nothing. It was just a rough night."

"Rough night?" Jenny asks. "Girl, please tell me you got yourself some dick."

"No, unfortunately I did not."

"Don't worry," Breanna says. She's started mixing up serum and face moisturizer on the back of her hand. "By the time we're done with you, you'll be sure to get some dick."

"Girl, you'll be swatting the dicks away," Jenny agrees.

Breanna's fingers work their way across my face, forcing me to close my eyes. I crack one eye open to see Jenny mouthing something to her sister.

"Can you guys do me a favor," I say, "and please stop saying dicks?"

A ping sounds from the kitchen and I practically jump out of my seat. I excuse myself to grab my phone, but when I check it, it's just a message from my driver letting me know he's on schedule. Shoulders hunched, I clutch the phone to my chest as I sit back down.

None of this goes unnoticed, of course, and both women start hounding me for answers on whose text I was so eager to read. Their questions make my head spin, so I stay vague and nudge the conversation back toward them. Soon they are the ones talking and I'm pleasantly distracted from all the hair tugging and face prodding. An hour and a half later, my face is a few ounces heavier and thick false lashes slice the world every time I blink.

I walk over to the mirror in the hall to take a look. It's a much nicer version of myself than the one I woke up to. My skin is smooth and even, my lips plumped and deep red. My eyes are big and refreshed, like I slept a full night. My hair is half up and teased with volume that brings out the angles of my face.

The sight is a confidence boost I didn't know I needed. I thank my friends, hugging them each in turn. They ask to see my dress again and I take them back to my closet and lay the dress out on the bed. The gown is made of deep red lace. It's long-sleeved but backless, with deep slits on either side. I loved the contrast between the peekaboo texture covering most of my body, while having my back exposed and my legs peeking out when I walk.

"It's gorgeous," Jenny says, running her hands down the sleeves. She glances at my arms, which are hidden inside my robe. "How come you always cover up your tattoos?"

I'm not prepared for the question, but I pull it off by shrugging. "Because it's personal," I say.

I practice my speech for another hour after Jenny and Breanna leave. Soon, it's time for me to get into the dress. I slip into the gown and put on my jewelry while looking in the full-length mirror.

The whole ride to the event venue, nerves flutter in my stomach. I check my phone twice, but there's still no response from Andrew.

Enough. This night could mark an important landmark for me. If I win the award and am allowed the platform of a highly publicized speech, it would help my business grow exposure beyond my wildest dreams. I'm determined to soak in the night.

The car rolls to a stop and a minute later, the door opens. I throw back my shoulders, lift my chin, and blow out a breath. *You've got this.* I head down the walkway and up the stone steps of the building.

When I enter the reception area, I stall at the door at the amount of people milling about. Strangers offer polite smiles, which I return as I pass. Everyone is dressed to the nines. Women with perfect faces dressed in breathtaking gowns, and confident men clad in sharp suits. It seems everyone has someone with them, making me even more aware of arriving alone. It's my first time at this event, but these are supposed to be my kind of people, like-minded successful professionals. I should fit right in. Instead, I'm sure I look like a fish out of water, overwhelmed and intimidated.

"You look lovely, Mila."

Tobias Kreisler comes to stand in front of me, dressed in his finest suit, a small smile on his tired face. I falter at the sight of him.

"Tobias? What are you doing here?"

He leans in and gives me a chaste hug.

"I'm here to watch you win, of course."

Any other day, the words may not have affected me as they

do now. A knot forms in my throat. I nod and a slow smile builds on my face.

"Thank you. God, I've been so worried about you—"

"This evening," he says, cutting me off without so much as raising his voice, "is not for that discussion."

We stare at each other, his eyes stern and unyielding.

"Alright…"

He extends an arm. I pat it before looping mine through it. Tobias knows most of the people in the room. He takes me under his wing, parading me around like a rare gem and introducing me with the fondness of a father.

We walk alongside each other, but I resist the urge to examine his appearance. It's not just our world we shape with our perceptions, it's the people in it too. I'll find evidence of whatever I seek on his face. I'd hate for him to catch me looking for hints of his condition.

Every so often, I catch myself scanning the faces in the crowd around me, searching for Andrew. As far as I can see, he's not here. It might be time I accept the fact he's not coming.

Half an hour before the award ceremony begins, we are ushered into the event hall where everyone settles behind round tables in front of the stage. Tobias and I part ways as I go to sit at my assigned table. I chat for a few minutes with my tablemates, who, not surprisingly, are all fascinating women. We fall into easy conversation up until the minute the first presenter is introduced.

Awards are doled out and graceful women swoop up to the

stage, hands to their hearts, speaking words of empowerment and hope. The energy in the room is electric, zipping between us all and gaining momentum. I'm inspired and awestruck by the company I'm in, by the words spoken from the stage. I experience it as a spectator, forgetting for several moments at a time to be nervous about the possibility of going up there myself. That is, until the award I'm nominated for is introduced. My name is called and applause erupts around me, sending my heart racing into overdrive.

SIXTEEN

COLE

EVERY PAIR OF EYES in the room is fixed on her.

It would be impossible to look away. She's breathtaking in her red dress, walking across the stage. It's the first time all night I've managed a clear look at her. I stare, trying to fit what I see in front of me with the memory of the woman I knew so well, I could still sketch every part of her in my sleep.

I thought I'd never forget her, but I realize now my memories are like faded photographs compared to the vision before me, like I've been slowly forgetting her without realizing. I don't know how that could be possible. There's no doubt in my mind she's the most beautiful woman I've ever seen. Except she's even more beautiful than I remember and that simple truth registers like a burn in my chest.

The train of her dress trails behind her, and each step reveals her legs through long slits up the sides. My gaze travels up the intricate pattern of lace, which allows hints of her skin to peek through. Every curve of her figure is a pang to my stomach.

The room goes still as Mila positions herself in front of the microphone. She stands tall, the way she always has, with the posture of a ballerina. Her high cheekbones are accentuated even further by her wide smile. Her brows rise over her almond eyes as she looks down at the award.

So familiar. And yet...she's different in ways I can't place. It's like walking into a room you haven't been in for years and trying to figure out what's changed. I'm standing here, trying to remember someone I've yet to meet.

Her mouth opens. I brace myself for the sound of her voice but am still unprepared when it echoes around me. It's like a punch in the gut after all these years, making the room shrink a few hundred feet in every direction.

"Thank you so much for this," she says, breathless.

The people around me wait patiently for her to continue. When she begins her speech, everyone can hear the words but only I know the details in between, the rich history I was part of for some time. I realize the woman in front of me is not a stranger after all. She could never be a stranger to me. I know her. I know her better than anyone in this room.

I hang back, careful not to step too far inside. A few people have already confused me with staff, asking for refills on their drinks. Wearing a black button-down shirt to an event like this was a tactical error. But I ignored the requests and the subsequent appalled expressions.

I didn't think I'd stay for as long as I have, stealing glances of Mila from between gaps in the sea of people. It's pathetic and not at all why I came here. All I wanted was to catch a glimpse of her in her seat and leave. I needed confirmation she was all right after what happened last night at the gallery. But instead of leaving when I should've, I remained rooted by the entrance from the moment I laid eyes on her.

She's closer to me than she's been in years. Steps away, words away. Words I promised myself I wouldn't say until she was ready to hear them. We all have an endless capacity for the truth, until the moment we're lied to and the truth becomes tainted. From there, that endless capacity shrinks down to a single shot.

The crowd erupts into cheers at her speech. I clap along with them before I can stop myself. Then movement in my peripheral catches my attention. Over to my left, a tall white-haired man gets to his feet and heads to the back of the room and down a straight path toward me.

Tobias Kreisler.

My hands curl into fists, tightening at my sides.

I hadn't realized he was here, though I should've guessed. He's always been Mila's sad excuse for a pseudo-father. Swoops in when it's convenient, disappears at moments when any real father would step up. I owe the biggest mistake of my life to him and his heartless games.

His face is warped by anger when he reaches me. He slows down his pace just enough to hiss at me as he walks past.

"*Outside. Now.*"

His shoulder clips mine, but I stay in place, not sparing him a backward glance as his loud footsteps fade down the hall behind me. Fuck him.

I cross my arms and lean against the frame of the archway,

keeping my eyes on Mila. She continues to speak, gaining lightness with every word. Applause cuts off her speech and her chest rises in triumph. She scans the room with more confidence now. Her eyes travel right past me, then fling back again.

Our gazes lock and I know, with every bone in my body, her insides rattle the same way mine do. She falters in her words, tries to talk, and falters again. My stomach drops. I should leave, but I can't move an inch. Not when her gaze holds me in place.

Several long seconds of silence creep into her speech. A rustle of movement spreads through the audience as people shift in their chairs, looking from each other to their surroundings. Most everyone looks right past me, searching for the source of the disruption, as though it couldn't possibly be me. But Mila's eyes hold on to me like I'm the only real thing in the room.

But then her gaze cuts away and I sink inwardly, as if someone snapped the strings holding me up. Mila recovers and picks up where she left off, though she's pale now and the words leave her lips quicker than before.

I shut my eyes. I never meant to ruin this for her.

I turn to go just as she finishes. Applause explodes from behind me. I'm halfway down the hall before the clapping dies out and the clicking of heels on the stone floor causes me to turn back. Mila's pace is steady as she heads straight toward me.

SEVENTEEN

MILA

SEEING HIM IS LIKE having poison flood my veins. Its rage and sickness distorting me into someone I don't know. My footsteps match the frantic pace of my heart. Cole's rooted to the spot, half-turned away as though not quite believing his eyes.

I come to a sudden stop a safe distance away. My chest rises and falls at quick intervals as I try and fail to catch my breath. All I see is red, and when I go to speak, my lips are stiff with anger, the words shooting out of my mouth like bullets.

"What do you want?"

"*Mila…*" He steps toward me.

A part of me shivers at hearing him say my name. His voice is rooted deep within me, wrapped in visceral memories of a time of ignorant bliss. A time of touches and whispers in the dark, and promises I believed without ever bothering to check if my feet were still on the ground.

But I'm not that girl anymore.

"Don't you say my name like that," I snap.

A man and woman walk past us, hand in hand, and they look from Cole to me as though sensing trouble. I straighten and glance around. There's half-a-dozen people scattered about the hall. This isn't an encounter I want to have in public, but what choice do I have now?

I relax my narrowed eyes, trying to dissuade the appearance of conflict. But it doesn't matter, I can't control the tension in my face. I take a few more steps in Cole's direction for the sole purpose of lowering my voice. I suck in a breath through my nose, my nostrils flaring.

"You have something to say to me, Cole?"

His downturned lips part for a second, making the smallest of movements as though words began to form but evaporated into thin air. Instead, he drags a hand across his mouth and down his chin. All the while, his piercing eyes consider me with slow deliberation.

The longer I stand here, the less stable I become.

"*Say it*," I grit out between my teeth. "I'm right here. Whatever it is you want to say, just say it to my face."

I take a breath in an attempt to regain my composure. My eyes burn under the intensity of my own glare. Blinking a few times, I scan our surroundings in time to catch sight of Tobias approaching behind Cole.

Damn it.

The last thing I need is to bring more attention to the encounter. Tobias walks around and stands beside me. Cole's shoulders stiffen, his head moves in a nearly imperceptible shake.

"I'm going to have to ask you to leave," Tobias says, his tone icy.

Cole snaps back in an instant. "I'm not going anywhere."

I go to step between them, but Tobias lifts an arm to block me.

"I can handle this," I say, aggravated at his attempt to manhandle me. Tobias is too busy staring down Cole to notice my reaction.

"Does she know?" Cole asks.

Tobias lowers his arm from blocking my way. Apprehension creeps across his face and his eyes flick to mine before settling back on Cole.

"Know what?" I ask.

Neither man responds. Not with words, but their bodies settle into a new power dynamic, with Tobias pulling back a fraction and Cole's shoulders squaring.

"You need to get out. Now," Tobias orders. "I won't let you ruin her life again."

Cole bites out a short, bitter laugh. "You're such a goddamn hypocrite."

Tobias touches my arm lightly. "Let's go, Mila." He's half-turned before he says my name.

"No." I shake free of his hold, my arms flinging back around as I set my hands on my hips.

"I want to know what the hell is going on."

Someone sets a hand on my back, making me all but jump out of my skin. My heart lodges in my throat when I see who's standing behind me. Andrew moves to my side, understanding dawning on his face as he assesses the situation.

He offers a tight nod to Tobias, who relaxes and says,

"Andrew, good to see you."

Someone calls Tobias's name from the entryway of the event hall and he lifts a hand to acknowledge them. He bows his head at me and says, "Come with me, Mila. He's not worth ruining your night over."

He holds out an arm, which I don't take. Whatever his intentions are, I've had enough of being managed. I stand with my arms crossed, staring at him. He knows I want answers, but instead of giving me any, Tobias nods to Andrew, as though passing a torch. This would be enough to get my blood boiling, but I've been watching Cole's expression since he set his sights on Andrew. It was like a train screeching to a halt. He pulled his head back in surprise then looked down to where Andrew's arm disappears around my back.

Tobias leaves, but Cole continues to stare at Andrew's arm.

"I suggest you go ahead and leave now," Andrew says, stepping up to him.

"I suggest you go ahead and get out of my face."

This can't be happening. To make matters worse, people are starting to pay more attention to us as they walk past. I smooth a hand down the front of my dress and take a long, steady breath.

"Both of you, that's enough. *Andrew, I've got this —*"

The last words grind out between my teeth, though I keep from raising my voice and drawing more attention to an increasingly tense situation.

Cole slips his hands into his pockets, unconcerned with the

hostility oozing from Andrew's posture.

"You don't look surprised to see me, Andrew. I'm guessing you've heard all about me. It's funny, man. Haven't heard about you at all."

"You haven't been around much, have you?"

"And you have?" Cole points between us. "What is this, Drew?"

My mouth snaps open in retort, but a detail of his question rattles in my brain. I glance back and forth between them.

"You two know each other?"

Andrew tenses beside me, his hand like a brick on my lower back. Cole's brows twitch in disbelief at my question, he opens his mouth, but Andrew cuts him off.

"It's exactly what it looks like," he says, taking another step toward Cole. Their proximity is now too close to be mistaken as anything other than antagonistic. Andrew cocks his head and adds, "She's with me."

Cole's face changes, muscles tensing as anger draws up in his eyes and pools there. He doesn't move, but his forearms twitch as though his hands clench in his pockets.

"Are you sure about that? Are you sure it's not me she's thinking of when you two have sex?"

My mouth drops open, eyes widening in panic and burning with mortification. All this time, my head spins at the rapid-fire way they respond to each other. These men clash around me as though I'm not standing right in front of them. Pretending it's somehow *for* me and not for their own egos, as if I'm some fragile creature without a voice and they're entitled to speak on my behalf.

Fuck. This. Shit.

"*That is enough,*" I seethe. But I go unnoticed even as I scowl up at them. They tower over me and I'm helpless to stop what's next. Never before in my life have I felt every inch of my five-feet of God-given height. Even with these heels elevating me nearly half a foot.

Andrew's fist hurls through the air and connects with Cole's jaw, sending him stumbling back into a table. Half empty champagne glasses from the cocktail hour tip over, crashing to the floor.

"*Stop it,*" I scream.

The hum of conversation that previously existed around us dies in an instant. Every pair of eyes in the room moves to Cole as he regains his footing and draws back up again. His green eyes are eerily calm as he flexes his jaw, rubbing a hand over the spot where Andrew hit him.

My hand flies to my still open mouth and despite the desperate urge to walk away from this, I can't remember how to move.

Cole takes slow steps toward Andrew again, his voice lowering as he says, "You're going to regret that."

EIGHTEEN

COLE

MY FISTS CURL TIGHT enough to send a jolt up my arms. The room closes to a pinhole and all I see is the motherfucker in front of me with the smug expression on his face.

Two strides and I've got the collar of his suit jacket twisted up inside my hands, pulling him with it. His hands rise up on either side to break my hold, but I'm prepared to shove him backward before he has a chance.

"*Stop it!*"

Mila's shaky scream makes us both freeze. One look at her face and my stomach clenches. She's trembling, her eyes wide in a helpless plea.

The audience we've garnered becomes apparent. Everyone who'd been walking about the hall is now gathering around us to see what's going on.

I release Andrew, dropping my hands to my sides. Mila shakes her head at us, disgust written all over her face. She glances down and to the right, as though resisting the urge to look around at everyone watching us, then turns on her heels and heads down the hall. The mutters of the crowd follow behind her, and a security guard approaches us.

Andrew eyes me like he's considering throwing another punch. I wish he'd fucking try. Instead, he looks back at Mila's retreating form, straightens his suit jacket, and takes off after her. I stand there for a moment, fighting the pull to go after her too.

"What's the problem here?" the guard asks when he reaches me. His tone is confrontational, seeking to escalate an already non-existent situation.

I don't answer him, too busy rubbing my aching jaw and watching Mila as she disappears around the corner with Andrew close behind.

"You need to leave," the guard says.

"I'm going," I say, but I stare at the spot down the hall for a moment longer. A flash of red reappears from around the corner, as if she's standing right out of sight. Andrew's probably got his hands on her now, trying to calm her down, whispering sweet apologies in her ear. The thought makes me want to punch a hole through the wall.

I slip past the dispersing crowd and push through to the nearest door. The night air lashes my heated face as I exit from the side of the building and walk toward the street. My phone buzzes in my pocket. I take it out and check the screen. Grant Kreisler.

I answer it without slowing my pace.

"Yeah?"

"Your ride is here, charming."

"How'd you know where to find me?"

"Mila Zelenko is at this gala. Where else would you be?"

"You got me there," I say. I turn the corner and head to the lot in the back of the building. I scan the line of cars as I approach, but none stand out. "Where are you exactly?"

"I'm parked by the fountain."

"There's no parking by the fountain."

"Then I guess you better hurry."

I hang up and walk back the way I came, turning the corner to the front of the building. I stop when the fountain comes into view. Just as I expected, a sleek black Maserati is parked in front of it. Grant leans against the side of the car. He's looking around for me and when he spots me, he spreads his arms wide in greeting.

"Flashy son-of-a-bitch," I say, reaching him.

Grant clasps my hand and pulls me into a hug.

"I think what you mean to say is, thank you."

"Yeah, that's what I meant. Good to see you're back."

I get into the car and Grant goes around to the driver side. He stops to admire a beautiful brunette walking past in a long, black gown. She turns her head in Grant's direction and a small smile grows on her lips. He stares after her for several seconds before getting into the car.

"*Fuck me*," he mutters under his breath. "I'd like to die with my face buried between her thighs."

He continues to stare as she strolls up the steps of the building. She glances over her shoulder again.

"Can we go?" I ask him, scratching at my brow.

He glances at me and seems to resist the urge to say something. Instead, he starts the car and zooms around the fountain and onto the street.

"When did you get back?" I ask him.

"This afternoon. Hope you don't mind having company, because I'm having people over this week."

"It's your place," I remind him.

"That it is." He taps on the steering wheel for a few seconds. "What happened back there?"

"What makes you think something happened?"

"Come on, Cole. I'm pretty sure that's not a hickey growing on your jaw."

I rub the side of my face again, not that the move makes it any less sore.

"Everything was under control until your father showed up."

"My dad's in there? He told me he'd be in Florida this weekend."

"Well, we know he's a liar."

"Watch it, man."

I turn to stare out the window. Even knowing what his father did, Grant's still wrapped around the man's finger. He worships Tobias just like everyone else in this city does.

"She has a boyfriend," I say.

"Who?"

"Who do you think? Mila."

Grant looks over at me a few more times before

responding.

"I thought Camille said she was single."

"Yeah, well, she was wrong. Mila's got Andrew hanging all over her."

"Who?"

"Andrew Pearson, from Milton prep."

"*Drew Pearson… No shit,*" he says under his breath. "Isn't he the reason you got kicked out? Shit, you think he's screwing Mila just to get to you? That's some cosmic karma to follow you all the way from high school."

"I'm glad you find it so amusing."

"Sorry, man. The guy definitely has a type: women who were in love with you first."

I set my jaw, tensing at the soreness, and stare out the window. I'm more bothered than I want to admit.

"Mila went to the exhibit last night. It was a disaster. I should've been there, Grant. I fucked everything up."

"Hang on. You finished the exhibit?" he asks, glancing at me as he drives. "Holy shit."

"Yeah. Holy shit."

"Only took you three years."

"Well, it took her a minute flat to tear one of the pieces down."

"I'm guessing that wasn't the reaction you were hoping for."

"No, it wasn't. She didn't get it."

I run a hand over my tired face.

Grant takes advantage of the lack of traffic and speeds

down the road. I can't afford to get pulled over, but Grant? He can afford anything.

"Why weren't you there?" he asks.

"I wanted to give her space to take it all in. I thought it would all make sense to her when she finished the exhibit. But she didn't. She never went into the last room."

NINETEEN

ANDREW

"MILA, WAIT. JUST HANG on a minute."

Ignoring me, she picks up her pace toward the sign for the women's restroom. I trail behind her. When she reaches the door, she pushes through and lets it swing shut in my face. But since the door is not, in fact, a force field against men, I push it open again and follow her in.

"*Get out*," she snaps, without glancing back.

I stay at the door, pressing my back against it as I watch her storm toward the mirrors. She sets her clenched fists on either side of the sink and bows her head, agitation coming off her in waves.

It's not a good feeling, knowing she doesn't want to talk to me. I could go, but I don't want her to be alone. I'd rather be here and have her lash out at me, than have her be out there with the coward. If he's even still out there.

I remain quiet, allowing her time to pull herself together. Mila shakes her head then lifts her sights to connect with me through the mirror. A storm of emotion twists her beautiful features into someone I barely recognize.

"You've been lying to me," she says, her voice low with

accusation.

"I should've told you I knew Cole."

"Why didn't you?"

"Because it was a long time ago, and by the time I realized he was your ex, it seemed pointless to bring it up. You were trying to forget him and I convinced myself it didn't matter because he was already gone. But the truth is, I'm not proud of what went down between us."

"Start talking. How do you know him? And what the hell happened between you two?"

I bring my hand up to the back of my neck before registering the ache spreading across my fingers. The guy's jaw might as well have been made of fucking steel.

"We went to Milton Prep together," I say, my tone flat. "I was there on grants and scholarships, one of maybe a dozen who didn't come from a rich family. Cole took me under his wing and...we were friends for a while. Until we weren't. We had a falling out."

"Shocking," she says, deadpan. "Let me guess, it was about a girl."

"It was, and it wasn't."

It was about a lot more than a girl, I just hadn't realized it at the time. I allowed my insecurities about being a charity case to grow into a massive chip on my shoulder. Cole bruised my ego and, being the hotheaded kid I was, I let my attempt to get back at him spiral out of control.

Mila watches me in the mirror and I can tell she couldn't

care less about a high school feud.

"You two need to grow up," she says. "I can't believe what you did out there. You put me in the middle of a fucking pissing contest on one of the biggest nights of my career."

"I know, I'm sorry—"

"*I felt so fucking small.*" She bites out a laugh. "First Cole showing up with his casual cruelness, like he had no idea what seeing him would do to me. Then Tobias cutting in like I'm some child. Then you, arguing over me like I'm some shiny toy for you to claim."

"I'm sorry," I say again. "You're right. I behaved like a child. I didn't need to use my fists to let your ex know you're with me now."

"I'm not with anyone but myself," she snaps.

I press my lips together, regretting my words, her anger rolling over me like barbed wire. She draws in a steady breath before straightening to take in her appearance. She sighs, her lips turning down, then leans in to inspect her reflection. My gaze lowers to the way her dress clings to her ass as she leans into her reflection.

I get the urge to slide my arms around her middle, to bring her comfort with my touch. The fact I don't is only a testament to her words. She's not mine. Despite the look in her eye on the night we danced like the world belonged to us. She'd leaned into my touch then, but something tells me she'd shrink away from it now.

She's thinking about him and I hate it. It's why I lost my

temper when he said what he did. It's the constant question gnawing at the back of my head, whether I'll ever be able to truly drive him out of her mind.

Of course she's not over him. I witnessed first-hand the struggle she's lived to even get to this point. She's never let anyone else in to take his place. She's never given anyone else the chance.

"I've got to go back in," she says.

"Do you really want to go back there?"

"Obviously, I don't. I can barely see straight I'm so goddamn pissed, but it'll look worse if I leave now.""

"Since when do you let yourself feel pressured to do anything you don't want to do, regardless of how it looks?"

She lifts a hand to her forehead. She's tense all over, trying and failing to hide how much seeing her ex has rattled her.

"You're right, it's almost over, anyway. It's not like I need to risk embarrassing myself any further."

I take careful steps over to her, and even when her gaze snaps up to mine again, she doesn't warn me off. I turn her around to face me and run my hands down the sleeves of her dress, the lace prickling my palms.

"Let's go," I say, brushing her hair back behind her ear. "I'll take you home."

"Fine, but just…I need a minute, Andrew."

"I'll be outside."

I step backward toward the door, watching her expression change. Her brows knit together and secrets swim past her eyes.

TWENTY

ANDREW

"MAYBE YOU SHOULD SIT for a minute and cool off some more before you break your house."

Mila ignores me.

A pot of boiling water rattles on the stove. I drum my fingers against the granite of the island countertop, where she banished me after the first time I tried to help.

"I hope you're hungry," Mila says, her expression grave enough to warn me against being anything but.

"I'm starving." I point to the stove. "Are we having a large pot of tea?"

My tone is playful, but she shows no signs of warming up. She slams the refrigerator door shut behind her and walks over to the counter. It's a strange sight. A woman clutching a head of cabbage and a bag of carrots while wearing a gown and five inch heels. She's so lost in thought I don't think she can hear the clacking of her heels on the stone tiles. I doubt she realizes she forgot to take her shoes off. She stormed into the kitchen as soon as we got through the door, mumbling things under her breath. I tried to stay out of her way, but when it became clear she planned on wielding pans around I tried to reason with her and almost lost an eye.

Mila arranges the vegetables on the counter across from me, setting them beside the ingredients she grabbed from the pantry. I have no clue what she's making, but I've never heard of anything good coming from boiled cabbage.

"You know, you don't have to cook, we can order something."

Her eyes snap up at me. "These vegetables will go bad if I don't use them. I've got a new grocery delivery coming next week."

I put my hands up. "Okay, noted. But, could you put the knife down when you talk to me?"

Again, my attempt to make her smile gets no reaction. Her face remains serious as she picks up some potatoes and begins skinning them like they insulted the motherland. She dumps the vegetables inside the boiling water, then pours chicken stock into it as well.

"What is it you're making again?"

She doesn't look when she answers, her eyes trained on the slow chopping of cabbage.

"Red borscht. It's a Ukrainian soup my mom used to make."

"Are you sure you need that much cabbage in it?" I ask before I can stop myself.

She pauses to look at me, eyes narrowed. "Do you have a death wish or something?"

I put my hands up and hold her gaze for a beat before she

turns away. She gathers up all the cabbage, heads over to the stove, and glares at me before she dumps it into the soup, daring me to stop her.

The steam from the pot wafts my way as she gives it a stir. Rich herbal scents wash over me with a sweet nostalgia I can't place. It doesn't smell so bad after all.

"I'm not trying to be a smart ass," I say. "I'm just genuinely curious if you always cook with stilettos on? Because that's fucking hot."

Her eyebrows draw in at my question. She stops to glance down at herself then back up at me. I can see she's considering taking her shoes off, but then she looks up at the cabinets and decides not to.

She opens a cabinet, closes it, spins around, and heads back to the pantry. After scanning the shelves for a few seconds, she slams the pantry door shut and heads back to the kitchen cabinets. She blows out a breath to move a strand of hair that fell on her face.

"What are you looking for?" I ask, sensing frustration boiling inside her hotter than the water rattling the pot. Sometimes I wish she would just yell outright, instead of steaming inwardly in an attempt to maintain her composure.

At my question, Mila mutters something that sounds like *flour*. She begins opening and shutting cabinets with more force than necessary. The last cabinet she shuts, bangs back as though an item shifted out of place. She opens it again and something falls down on the counter and explodes into a cloud of white dust.

"*Motherfucker!*" Mila screams.

She throws her hands up in the air, shaking with anger and sending more flour swirling into the air around her.

I rush over to where she coughs and splutters. Her face, her hair, her dress, everything is covered in flour. Brushing a hand over her face, I wipe away some of the white powder from her eyebrows.

"You found the flour," I whisper.

I pull my lips inward to form a tight line.

"*Andrew,*" she snaps, her eye twitching. "This is *not* funny."

I nod, mustering a serious expression only because I'm holding my breath. I tuck a white strand of hair behind her ears and stare at her. She has no idea how bad it really is.

"I'm sorry," I say.

Mila sighs and a puff of white lifts from her chest and hovers over our faces. A slow wheeze of laughter escapes me. Just when I think I'm in trouble, a grin splits across her face and laughter erupts from us both at the same time.

We laugh for a long time, me much harder than her. But when our laughter dies out, Mila lifts a strand of her now-gray hair then looks down at the soiled sleeves of her once-beautiful dress.

"*What a fucking night,*" she says, throwing her head back with a groan. "I should go take this dress off."

"I can help with that," I say, but when she squints up at me I pull on an innocent smile.

She lets out another sigh and backs into the counter, her shoulders sagging.

The rejection stings more than it should.

"I'm still mad at you. You know that, right?"

"I know. I meant it when I said I was sorry about tonight," I say. "I'm sorry for not telling you I knew Cole. I'm sorry for the role I played in upsetting you. I just...I don't know where we are, Mila. You and me. It's hard to read you, sometimes. I don't know what you want."

She covers her eyes, mouth opening and then closing again.

I draw in a slow inhale, dreading whatever thoughts are swirling around in her head. I have the strong suspicion I'm not going to like what she's about to say.

"I want everything to go back to the way it was," she blurts out.

My response is a slow blink, my chest rising and falling at steady intervals as silence settles between us.

She goes on before I can speak. "I've been kind of a mess, if you haven't noticed. This time of year...it always screws with my head. If I'd been thinking straight, I wouldn't have kissed you. Because you mean more to me than the mindless urge for physical contact."

I step in front of her, setting my hands on her waist. She shifts and flour dusts the sleeves of my suit. She looks up at me and I wipe more flour from her cheeks. Not that it makes a difference.

"Mila..."

"Drew, we can't do this."

Even before the words leave her lips, my heart begins to race in my chest. I draw my arms around her middle slowly, giving her time to react.

She doesn't pull away.

"Things with you are never easy, Mila. I get that, but I don't care. I don't care if I've got to walk uphill the whole way to make it work. I want you."

The delay in her response weighs heavy in the silence.

"I don't want to lose you," she mutters. "Every relationship I've touched since Cole has turned to dust in my hands. I don't think I know how to give myself to someone again. And I don't want to hurt you."

"You couldn't hurt me, not unless I let you. Look, I know Cole being back is messing with your head. But I'm here, Mila. I've been here this whole time and I'm not walking away now."

"I don't know why I let him get to me like this."

The words are low and fast, like a thought escaping her lips. They weren't meant for me to hear.

"He makes you angry because he's everything you're scared of."

"I'm not scared of him," she argues.

"That's not what I mean," I say. "You're scared of the unknown and the unpredictable. You're scared of who you are around him. You're not yourself."

I lean back to look at her. She nods but remains silent, gaze cast downward. I run my hands over her arms. I ignore the clouds of flour hanging in the air around us. It's strange, but I don't think we could've had this conversation if she weren't covered in white powder.

"I should go clean up," she says.

I take a step back and glance down at my suit, which now matches her dress in patches of white.

"Stay here and keep an eye on the soup. But don't touch it." She blinks up at me all serious-faced for a few seconds, then adds, "Why are you looking at me like that?"

I try not to grin, but the concern on her face is too genuine not to.

"You look like an angry ghost and it's so sexy, it's killing me."

"Are you kidding?" she asks. "This is turning you on? I look like something that's about to be deep fried."

I shrug. "Yeah, I mean, I don't know what else to say. It just works for me."

Her gaze flicks to the ceiling. She points to me, then to the soup. I watch, amused as she turns on her heels and walks away. Wisps of flour follow her movements out of the kitchen. When she disappears down the hall, I roll up my sleeves and get to work cleaning up the mess. It's a task that proves to be tedious and yet, not enough to distract me from the knowledge Mila is currently stripping off her dress just a few rooms away. I ignore the nagging in the pit of my stomach. The one that's been growing since last night when I picked her up from the exhibit.

I can lie to myself as good as the next guy, but there's no

escaping a truth that insists on pelting you in the face. It's one thing to not be over your ex, and another to have him actively trying to get you back. It doesn't matter if my ego is bruised that she's not over him — it's not about me anymore. It's about making sure Mila doesn't get sucked into Cole's orbit again. I'd catch a grenade for that woman. I'd let it splinter me if it meant keeping her from getting hurt.

TWENTY-ONE

MILA

THIS IS THE TIME of year I dread the most. Not only is it the anniversary of the wedding I never had, but it's also the anniversary of my mother's death. She passed away three years and a month from the day Cole left.

The events have layered over each other, making it impossible to think of one without thinking of the other. And every year as this week approaches, I'm trapped in a mood I cannot control. It's hard to face the reality of wounds never quite healing.

It's frustrating to accept we only move in circles. I don't want to believe it's true, but every year around this time I begin to see Cole's face in every crowd. I hear my mother's voice in the dead of night. They haunt me together, driving me to obsess over the things I should've said, or the questions I could've asked. And though I've never been able to escape this pattern, or even brace myself for it, I've done this enough to know there's a point where the spell breaks and I'm allowed to repress the memories again and move on. At least for another year.

This year is different. This year Cole's face is no longer a mirage in the crowd. His haunting is no longer a nightmare in the middle of the day. It's real. He's back. He's here.

I wake for the second morning in a row weighed down by bitterness and resentment. There are lots of people I want to blame, but the truth is there's no one to blame but myself. For the last few years, I convinced myself I didn't need answers. It's easy to tell yourself you don't want the things you're sure you'll never have.

And now, as I dress for work, I realize I'm done pretending. I let my pride get in the way for too long. I've never been able to shake off the way I broke down on the phone with Grant all those years ago, begging him between pathetic sobs to tell me what happened. Grant wouldn't tell me, and it felt as though I'd been dropped for a second time in just as many days by yet another man I thought I could trust.

I closed up after that, hating what the pain did to me. I refused to show my weakness to anyone in such a raw way ever again. It was the worst kind of torture, to be surrounded by people who wouldn't tell me what they knew. So I pushed away those I could, and pretended to be okay with those I couldn't.

I ask my driver to take a detour this morning on my ride to work. We get caught up in traffic and I sit in silence, plotting the way I will get answers. We ride over the Brooklyn Bridge, leaving the city behind us.

We arrive at our destination, coming to a stop along a street lined with small shops. I find the one with the rose-gold sign and white script lettering.

Bakeology Cafe.

I get out of the car and I'm overcome by the decadent aroma wafting out onto the street. I follow the scent inside, powdered sugar with hints of fruit and vanilla. The smell alone is enough to sag my tense shoulders, but the view inside is a small oasis from the city street.

Slab and cement are replaced by bright and cheerful colors. Sounds of traffic are exchanged with the chatter from customers in a little sitting area across the counter. A long row of tall display cases boasts an impressive array of cakes, pies, donuts, and other pastries.

I move farther inside, catching the attention of a fresh-faced young woman who flashes a huge smile and asks what I would like to order. I start to tell her whom I'm here to see, but a figure at the open doorway to the kitchen catches my attention.

Camille steps behind the counter wearing a white apron. She stops dead when she sees me, both surprise and worry ticking past her face.

"Hi, Camille." I offer a small smile despite losing the warm sensation I got when I first entered the bakery. She looks no better than the last time I saw her. "Can we talk?"

She hesitates before nodding.

"Of course, yeah, come on back."

She glances away and undoes her apron with clumsy hands, setting it somewhere behind the counter. I follow her down a short hall, past where several of her employees mill about, and into a small office with an oversized window overlooking the kitchen.

Camille closes the door behind us and offers me some coffee, which I decline. She then offers me some pastries, which I also decline. She sits on the edge of her desk and crosses her arms as though she's cold.

"Did you go?" she asks, biting at the corner of her mouth.

The question is innocent, but the show of nerves is the only evidence she knows why I came to see her. The whole ride here I'd been assigning blame to Camille for misrepresenting the exhibit to me. After all, hadn't she been the one to tell me it would bring me closure? Hadn't she insisted it would be the best thing I could do?

I sigh, shaking my head. "Yes, Camille. I went. I saw it all, and I want to know why you sent me."

My voice is calm. I expected to speak to her in a clipped tone, reflecting my frustration toward her. But as I stare at her now, it's hard to do. Camille seems fragile, a shadow of the woman I used to know.

"I — Was it bad?"

I shut my eyes at her question. Of course. Of course she hadn't seen the exhibit herself. She sold me on going when she had no clue what it was about. Had Cole lied to her?

"It was bad, but I'm fine now. I just want the truth. Why did you lie to me? Why did tell me it would bring me closure? Was it because it's what he told you to say?"

"I lied. Cole never sent me an invitation, he only sent me to deliver yours."

My mouth is slow to part. "You…you said he—"

"He wanted you to go on your own, he never asked me to convince you. I just…I know you and I knew you wouldn't go. I was trying to fix everything."

"What's everything?"

She stares at me, unblinking, her eyes wide and glossy.

"You…and him…it's my fault, Mila. Everything is my fault."

I shake my head, not understanding. Camille wasn't with Cole on the day of the wedding. She was with *me*. She had no idea what happened to her brother, I watched the genuine shock on her face. She might have pieced together the events later, but if she did she kept me in the dark.

"*What are you talking about?*"

"I wasn't a good sister. Growing up, I never protected him from my world. I should've been more careful. I should've…"

I let out a small breath, impatient. I'm familiar with Camille's remorse. She told me long ago how much guilt she carried over Cole's troubled teenage years. How long would she carry that around? He's a grown man now, just like he was when he left me.

Camille looks to the ground and blinks a few times. Her arms are still wrapped around her, and she shifts where she sits as though she'd much rather stand.

"Camille?" My tone is soft, but with a small plea for her to look at me. She does, and I take a step closer and set a hand on her shoulder. "You don't have to fix anything. Cole can't hide behind his childhood. No one made him do the things he's done as an adult. So please, stop looking so guilty. I don't blame you for anything. Except lying to me. That was shitty."

She nods, biting out a laugh. "Yeah, I know. I just wanted to make sure you went. It meant so much to him. He didn't want anyone to see the exhibit until you did."

I grind my teeth to keep from telling her what I think of that. It meant so much to him that I experience his cruel feelings of entrapment?

Camille glances up and notices my face. "Did it not help, at all? Did you not get any answers?"

"Oh, yeah. I got answers."

Just not the ones I wanted.

We watch each other in silence. Every second dread spreads across my insides at the question I know I need to ask, and the answer I know she will give.

"I hope you don't mind me asking, but are you okay? You don't seem like yourself."

"Huh?" she asks, true confusion in her eyes. "What do you mean?"

"You just…you don't seem like yourself. You seem…"

It's hard to say. Not because I don't have the words, but because we are no longer the friends we used to be.

"I haven't been taking care of myself," she says, nodding at her own words. "I've been working too hard, not eating enough. I get obsessed sometimes."

"Okay, okay." I nod too, because I want to believe her.

"You'd tell me, right? If you needed help?"

Her eyes snap to mine. "No, we've got plenty of help."

"I'm not talking about the bakery."

She turns her head a fraction, as if wanting to look away from me, but her eyes remain locked onto mine.

"I better get back to work. We've got a huge catering order to fill this morning."

My mouth opens but what I want to say is lost in the sudden chill between us. I came here because I wanted to blame her for my decision to go to the exhibit. I came here hoping she'd admit to being in on the torture. But when I turn from her to leave, there's a weight in the pit of my stomach I can't place. Maybe it's the difference between who we used to be back when we told each other everything and the strangers we've become. Even with our feeble attempts to keep in touch, it's never been as obvious that we won't ever be the same. And it's my fault.

I make my exit, but not before purchasing a box of sweets for the office. I thought I'd leave feeling better than I had when I woke up this morning, but I don't. There's an unsatisfying swarm of emotions deep in my belly, each too uncomfortable to hold on to long enough to identify.

TWENTY-TWO

MILA

I STALK INTO MY office, frustrated by my own mood, and embarrassed by the glances from the people I pass on my way to the elevators.

Have they seen a video of my humiliating speech?

My stomach sinks further. There's also the possibility of a video featuring two men fighting over me like idiots.

My mood is hard to bury around Andrew. I know I shouldn't dump it all on him, but seeing him right now only reminds me of the most embarrassing night of my life. He knows I'm going to need a little more time to get over it. My professionalism toward him is colder than usual when he joins in on an afternoon meeting with a client. I catch him eyeing me for longer than necessary. When the meeting ends, he walks the client out, engaging in the small talk I've never been good at.

Andrew returns to my office a few minutes later.

"Hey, Mila, I forgot to mention…I was looking through my calendar and I don't see any room for that appointment you made."

I stare at him, my head tilting in confusion.

"The appointment," he insists. "*You know*, to be mad at me

for the rest of time? Yeah, I checked and I just don't have time for that."

The teasing catches me off guard and I almost crack a smile. He's getting me right where I'm weakest, my guilt over my own bad mood. Damn it if the guy doesn't know me like the back of his hand.

"Alright, then," I say, leaning back in my chair. "I guess I'll have to shorten your sentence."

"*Would you?* That would be great. You've been cold as ice with me all morning. I'm freezing here."

"Let's make this all about your feelings then," I say.

"Can we?"

Again, I almost smile. The block of resentment I've been trying to hang on to out of principle already pooling at my feet.

"You're a baby. I've been mad at you for barely a day. I've been known to stay mad at people for decades."

His expression softens a few degrees, and so does his voice as he lowers it a notch. "I know you have every right to be pissed at me. But I miss touching you."

I glance down at his chest, then back up to his eyes. I miss touching him, too. Just a few nights ago we'd been right on the cusp of something more, something real. Now it all seems further away. I want to pull it back in. But I also want to push it all away.

"Come here for a minute," he says. "I've got something to show you."

His playful tone brings on the vision of his hands on my

body. Of our desperate kiss. Of me on his lap and his erection pressing against me.

My eyes narrow and drop to his crotch before I can catch myself.

"*No*, Mila, not that. Though I like where your head's at. I'm talking about something in the break room." He waves me over. "Come on, I'll show you."

I muster up the energy to get to my feet and around the desk to reach him. He sets a hand on the small of my back and guides me out into the hall. We're quiet the whole walk. Andrew crosses through the door first, and when I follow, cheers erupt across the room. I blink at the sight of my employees crammed around a cake. Both of my hands fly to my chest.

"Wow," I say.

"We wanted to make sure you knew how proud of you we are," Andrew says.

I make my way around the room, thanking people and hearing their kind praise. A genuine smile creeps up on my face and my spirits lift a fraction. We eat and chat amongst ourselves for well over half an hour. Afterward, Janet walks me back to my office to discuss tomorrow's schedule. As we enter, she mentions watching my speech.

"Was it painful?" I ask in a flat tone, hiding my concern.

"What do you mean?"

Her confusion is too genuine to pass as politeness to spare my feelings. We move behind my desk and she pulls up the video on my computer. At first, I'm sure she's got my speech confused with someone else's. But then the video loads with the image of me in my red dress, my cheeks flushed. I cringe, waiting for the moment when I spot Cole standing in the back of the room. I wait, and I wait, but the moment doesn't come. What plays in front of me is a smooth speech with no interruptions, my stuttering edited out. My pattern of speech accelerates toward the end, but the way it's edited makes it seem like I do this because I'm running out of time, and not because my heart is punching a hole through my ribcage.

I sit back in my chair, disbelief and gratitude swelling up in my chest. I didn't realize these speeches were altered. Edited so well between shots of the crowd, you wouldn't be able to tell unless you watched the speech live. It's a small consolation that the hundred and twenty-five thousand people who watched the video didn't have to witness what really happened last night.

I wish I could have my memory edited as well.

Picking up the schedule Janet dropped on my desk, I tap the end of a pen to one of the names.

"Hey, Janet?" I call out as she steps into the hall. "What is this lunch meeting with Grant Kreisler tomorrow?"

"His assistant called first thing this morning asking for your next availability. It sounded urgent, and he said you've been waiting to hear from him."

I nod. "Yes, thank you."

I watch her walk away before turning my attention back to the schedule. The request could only mean Tobias came to a decision about his son's inheritance. But would Grant be ready to discuss PR strategies this soon? He should take time to process his father's news. Regardless, I dread having to speak with him. Now that I know Cole is back, Grant Kreisler's name has moved to the position of the second-to-last person on this earth I want to see.

Those two have always been attached at the hip, and I've never understood why. Grant lives for thrills and immediate pleasures. And though I've heard of Cole's wild days, the man I knew seemed grounded and not as sheltered by his family's fortune. I'd been drawn to the deliberate way he lived his life, taking everything in as if fearing he could drift away at any moment. Then again, he did just that. And come to think of it, Grant Kreisler might be the only person who knows exactly why.

TWENTY-THREE

COLE

MY EARS RING WITH the words chanted around me, the ones rumbling from my own throat. When I finish, the final words leave a bitter taste on my tongue. I don't want serenity tonight. I don't want to accept the things I cannot change.

I sit with my legs parted wide, my forearms resting on them and my head bowed toward my hands. There's a man to my right and another to my left. We sit in a close circle and though the floor is open for sharing, silence stretches out between us instead. It's a comfortable silence, the type needed for someone to muster the fortitude to speak the traditional opening line.

The one we've all said aloud countless times, but never seizes to ground me in its truth.

"My name is Ethan, and I'm an addict," says a deep baritone voice.

I glance up, surprised to see who the sound came from. Ethan's come to the last three meetings without uttering a word. Not that I have either. I've been going to different meetings for years, back in Chicago and here in New York. But I've never been one to share much.

I get more out of listening.

Ethan shifts for a moment, as the attention in the room settles on him. His eyes sweep across the rest of us, their light blue hue a sharp contrast to his deep olive skin. His white t-shirt hangs on him, making him look younger than he already does. He clasps a hand over his opposite arm, fingers twitching over his skin. In that movement, I see myself in him. I can imagine the way his skin is crawling.

I felt the same way the first time I went to a meeting. Until I realized this isn't a place for shame. It's a place of strength. A place for self-awareness and reflection.

Ethan lowers his gaze to the floor between us before speaking again.

"I almost used last night. It's been four months and I was doing pretty good. I put all my energy into my poetry, you know, just getting all that poison out of me. I'd wake up in the middle of the night shaking, and I'd just grab a pen and start writing until the words came out steady. That was really working for me..." He pauses, nodding at his own words. His gaze darts around the floor. "Last night, I went to a jam session—it's where I perform my poems, because saying the words out-loud was helping too. But then I saw her again. Olivia—she's my ex—she was there, on the stage. I don't think she even saw me, but she stood up there and just slaughtered me with her words like she hoped I'd hear them." He rubs his arm. Silence rings in the room, and nobody moves. "I've tried to stay away from her, you know, because...because I'm no good for her. And I just ruin her. I ruined her. But she came looking for me last night, and I don't know, man…I don't know if I can forget I need her. Because she's the one thing I want more than heroin. But she's also the one thing that can break me enough to get me to start using again."

He stops abruptly, looking around at the rest of us. There's not a single ounce of judgment on anyone's face. No one speaks, but a few people offer him nods of encouragement.

Outside of this room, these men are strangers. But in here? We share the same struggle, a fight we endure every single day. Despite how different our stories may be, this is a safe place to speak about our deepest hopes and desperations. It took me a long time to realize this type of vulnerability can only come from a place of courage. Recovery requires courage.

"Anyway," Ethan starts again, running a hand over the back of his neck. "That's it. I just, I just wanted to say I really wanted to use, but I didn't. I'm still clean. Thanks for letting me share." He mumbles the last words.

"Thank you for sharing," the room erupts in chorus.

I try to join in, but my mouth has gone dry.

Everyone goes quiet. I glance down at my hands as Ethan's words continue to burrow under my skin in the silence.

There's no pressure to fill the lull, even as entire minutes tick past. It could stretch out for the rest of the hour and we would know our time was better spent here than it would've been anywhere else.

I clear my throat, then hear myself speak.

"My name is Cole, and I'm an addict…"

A few people look up at me, the thinly veiled surprise on their faces reminding me I rarely speak. But it's been a while since I've had as much on my mind as I do tonight.

"I've been sober three years. I didn't realize until just now, listening to Ethan, it's been my art keeping me clean." I pause, meeting his eyes. He nods then looks away. I go on, "He's right. It does help to get all the poison out of your head. I started out like him, just wanting to do something with my hands when the cravings hit. I started making things I never knew I could, and it grew into a lot more than I imagined it would. I started my own business. I even designed an exhibit to showcase everything I'd been working on. When I finally finished, I realized there was only one person who I really wanted to see it. She's a woman I hurt badly. And for a long time, I wasn't strong enough to face her, even if just to apologize. Seeing her again would've shattered me, undoing all my progress. But I'm finally in a good place. I'm finally strong enough to show her what's inside of me." I swallow, then shake my head. It's strange, the slow build of energy coming over me as I speak, as if a truth I never expected is now piecing together in my head, one syllable at a time. And something's shifting in me. The hopelessness is settling into determination. The pain into fuel. "I didn't come here to get her back. Honestly, I never thought I could. Even when I was with her, I knew I didn't deserve her. I still don't. But last night, I saw her again for the first time in years, and I swear it was like stumbling right off the edge of everything we used to be. She wasn't the woman I remembered. She was...more. And yet, she was familiar enough to remind me of why I haven't been able to move on." I stare at the floor, my own words washing over me as if someone else had spoken them. "She's with another guy now, but I don't think she loves him. And I know I didn't come to get her back, but now it's all I can think about. If there's a chance she'd forgive me for what I did, then I can't walk away. Because it's been eight years, and I still can't get her out of my system."

TWENTY-FOUR

MILA

FOR WHO KNOWS HOW long, I've walked through the streets of Manhattan without the slightest inkling that Cole moved through them as well. I was doing just fine then, and I'm going to be fine now. The city is big enough for the both of us, and if I've gone this long without running into him, I can go twice as long without ever having to see him again.

I pack my bag with pens, my tablet, and a notepad, and head out to my meeting with Grant. Outside, the sun glows from behind the thick white clouds, making the overcast skies impossibly bright.

I reach the cafe where Janet arranged for us to have lunch. He's not here yet, but I'm not surprised, the guy's never been known for his punctuality. I order a coffee and a sandwich and sit by the entrance. I busy myself checking through emails on my tablet.

The door chimes behind me for the third time since I've sat down. I resist the urge to check to see if it's Grant. He's five minutes late and I suspect he's not showing up for at least another five. What he'll find when he gets here will be of his own doing. My annoyance is bubbling up by the second.

The rush of air from the closing door brings with it the traces of a scent that knocks into me, sending chills up my arms. I freeze with the cup of coffee halfway to my mouth then set it back down without taking a sip.

Cole appears before me. Even with the warning of his cologne, I'm not prepared to see him. Words lodge in my throat and my entire body locks up.

"Don't go," he says, sitting in the chair across from me. He leans forward and sets his arms on the table. *"Please stay."*

The low rumble of his voice drowns out the background noise like he's pulled me underwater. My reactions slow, my gaze traveling up his arm and along the intricate designs tattooed there. I'd forgotten how beautiful they are. I used to trace them with my fingers, asking him to tell me what each tattoo meant, even when I already knew.

Cole bows his head and peers up at me from underneath furrowed brows. Piercing green eyes lock me in place for several seconds before I manage to break away. Sound rushes back to my ears and my pulse quickens. There's a warning rising in the back of my mind, urging me to maintain my composure. I won't let him make a scene. Not again.

"I take it Grant isn't coming."

"I'm sorry, I knew you wouldn't come any other way."

"Then maybe you should take a hint, Cole. I don't know who the hell you think you are, crashing my speech at the gala, using my clients to trick me into meeting you."

I manage to keep my voice even, despite the tightness in

my throat. I get to my feet and reach over him to grab my bag. His hand clasps over mine and my breath stalls. He stares at the spot where my sleeve hikes up and my tattoo peeks out.

"I didn't think you'd ever get a tattoo," he says, with slow disbelieving amazement in his tone. He tries to nudge the sleeve farther up. "Does this run all the way up your arm?"

I tear my hand away and use it to adjust the strap of the bag on my shoulder. My throat is closing up.

"What do you want from me?" I snap.

His eyes, they've always been more expressive than most. They're such a clear green, offering no room for his thoughts to hide. The way he stares at me now flips my stomach on its end, and when he speaks, it's like his throat is closing up on him, too.

"God, Mila, I still can't get over seeing you, every time it's like I can't breathe."

"Spare me," I say, already half turning away.

"I came to talk to you about the exhibit."

The words latch onto me, forcing me to face him again.

"You really want to talk about that? You really want to talk about what a cruel joke that was?"

"There's more, you didn't see all of it."

"I don't need to," I grit out between my teeth. "I got the message. I don't need to see more of how suffocated you were with me, how trapped you felt. I fucking get it."

"*No, Mila.* That's not what I was —"

He jumps to his feet and reaches out, a hand extending toward me. I jerk back and hit the edge of the table, then straighten.

"Don't you get it, Cole? I don't want to see you, I want you gone and out of my life for good."

I spin around and rush to the door, pulling it open to inhale a rush of fresh air. But before I can step through, Cole calls out to me.

"Mila, wait —*Just please*, ask Tobias what he did."

TWENTY-FIVE

COLE

A WOMAN LAUGHS FROM somewhere inside the suite. Out in the hall, I pause just short of opening the door. Another voice comes in and the muffled conversation gives me the impression it's safe to enter. I punch in the code on the keypad and step into the vast living room.

It takes me a few seconds to spot Grant.

He's sitting in the center of one of the long leather sectionals, legs parted wide. He holds a drink in one hand and has an arm draped along the frame of the sofa. A woman I've never seen before is sitting beside him. She's propped up on her knees, staring down at him as she speaks. There's a large smile plastered across her face and the purple dress she's wearing has rolled up closer to her hips than her knees.

The heavy door closes behind me, and Grant's and the woman's eyes snap to mine.

"There he is," Grant calls out, raising the drink in my direction.

"Oh, you're right, he is cute," the woman says, loud enough to ensure I don't miss it. Her high-pitched tone pierces my brain like pin needles.

"I'll be out of your way in a minute," I say, raising a hand in greeting.

"Don't be ridiculous," Grant half shouts. "Come join us."

I ignore him, heading down the steps of the entry hall into the kitchen. They remain in sight. There's nowhere to hide in the massive open living space until I can disappear into the guest bedroom. But first, I pour myself a tall glass of water.

Mila's words still ring in my ear.

Seeing her earlier, I couldn't find the words I'd planned to convince her to let me take her back to the exhibit. Her words slashed away at me like razor blades. But there was something in her eyes I recognized. I saw how jaded and closed off she'd become. Just the way I used to be. Then I glimpsed her tattoo, the cryptic words running up her arm, and a larger picture fell into place. I'd heard she's been collecting art for years. I'd heard of how she'd quit her job to risk starting her own business—a dream of hers, but a huge risk the Mila I knew would've never taken.

I see so much of myself in her now—and the crazy part is I've become a lot like her too. I've sought to root myself in a responsible, predictable life. I've grown ambitious and I've found my calling, the way she always wanted me to.

What I saw today knocked me to my knees.

She and I, we are showing symptoms of each other.

"Hi there, you must be Cole."

I blink at the intrusion and turn toward the soft voice behind me. Another woman stands there. She must've reached the kitchen from the bathroom at the other end of the hall.

She tucks her long dark hair behind her ear and extends her hand to me. I give it a gentle shake before pulling away.

"I am, and you are?"

Grant approaches from the living room, the first woman following close behind.

"This," he says, "is Ingrid. She's been *very* eager to meet you."

A pointed silence falls over the room. I give Grant a look and he responds by tilting his head and widening his smile.

"I was an intern at your father's company in college," Ingrid says, smiling. "I was telling Grant here that I—"

"Excuse me." I set a hand on her shoulder, cutting her off. "I need a word with my friend, if you don't mind."

"No, of course not." Her smile falters as Grant and I walk past her.

We head down to the nearest room, his home office, shutting the door behind us.

"What's the matter?" he asks, unconcerned. "I thought for sure you'd like her. She's your type."

"What, you think I'm going to fuck some random woman you brought over?"

"Don't be presumptuous, Cole. No one said she came here to fuck you." The ice in Grant's scotch knocks against the glass as he brings it to his lips, before hesitating. "Although, she probably did come here to fuck you." He takes a mouthful of drink and swallows it back. "You should've seen her eyes light up when I mentioned your name."

"That's great," I say. "Tell me, Grant, do you really enjoy screwing women who only want you for your money?"

"Predictability is an asset, my friend, not a liability. I never go into a situation until everyone involved knows exactly what it is." He tilts his glass at me. "Don't look at me like that. They're the ones hoping to use me. I'm just giving them exactly what they ask for." He heads to the door then glances back to add, "And Cole? You should hear the things they ask for. Might be something you want."

"What I want isn't out there."

Grant shuts the door again and turns in a slow half circle to face me. He seems to debate his words in silence before speaking.

"*What are you doing, man?*" he asks, his tone serious for the first time. "You said you weren't trying to get her back."

"I wasn't."

"So what the hell changed?"

"I went to see her and…I can't explain it, man. But there's something still there, in her eyes."

"You're kidding, right? You said she's with Drew."

"I don't care."

Grant drags one of his knuckles over his brow.

"Listen, I'm just watching out for you. You know what happened last time you got all hung up on her. You were the one who said the only thing you cared about was making sure she saw the exhibit. She did. It's over, man, walk away."

"She didn't see the whole thing."

"*For fuck's sake.*" Grant drops his hand to his side. "What would it change, Cole? Honestly? One more room of the exhibit, what difference would that make? It's not going to change what you did."

"No, but it will change the way she sees it."

"And what does that matter?"

"It's all that matters, Grant." I glance away, then gesture toward the door. "Just go. Have fun. I know you don't understand why I don't want to join you. And I don't blame you. You've never felt for someone the way I do about Mila."

He stares at me for several long seconds, his lips drawing into a flat line.

"You're right," he says, facing the door before I catch the rest of his expression. "And looking at you now, I hope to God I never do."

TWENTY-SIX

MILA

I LAY AWAKE ALL night, replaying the moment Cole appeared in front of me at lunch. Over and over again. And when my guard lowers from exhaustion, I catch myself savoring the sweet ache accompanying the memory of his face.

The night of the gala had been a blur, too much for me to process very much of him, but this time it was as though everything moved in slow motion. His face was so close, just on the other side of the table. He sucked all the air out of the room and made my head spin with the intensity of his green eyes.

I hate to admit it, but Cole looks as good as the day he left me.

I've tried so hard to forget his face, forget what it does to me.

Ask Tobias what he did.

It's been a long time since I shut the door on my questions just so I could go on with my life. I've ignored the demons banging against it. But now? The door's creaked open and I don't think I can close it again.

To unravel a ball of yarn you start on the outside, on the most accessible strand, and work your way inward. It's the same with the truth. There's only one truth, and that's the truth in its entirety. Anything else is glorified fiction.

Another morning dawns and I head out on yet another detour. This time, I'm determined not to leave until I get answers.

I find Tobias Kreisler lounging in his expansive backyard. He's wearing a robe and staring past his pool, toward the wall of manicured hedges lining the perimeter.

"Good morning," I say from the patio doors.

He doesn't turn, just simply lifts a glass of clear liquid to his lips and takes a sip.

Somehow, I doubt it's water.

"You're a hard man to reach," I go on. "You disappear when you don't want to be found."

"And yet you managed to find me when my own son still thinks I'm out of the state."

He knows the only reason I'm here is because he wanted me to be. He answered my call, something he refused to do for days before he dropped in on the gala. Since before I even had the nagging question of what happened between him and Cole.

"How do you feel?" I ask.

"Some days? I think for sure the doctors are wrong. Other days...are for vodka..."

He trails off and for a moment I think he's forgotten me. But then he waves me over. I walk around to face him, my hands clasped in front of me. I don't know the details of his diagnosis, and if he hasn't shared them with me by now it's because he doesn't intend to. It stings that he can hold me at arm's length, even after being a part of my life for so long.

"You still haven't told Grant, have you?"

Tobias lifts the glass again, but instead of taking a sip he stares at it.

"I will do everything on my own time. No one else's. But I don't want to talk about that."

"Good thing, then, because I'm not here to talk about Grant." I straighten, hardening my resolve. "I think you know exactly why I'm here."

"You're here because you've finally realized I haven't been truthful with you."

"Oh?"

He continues to look past me, his eyes tracing the scenery around us as though seeing it for the first time. Somewhere on the property, a lawnmower is running, and the scent of freshly cut grass permeates the air.

"I always wanted a big family, more kids. Not to say I'm not thankful for Grant, because I am, but sometimes I wonder if he would've turned out differently had there been more influences in his life."

"I'm an only child and I turned out just fine."

"Yes…yes, you did. But your mother was an exceptional woman, and she raised an exceptional woman. I, on the other hand, did not do so well with my own son. Or even with you. I promised your mother I'd keep an eye on you after she was gone, but I've been trying to look out for you much longer than that. In ways I suspect you already know, or you wouldn't be here right now."

His eyes connect with mine for the first time since I walked out here. There's remorse swimming in his expression, along with all the signals I read when he came into my office to deliver his awful news. Only then, I had misunderstood their meaning.

"I wanted to tell you then," he says, "but you weren't ready. I'm going to tell you now, but I warn you—you're not going to like it."

"Speak your truth and let me decide how I feel about it."

"Fair enough." He exhales and his shoulders sink as though his entire body might deflate. "I never liked Cole for you, Mila. For the life of me, I never understood what you saw in him. He had a history, a reputation before you two met. I'm sure you know. Drugs. Arrests. DUIs. You didn't know him back then, Mila, but I did. Even after he got clean, I could just see it in his eyes. He was unstable. I never trusted him, never liked him being around my son."

"This isn't news to me. It's no secret you and Cole didn't get along."

"I want you to understand. Cole…he was a lot like me. He was exactly like me. I could see his greed, his wanting of things he didn't deserve. I could see how he would ruin you the way I… the way I ruined the only woman I really loved." He swallows back his words, then more of his drink. "That's what men like us do, Mila. We sabotage the good in our lives."

I remain silent, the discomfort deep in my stomach

growing by the minute.

Tobias throws back his drink, sets the glass down, and stares at the space between us like someone looking through time and into the past.

"Right before the ceremony, I asked Cole to come see me. He did and I think he knew why. I only told him what I'm sure he already knew—that he didn't deserve you, that he'd drag you down with him and ruin you. I wasn't the only person who felt this way. And he knew, he knew everyone was rooting against the two of you. He knew every person sitting out there secretly believed you were making a huge mistake. He didn't care. He was going to marry you, anyway."

His words take me back to my wedding day, to the faltering smiles of my bridesmaids that greeted me when I opened the double doors of my bedroom suite. I knew not to expect a room buzzing with excitement at the prospect of me walking down the aisle to Cole. But the abysmal energy that rushed in on me from all directions was a punch in the gut.

Nearly every person in that room had, at one point or another, questioned me about my decision to marry Cole. But a person's understanding is limited to their level of perception. So how could I convince them of something so intangible? Of an experience wrapped up in moments I could never share with them. Moments no one would understand, for all their intensity and passion, the slow crescendo tumbling into a blissful free fall.

I blink away the memories as Tobias narrows his eyes, polishing off the dust on his own recollections.

"Cole didn't like what I had to say," he goes on. "Things got heated and he started losing his temper, spitting insults at me and insisting I was wrong. Insisting he'd never hurt you. I thought the matter could be put to rest rather easily. I handed him fifteen grams of heroin and I told him to choose, then I walked out of the room. He—well, you already know what happened."

My mouth hangs open. Tobias's confession snatches the breath from my chest and the echo hits me with twice the force. The image of Cole's face materializes in my mind as though I had seen it myself. Trembles work their way up my body and my voice is low and shaky when I speak.

"You gave heroin...to an addict...?"

"Mila, he was weak."

"Do you think he didn't know that?" I blurt out. *"He knew* he was vulnerable and he worked hard to stay sober. Cole didn't even want a bachelor party. He didn't want to brush up against anything resembling temptation. *Damn it*, Tobias. *How?* How could you do that?"

"I didn't make him do anything. No one put a gun to his head—"

"You gave *heroin* to a recovering addict," I repeat, slower this time because my heart is pounding in my ears. "On the biggest day of his life."

My surroundings cloud at the edges of my vision and I'm forgetting everything I know about Tobias, forgetting the connection I thought we shared. I'm looking at him now, and I don't recognize him at all.

"I'm not proud of what I did, but I was right to do it. He wasn't ready, Mila. Sooner or later, he would've relapsed and you were going to get dragged into one hell of a mess—"

"It would've been *our* mess to solve. Not yours. It wasn't your decision to make for me. How dare you think it ever was?"

My words cut through like a whip and Tobias remains with his mouth parted. I wait for his response, a part of me hoping he will argue, hoping he would give me a reason to unleash the full wrath of my resentment. But there's no fight left in his eyes.

"I've done some terrible things in my time, Mila, but I've always prided myself in knowing they were necessary for the greater good. But I've watched you over the years, and I've seen you become a shell of who you were, despite achieving everything you set out to do. I've seen you push everyone away, including me. I've come to realize through the clarity only a death sentence can bring us—In trying to protect you...I might have been the one who ruined you."

I set a hand to my stomach, the contents lurching from side to side and making me ill. I can't stand to look at him for another minute. He sat back for so long, watching me hurt and denying me the answers he held all along.

"I have to go," I say, half turning from Tobias.

"I knew you wouldn't be pleased with me when you found out. I knew one day I would have to tell you. But in my selfishness, I hoped the end of my days would come before I had to admit this to you."

A coldness beyond my control creeps across my heart. I

don't want to feel like this toward Tobias, I want to forgive him right now before walking away. But I just can't, it's just too much for me to take in.

There are a lot of things I wish I could say to Tobias, but I turn my back on him and head back through the house and out the front door. I tell my driver where I want to go, but even as it leaves my lips, the address feels foreign on my tongue.

New questions replace the old ones.

Why did Cole leave instead of telling me the truth?

Sometimes it's not the act, but the covering up of the act that's worse. I might have been able to forgive the relapse, but how can I forgive him for disappearing?

It's a long drive back into the city. The worst part is, even after reaching my destination, I have to wait on the elevator as the numbers tick past and I climb all the way to the top. Finally, the elevator pings to a stop and the doors open.

I've never gone looking for Grant. I've never cornered him in person to demand answers because I knew he wouldn't tell me anything Cole didn't want me to know.

This time it's different.

This time he'll have no choice.

TWENTY-SEVEN

ANDREW

I SHOULD KNOW BETTER than to go looking for it, but I flip right to the end of the paper and stare at my ex's picture among the slew of garbage headlines she doesn't deserve to be a part of. It's like a part of me enjoys watering the seed of self-loathing sitting right in the center of my chest.

Tearing my gaze away, I shut the paper and stare at the trashcan, but instead of throwing the paper out, I clutch it tighter and head to the front desk.

Janet's on a phone call, but I hang out waiting for her to finish. When she notices me, she grows self-conscious, biting her lip and tucking her hair behind her ear. Not unusual behavior for her, at least around me.

"Everything alright?" she asks me when she hangs up the phone.

I smooth out my face, realizing my expression was taut. Her eyes lower to the newspaper I set on her desk.

"Can you cancel my subscription to this?"

Janet tilts her head. "Uh, it's not...it's the office's paper."

"Right," I say. "Cancel the subscription."

"But, Mila—"

"She'll be fine with it."

Janet blinks a few times, making me aware of how I'm coming across.

"I'd appreciate it," I add, softening my tone.

Still, she eyes me with curiosity, her gaze softening along with my voice. She catches herself and glances down at her notepad. As she scribbles a note, she mumbles something that sounds like, *I'll see what I can do.*

The tension in my chest relaxes. I glance over my shoulder at Mila's office door, which is ajar, then at my watch.

If it were any other day, I wouldn't think twice about the fact Mila has been out of the office all morning. But it doesn't sit right with me today.

Just yesterday, Mila returned from her lunch meeting upset. She told me behind closed doors how Cole tricked her into meeting with him alone. To say it pissed me off would be an understatement. I told Mila I would talk to him, but she blanched at the idea. She insisted the best thing I could do was stay away from him, and I agreed, but only because I'm on thin ice with her as it is.

I called her late this morning to fill her in on a meeting she'd been waiting for me to have, but her phone went straight to voicemail. It's not like her to be unavailable during the workday. The inkling something is wrong has only grown as the day has yielded no sign of her.

"Do you know where Mila is?" I ask Janet. "I've been trying to reach her all day."

"She's been out in meetings."

Multiple meetings might account for her phone being off. Sometimes she turns it off and only checks it between appointments.

"Thanks," I say, starting to turn before I think of something else. "Do you know who the meetings are with?"

"Yes, the Kreislers."

"Kreislers. As in both of them?"

"That's right."

I stare past her for a few seconds.

Hearing she's meeting with the Kreislers makes me wonder if it could be another trap.

Would Mila fall for it a second time?

"Hey, Janet?" I give her a small smile and her eyes grow a fraction. "Could you do me a favor? I've to get ahold of someone but I don't have a number for them."

"Sure. What's the name?"

"The name is Cole Van Buren, he's the owner of an exhibit here. I've got the address of the gallery if that helps."

Janet nods and jots down the information I give her. Her gaze fixes on her computer screen as her fingers tap away at the keyboard.

I know how badly Mila wants to handle everything herself. But she continues to undermine the effect her ex has on her. This might just be the one thing that drags her under. Being independent isn't the absence of outside support, it's knowing when to ask for it. She understands this in business, but in her personal life she's always been defensive of anyone stepping across the parameters of her independence. It's part of what I like most about her and part of what drives me crazy.

"I found something," Janet says.

I come around the desk to look over her shoulder at the address and number she's pulled up.

"What's that?" I ask. "Is that a residence?"

"No. It's a business, but this is a different one from the one you gave me."

I tap the desk, staring at Janet.

I'd been holding out hope Cole was only in the city on a temporary basis. But it's not just the exhibit he's here for. He's got another business here, an excuse to stay as long as he wants.

The discovery only solidifies my decision.

"Put the call through to my office," I tell Janet.

Janet swallows, and I think she knows exactly who Cole Van Buren is and why I'm trying to reach him. Mila will be upset when she finds out, but I'm willing to risk that. The alternative is to watch her unravel again when he's done playing his games.

TWENTY-EIGHT

COLE

TODAY IS ONE OF those rare days I'm grateful not to have to stare at her face. I work instead on the thick strand of hair swirling overhead. It blends from black to gray as it transforms into a tiered skyscraper. The brush moves in long strokes as I add color to the sketch of the building. I take careful steps down the ladder as I move back downward.

For a moment, I forget where I am. The cars honking and people yelling in the distance fade an octave as I watch the way the thick gray paint adds fresh color to the dirty wall, giving it new purpose.

"Mr. Cole!"

The urgent shout breaks my focus. Sounds of feet scurrying across the cement bring my attention down to where my students are supposed to be painting. Instead, they are rushing across to where one kid shoves another one for what looks like the second time.

"Shit," I mutter under my breath.

I hurry down the ladder, keeping my eyes on the spot where Mannie and Aidan stare each other down, inches apart.

"Say it again, bitch," Aidan says. "I fucking dare you."

Concern flickers across Mannie's face and for a moment, I'm sure he'll back down. He's at an obvious disadvantage being the smaller of the two. But then Mannie looks around at everyone watching him. To these kids, backing down from a fight is worse than getting your face pummeled.

Mannie shrugs, tilting his head to the side. "I said, your mom's a fucking —"

I reach them just in time and pull Mannie back by the shoulder.

"That's enough," I say. "Someone tell me, what happened?"

A chorus erupts at my question, where everyone around me tries to give an account of the events, sprinkled with swear words and personal opinions irrelevant to the current situation.

I put up my hands. "Quiet, quiet. Okay, look. I need you all to get back to it, this mural isn't painting itself."

Everyone slowly disperses.

"Mannie, Aidan, not so fast. You two, come here."

They both sulk to a stop. Crossing their arms, they approach me, but both avoid my eyes. It's easy to forget just how young they are. These kids look like they could be finishing up high school, but they're barely thirteen.

I lower my voice when they reach me.

"What's going on with you two? I thought you were friends."

"I'm not friends with that punk ass —"

"No, no, no," I say, cutting Mannie off. "If you're going to diss someone, you're gonna have to get real. None of this generic crap. Mannie, why are you really mad at Aidan?"

The boy shrugs, staring past me.

"Aidan?" I ask. "Why are you mad at Mannie?"

"Because he's a punk ass bitch—"

"Alright...maybe you two need to mull over exactly why you're angry before you start beating each other's faces in. Does that sound reasonable?"

Both kids shrug. I know I'm not bringing my A-game at the moment, but the least I can do is send them home with their noses intact.

"Mannie, you go wash the brushes—"

"*What*? That's some bull—" he starts, cutting off when I raise an eyebrow at him. "Man, whatever."

Mannie stomps off to the stash of used brushes. I turn to Aidan, who's staring past me with a hardened expression on his face. It would've been easier for me to send Aidan off by himself to clean the brushes, but he's the most difficult kid I've got. The one everyone else has given up on. The last thing he needs is to be sent off on his own when he's upset.

"Come on," I say, "I need you on the ladder."

He had already started shaking his head, dismissing my request, until it registered. His eyes grow incredulous. "You want me up there?" He points to the wall above the ladder. "Thought we weren't allowed on the ladder."

"You'll be fine, don't be scared."

Aidan's lips turn up. "Never said I was scared. Just thought you had rules and shit."

"I do. And sometimes I change them…and shit."

His smile threatens to widen but he holds it back.

I set a hand on his shoulder and usher him toward the wall. We stand in front of it in silence for a few seconds, watching the others recommence their duties. Half-a-dozen kids wield paintbrushes over the side of the building, the mural coming to life with every brush of color.

"Alright, everyone, listen up," I say. "Aidan here is going to risk breaking his neck on the ladder. Anyone have a problem with that?"

I thought there might be some groaning about wanting to climb the ladder too, but those who turned sluggishly toward me as I spoke go back to painting without saying a word. I guess I overestimated the ladder's appeal.

"I'll take that as a no," I mumble.

Aidan and I stare up to where the woman's hair twists into the Manhattan skyline. I point to the highest skyscraper. "You can finish that one up."

"For real, Mr. Cole?" Aidan asks, his enthusiasm peeking through before he manages to contain it. "Yeah, alright."

I hand him the wet brush and he gets to the top of the ladder. Aidan fills in the first layer of paint with careful deliberation, making sure to not get any paint outside of the sketched margins of the building.

"You're doing great," I say.

"Yeah, whatever," he shoots back.

I shake my head. As dismissive as he pretends to be, I

remember how good it felt to be told I did something right at his age. Because the truth is, I rarely got told I did anything right. People like Aidan and me, everyone expects us to fuck up. They expect it so much they encourage it in the way they accept it, as though it's all we're capable of anyway. No one tells a kid like Aidan he can be better, they only remind him of how bad he is.

"Yo, Mr. Cole?" Aidan says, eyes on the brush. "Who's this girl you keep drawing?"

I stare up at him.

He points down to the image of the woman on the wall beside me.

"The girl in your murals. Is she your daughter or something?"

"Why would you think she's my daughter?"

"Because she's little and she always got something bursting out of her, like she's having a fit."

"I don't have any kids," I say.

"Ah, I got it wrong."

"You can't get art wrong. Art is whatever you want it to be."

Aidan nods, lowering the brush to admire his work. He scratches his nose with his forearm, the brush dangling from his hand.

"What do you want it to be?" he asks.

I blanch at the question and he notices.

"My bad," he says. "That was a dumb question."

"No. No, that was a great question. When you make

something, Aidan, there are only two things that matter: what *you* want it to be and what it makes other people feel. That's it."

Aidan stares past me toward the street as though mulling over my words.

"You just look so old," he says, "thought for sure you had a couple of kids."

"I'm not old."

"You old, Mr. Cole. What are you? Thirty?"

"Get back to painting."

Aidan starts to turn his attention back to the mural but something catches his eye on the street behind me. He points with the brush and asks, "Who's that guy?"

Several people walk along the street, but it's easy to tell who Aidan is referring to. A man emerges from the line of parked cars. He stands out like a sore thumb in his sharp black suit. Even at this distance, our eyes connect. He follows along the broken fence, past an overturned shopping cart, and enters the parking lot. I frown.

"That's an old friend of mine."

TWENTY-NINE

MILA

"MILA ZELENKO, TO WHAT do I owe this grand pleasure?"

The mild amusement on Grant's face is something I'm familiar with, but it annoys me all the same. I glance down at his business attire. His tie is loosened and he's not wearing a suit jacket. He's either getting ready to go out or just getting in.

"You don't look surprised to see me," I say as I move past him.

He closes the door behind me as I step farther inside, taking in my surroundings. Nothing much has changed in the near decade since I was last here. Neutral colored furniture glows under the light of the sun, which shines in from nearly all directions. It's dizzying at first, after walking in from the dimly lit hallway.

"I thought you might end up here at one point or another," he says, fixing his tie. "But if you're looking for Cole, you just missed him."

I blink a few times before recovering. Of course Cole is staying here. I shouldn't be surprised, yet my stomach did a flip at the thought of unintentionally coming face-to-face with him.

"I didn't come here looking for Cole. I came here for you."

Grant's carefree expression slips a fraction. "How can I help you?"

He heads into the living room toward a suit jacket draped over one of the chairs. I stay where I am, crossing my arms and eyeing him carefully.

"You can help me by telling me what happened to Cole on my wedding day."

Grant hesitates as he reaches for the jacket, head turning enough to put me in his peripheral. He picks up the coat and slips his arms into it, keeping his back to me.

"I already know what your father did," I say. "Now I want to know what happened after."

He turns back around, letting me spy the incredulous look on his face.

"My father told you? Wow. I thought he'd die before he owned up to that one."

I swallow at the casual way Grant throws around the idea of his father dying. I'm sure his father is immortal in his eyes. Grant misses my reaction. He straightens the front of his suit and clasps the first button before walking over to me again.

"Sorry, Mila. I don't think I should be the one to tell you."

He tries to pass me but I step in front of him.

"Really, Mila? You're like four-feet tall. What are you going to do? Fight me? Come on, get out of my way."

"No." Arms still crossed, I stare up at him, eyes narrowed, nostrils flaring.

"You can't face him, can you? You don't want to hear it

from him."

"I'll decide if I want to talk to him, if and when I have all the facts," I say.

The idea of it makes me nauseous. Nothing I've learned changes what I went through all those years. But it doesn't matter anymore.

Grant looks off to the side and shakes his head, then drags a hand across his mouth.

"It's not like he remembers much of it anyway," he mutters.

"I know you found him, Grant. I want to know the rest of the story."

He nods, still looking past me. His chest falls on a resigned exhale.

"My father called Cole up to his suite to have a talk with him," he says. "When Cole didn't come back, I went looking for him. I found him sprawled out on the floor. It was fucking scary. I thought he was dead, and I didn't know what to do. His father came in after me and saw him too. He arranged for Cole to be snuck out to the hospital. There was some press covering the wedding and he said he didn't want a scene. I thought he was trying to protect you and Cole from the embarrassment, but it became clear later all he cared about was covering his own ass, protecting his company name. It took years of public relations to fix Cole's image and his father preferred for everyone to think Cole walked out on you rather than to know he'd relapsed. Cole was in no condition to weigh in on the matter…"

I wait, but he doesn't continue.

"There's more. What happened after?"

He shrugs. "Cole was in the hospital for a few days, then his father took him straight to a rehab somewhere out west. That's all I know. I didn't see Cole until almost a year later. He disappeared again on and off. I don't know what he was up to, but I know he wasn't doing well. Not until three years ago."

Camille mentioned the same time frame before.

"Three years ago? What happened three years ago?"

"Look, if you want to know what he was up to, you'll have to ask him."

"Did Camille know this whole time?"

"No. Cole's father didn't trust her. She didn't find out until Cole told her himself, almost a year later when he first came back to the city."

I hold still even as traces of a shiver pass through me. I don't want to think of all the times Cole came back and didn't bother looking for me. It only makes me angrier with him. Because why now?

By the time Camille had found out what happened from Cole, a year after he left, I'd already pushed her far away. As the months passed, I grew bitter toward her. I thought she knew more than she let on. It never occurred to me she'd been in the dark all that time, too. Cole's father never accepted her as his daughter, but the cruelest part is her own brother ghosting her for a year.

I remain rooted to the spot for a few seconds. Grant passes me, but pauses at the door. He waits for me there, watching as I come back to my senses and approach him. He tries to open the door for us, but I take his hand in mine and force him to meet my eyes. His expression goes slack as his gaze moves from my face down to where my hand rests over his.

"Why didn't you tell me, Grant? Why would you let me suffer in the dark?"

He glances down then back up at me, with a slow regretful shake of his head.

"Cole didn't want you to know. It wasn't my place to tell you. I'm so sorry, Mila."

I go still, my hand dropping to my side.

I'm so sorry.

The words have an effect I don't anticipate. I wasn't aware until this moment how much I *needed* to hear them. This is why I haven't healed. There hasn't been a moment where anyone acknowledged any wrongdoing. There hasn't been a single moment of clarity or remorse. No moment where I could admit my own role and forgive myself.

I knew Cole was an addict, but of all the things I'd worried about, that was not one of them. He'd been sober for over a year when I met him, and he seemed so intent on staying that way, doing everything he could to weed out the negative influences in his life. Simply put, I thought he loved me more than the drug. I was a stupid, stupid girl to think love had anything to do with staying sober.

Grant's apology is a tiny chip in an iceberg, but it causes a crack that runs down and makes me realize how deep this goes.

THIRTY

ANDREW

THE KID ON THE ladder is the first one to notice me. Cole turns to look, and even from a distance I can tell he's not pleased. He stands by a mural on the side of the building. It's incomplete, but the sketch is visible enough for me to make out the profile of a woman.

One by one, each of the kids turns their attention from the mural to me. Every single one of them eyes me with distrust, as though the suit I'm wearing is a sign of trouble.

Music plays from an apartment nearby, loud and energetic, but it feeds into the tense silence of the parking lot. Cole sets down whatever was in his hands, says something to the kid on the ladder, and heads in my direction. I stop at the edge of the sidewalk and wait for him to reach me.

"What do you want, Andrew? I'm working."

"I have just one thing to say and then I'm gone," I say.

"See those kids back here?" he asks, nodding to the parking lot behind him. "They're my responsibility. So, how about you take ten steps back and thirty steps sideways?"

"Don't worry, I promised Mila I wouldn't punch you again."

"Is that right?" he asks in a flat tone. "And here I was really looking forward to showing you what happens when you do."

"Don't go looking for Mila again. Stay away from her."

Cole glances away and laughs. The sound grates on my nerves worse than his unconcerned posture.

"You think this is funny?"

"Yeah, man," he says. "I do think this is funny, and I'll tell you why. You came all the way here to—hang on, how'd you find me, anyway?"

"Your receptionist is eager to tell strangers where you are. You should probably get a new one."

Cole picks up again as though he didn't hear me. "You came all the way to tell me to stay away from Mila? But what are you going to do when she comes looking for me? Are you going to warn her against coming near me? Because I'm sure you're aware no one tells Mila what to do."

His question takes me off guard, but I recover.

"What makes you think she would come looking for you? She hates you more than ever, last I checked."

He doesn't answer right away, just looks at me. He looks at me the way he used to when we were in school. In the same condescending way of someone who has seen much more, and knows much more than me. And frankly? It fucking pisses me off. My fingers twitch, craving to curl into fists.

"She's going to come looking for me when she finds out the truth of what really happened."

"Yeah? And what's that?"

He doesn't answer at all this time, just tilts his head up and stares at me.

"You left her. Unless you were kidnapped by the Italian Mafia, you're not coming back from that. Not after eight years. I was there for her, by the way. I watched what you did to her. I'm not going to let you do it again."

"What—did you go looking for her after you heard what happened? Are you really that petty?"

"She came into a bar looking for someone to scratch an itch you couldn't. I didn't know who she was. If I'd known she was your ex, I'd have fucked her right then," I spit the words out just to get to him. I don't mean them, but they feel wrong all the same.

Cole's jaw flexes, but when his brows lower over his eyes, I realize my mistake.

"But you didn't, did you? And you still haven't. Isn't that right?"

A word begins to form on my lips, but the sound doesn't follow.

Cole nods, a slow smile building on his face.

"Yeah, *see*. I caught on to that. You're not really with her, are you? You just want to be. You always had a thing for the ones that wanted me first."

"You always were a spoiled asshole."

"And you? You always worked hard to bring me down like it would make you a bigger man. But look at you, still the kid I knew in high school. Still pining after a girl that doesn't even want to be with you."

I bite out a laugh, half turning from him to regain my composure. Because I swear to God, I'm going to drive my fist into his face again.

I turn back to him and take a step closer even when I know I shouldn't.

"You have no idea what you're talking about," I say.

"Don't I? You come all this way, acting like she belongs to you. But if you really knew Mila, you would know she's not the kind of woman you claim. She's the kind of woman who claims you."

I take several steady breaths, reeling myself in. He's got me worked up while he seems unaffected. The kids behind him are walking toward us, anticipating a fight.

"I just came to tell you to stay away from her."

"Why? Because you think you have a chance? You say you've been there for eight years and you're just now realizing you want her? Bull-fucking-shit. What is this really about? You can't overlook someone like her for eight years."

"Are you fucking kidding? That's exactly what you did."

Anger flashes past his eyes and though it brings me satisfaction, I brace myself for a fist to come hurling toward my face. But Cole doesn't make a move. Instead, he puts his hands in his pockets.

"Don't tell me what I did, I know exactly what happened. And soon, Mila will too."

"I'm serious, Cole, *stay away from her*," I say through gritted teeth.

"What are you going to do? You can't spread a rumor this time, you can't get me kicked out of school to get me out of your way." He shakes his head with a bitter laugh. "You fucking knew those drugs weren't mine. You knew I was only keeping them from Camille —"

"I didn't spread the rumor."

"Oh, no. You only meant for the girl to know. Right? You only meant to look better than me in her eyes. But did it work? Did you get the girl? Because I don't think you did. It didn't work then, and it's not going to work now, brother."

"Don't call me *brother*. We're not friends, Cole. I don't think we ever were."

His gaze darts across my face, and realization dawns in his expression. All my layers are out in the open with my inability to contain my frustration, and Cole's using my weakness to read me like no one ever has before. His smile falters. He looks down for a moment then back up.

By the look in his eyes, he can see the secret guilt behind my hatred. The remorse I carry about everything he went through after what I did. I ruined his life, then. Back when he was supposed to be one of my closest friends. But this isn't about that. This is about what he did to Mila.

"You should go ahead and walk away, Andrew."

The kids are close enough to hear us now, they jeer and snicker to each other. Cole glances down and shuts his eyes for a second, frowning. This isn't what I wanted, either. I put my hands up, more for the sake of the kids.

"It's over, Cole. Let her go."

He doesn't respond. I back away for a few feet before turning and heading down the block to my car. I'm flooded with dread when I yank open the door. Cole Van Buren has always been Mila's greatest weakness, and the one person with a proven capacity to shatter her. He's also one of the most defiant people I've ever known. In trying to warn him off, I might have just enticed him more. I might have just made everything worse.

THIRTY-ONE

COLE

"I ALREADY TOLD YOU, Cole, I don't do meetings," Camille says before nodding to the box beside the register. "So take your donuts before I change my mind and charge you for them."

My sister stands behind the counter, her attention on the notebook she's scribbling in. It's the third time she's written the same number down and she thinks I haven't noticed.

I'm tired and it's only a quarter past five. This is the second time today I've had to argue with someone I don't want to argue with. At least this time, there are no kids present to witness it.

"Come with me tomorrow night," I say. "You've never been to a meeting, you should at least see what it's like."

Camille shakes her head at my suggestion, her face hollowing out as she sucks in her cheeks. She's lit by the glow from the kitchen behind her. All of the other lights have been turned off. From somewhere in the building comes the soft clanking of cooling equipment. The eerie sounds of a store after hours.

"I'm busy, Cole," she says, still not looking up. "I've got so much to do. I'm looking to hire an assistant manager to help me run this place, but finding the right candidate has been more time consuming than just doing it myself."

Her energy is light, so at odds with her appearance. I swallow back the guilt creeping up. It's been months since I've seen her face-to-face. When I called to ask her for the address of Mila's office, Camille had offered to pick up the invitation from my studio and deliver it in person. I figured she just wanted an excuse to reconnect with Mila herself.

I wasn't there when Camille came by. Had I seen her like this, I would've worried sooner. I put my hands in my pockets and bow my head in front of her.

"You're using again," I say, and brace myself for what comes next.

Camille freezes for a moment then sets down the notebook and slams the register closed, her light energy zapped in an instant.

"Did you come here to make accusations?" she snaps. "I thought maybe you came to visit me for a change. You know? The sister you wish you didn't have."

I tilt my head, my mouth falling open in surprise.

"Oh, don't look so confused, Cole. Do you really think I don't notice you avoid me like the plague? You come in and out of the city and never once do you stay with me. Then you finally call me and it's for a favor? Do you realize I'm the only one in our family that gives a fuck about you? I wonder why I bother."

The sting of her words settles, but I keep my voice even, calm, as I hold her gaze.

"You know I care about you. You know why I had to keep

my distance."

"Right. Because I'm such a bad influence. Because I ruined your life." She speaks in a sardonic tone, but pain rims her eyes.

I swallow, shaking my head, discouraged at my inability to respond. What could I say? She's always felt guilty for being the one who introduced me to drugs. They weren't a big deal to her, she was just a fucked up kid herself, who'd managed to use for years without our parents ever noticing. She kept up her grades and seemed fine. But me? I fell right down the rabbit hole and never recovered.

"I'm worried about you," I say.

She bites out a laugh and heads through the open doorway to the kitchen area. When she glances back, she seems both pleased and upset I've followed her.

"I've been taking care of myself for way longer than you have. Look, you should go. You're starting to really piss me off. If I didn't know better, I'd think Mila sent you. She was on the verge of accusations the other day—"

The name distracts me, pulling me onto a different track.

"Mila came to see you? When? For what?"

She looks to the ceiling, thinking.

"It was Monday morning. She was angry with me because I convinced her to go to your exhibit and it mind-fucked her halfway to Long Island."

"What did she—" I cut myself off, shaking my head. "Okay, look, forget Mila. This is about you coming with me, just for one night."

"I already said no. Why are you suddenly worried about me? I'm sorry to break it to you, little brother, but I'm not the one with a problem. How many times have I been sent to rehab? Hospitalized?" she asks, waiting. "No, I mean it. Tell me. How many times?"

"None."

She points to me, pleased.

"That's right. Not a single time in my whole life. I've always managed to keep my shit together, Cole, so stop projecting your issues onto me. Look around. This is my business. I run it all by myself. I'm *fine*."

"You're not fine. Look at you, you're wasting away. And the way you're acting—" My heartbeat picks up. "Are you high right now?"

She shakes her head, glancing away from me.

"I'm feeling good, Cole. I'm not you, I know my limits." She gives me a pointed look. "Now do me a favor and get the fuck out of my bakery."

I turn from her, every step I take echoing in the silence. Before I reach the doorway, she sighs, then whispers, "*I'm sorry.*"

I go back to her, hoping to latch onto the window of opportunity, but it only ends in yet another circular argument. We end up back at the same place, with her ordering me out of her shop. I leave, knowing I'm not getting anywhere with her this evening.

When I step onto the street, I pull out my phone and dial Grant's number.

"Did you go see her?" he asks, by way of greeting.

He'd been the one to warn me she was looking worse for the wear when he ran into her yesterday.

"I did. You're right. She needs help, Grant. I've never seen her like this."

Camille's always been a high-functioning addict. Hardly anyone has suspected her drug use, and those who figured it out never worried because she's never shown the typical signs of needing help before. It's been easy to tell myself she was fine. I don't know what she's doing now but whatever it is, she's in way over her head.

"She didn't listen to you?"

"No. And apparently, she didn't listen to Mila, either."

There's a moment of silence on the other end of the line, then Grant says, "Maybe get ahold of your parents?"

I scrub my hand over my face. "She's walking a tight rope, Grant. They would send her right over."

"Yeah. Yeah, you're right. But you can't force her to get help. You know that better than anyone."

"Maybe this isn't a one-person job," I say, an idea dawning on me. "Maybe it's a three-person job."

"Meaning?"

"An intervention. You, me, and Mila."

THIRTY-TWO

COLE

MY MUSE HAUNTS ME most when my brain is full. She's elusive and tantalizing, showing up at unexpected moments and dangling ideas in odd brushstrokes and bright colors until I have no choice but to make the thing in my head come to life. Sometimes it's a painting, sometimes it's a sketch of ideas for an exhibit. I only finish half of what I start and can only stand to look at a quarter of what I finish.

I head to my studio right from Camille's bakery and work for an hour, until a knock on the door interrupts me.

I frown.

No one bothers me here. I rent this space out exclusively to work. It's away from the office, where I run my outreach nonprofit. It's away from the exhibit, which is still closed to the general public.

I lift from the creaky chair in front of the canvas where I've been sitting for hours and head to the door. I'm sure it's Grant coming to talk to me about what I said to him on the phone about Camille. I wouldn't be surprised if he came all this way to tell me he didn't want to be involved. Grant hated having to talk about uncomfortable things.

But when I pull open the door, the person framed in the doorway is not Grant.

My head pulls back in surprise and I'm dumbfounded for a moment, sure I've fallen asleep while painting and am imagining her appearance. It's Mila.

"Can I talk to you for a minute? Grant told me you'd be here."

I've been waiting to hear the first part of her statement for a long time, but the small bubble of hope in my chest pops at the realization she's here to talk about Camille. A greedy, selfish part of me hoped she'd come to talk about us.

"Of course," I say, stepping aside to let her in. "Come in."

The entry hall is narrow and she passes just a few inches from me. A deep, intoxicating scent follows her in, wrapping around me just as it did the first time I met her. I used to think it was perfume, but she told me once it was her shampoo.

Mila walks all the way down the hall and into the large open space of my studio. She looks around from one unfinished piece to another, lips parting.

I run a hand over the back of my neck. The majority of the pieces here weren't meant for anyone's eyes but my own.

"I assume you're here because of Camille," I say.

She stares at me, eyebrows furrowing.

"Why would I be here about Camille? Did something happen to her?"

"No. You said Grant sent you—"

She blinks a few times, confused, then hesitates.

"I went to see Tobias before work today. And I talked to Grant, too. Obviously. I know what happened the day of the wedding."

The meaning of her words presses on me from every direction. A familiar gnawing of shame grows within me. It comes from the shadows where I banished it. What I need to focus on is the guilt. Guilt is my friend. Guilt gives me a problem I can solve. Shame does nothing but make me hate myself, and hating myself is always the beginning of the spiral downward.

My mouth opens then closes again. She stares at me, waiting. How long have I waited to tell her everything? Now here she is and the words lodge in my throat. It's not that the words are hard, there are only two I need to say. But the scary part is what happens after.

"I'm sorry," I say, "I'm sorry for everything I did that day. But mostly, I'm sorry for everything I didn't do every day since."

She gives me a small, tight nod, her face serious.

Mila's small but has always had a presence to her. Even now, standing in this vast room, surrounded by canvases up to three times her size, she manages to be the biggest force in the room. Everything radiates out from her, everything begins and ends where she stands.

"I don't know how to feel." She sighs, crossing her arms. "I thought those words would make it better, but they don't."

"I know they don't, I just needed to say them."

She takes a breath and begins to speak, calm and collected, but cold and detached.

"Hating you is easy, Cole. I did it for years. But now? Hating you makes me hollow. So now I have nothing. No hate, no peace. Just…emptiness. And I don't know what to do with that."

We stand closer than the night of the gala, but still so far apart. The distance is worse than not seeing her at all. Because she's right here and yet, by the look in her eye, it's a gap I can't breach.

She might as well be a million miles away.

My chest rises with a deep breath. I'm unprepared for this. For this moment. I wanted to know what to say. But words have always been my enemy. They fumble from my mouth, or get stuck rattling around in my brain. Only a brush brings them out, only props give them sound.

"I'm sorry," I say again.

"Yeah, I know you are." She scans our surroundings again. "The exhibit, it wasn't about me, was it? It was about you."

"It was about addiction."

She nods, as though she'd already guessed as much.

"It was about everything I went through to get back here."

I point to the ground at my feet, but then regret it because I fear she's going to misunderstand what I mean. And she does.

"But this isn't your first time back, is it?"

"No. But this is the first time I had something to say."

"The exhibit."

"Yes. I spent three years on it. At first, I didn't know what I was doing with it. It seemed to be just a means to an end. The end being a distraction. But it took shape, became a story. And when I designed the last room, I was covered in paint and you were up on the wall."

She shakes her head. "You mean the first room."

"No. That was where I ended. But I knew it was where the exhibit would begin. I'd walked backwards through everything without even realizing it and ended with you. It always went back to you. I knew you were the only person I wanted to show it to."

"I'll be honest," she says. "I hated it."

I almost laugh, despite the somber mood between us.

"No, I get it."

She watches me with curiosity.

"You said there's another room."

"There is. It was the first room I finished. But it's where all the pieces fall together."

"The first room is the last room you did, but where the exhibit begins. And the last room is the first room you did, but where the exhibit ends?"

"I know. It's…"

Her eyes move from me to the canvas behind me, the one at the center of the room. The painting I'd been working on when she walked in.

"What's that?" she asks.

"What does it look like?"

She stares at the incomplete work, and I doubt she'll be able to make out what I was trying to do. But when her eyes connect with mine again, the ground shifts beneath my feet. There's a flash of something there, just like there was the night of the gala and the day I glimpsed her tattoos at lunch.

She hesitates before answering.

"It looks like me."

THIRTY-THREE

MILA

COLE SEEMS MORE SHOCKED than I am at what I said. I'm not sure why I think the painting is of me. There's no face, no definitive figure or even the vague impressions of a person. No, it's all colors and curves and texture. It's nothing, really. Nothing that I could make out for certain. And yet, it's me.

I can't explain it.

I take a few steps toward the canvas but pause to look at Cole. He reads my thoughts, somehow, and nods.

"You can touch it."

"Is that paint wet?" I ask.

"Doesn't matter, Mila. Go ahead. Touch it."

I do. I step right up to it and press my fingers to the thick coat of purple paint. My fingers come away stained, but the painting appears untouched. Because the brushstrokes are chaotic, the colors a stunning and mesmerizing swirl of emotions. How could this have come from the inside of his head, when this painting looks the way I felt when I saw him the night of the gala.

Cole steps up behind me. I sense him before he speaks. The hairs on my arms prickle awake at his proximity.

"How did you know it was you?" he asks.

"I don't know. It just...it's like a feeling painted on a canvas. I just don't know how that's possible."

"I don't, either," he says, his voice so close I'm sure our faces would be inches apart if I turned around.

But I'm scared to. I'm scared to feel. And this painting, it's a cruel reality of everything inside of me. Worse, still, is the fact Cole would know. Does he know me so well?

He goes quiet, and I'm scared to check if he's gotten closer because I'm not sure how I'd feel about that. He's barely said anything, hasn't laid a single finger on me. And yet it's already like he's got his thumb and forefinger at my seams, ready to unravel me. I need strength to gather myself. I'm not me around him, I'm something else.

Something more.

"I should go," I say, even though I don't move.

"You don't have to go. Have you had dinner?"

I hesitate.

"I'm guessing you haven't," he says. "I remember when you'd get too busy and forget to eat. There's a small place, just a few blocks over. We can talk."

For the first time, I'm glad he's standing behind me so he can't see the way I shut my eyes.

Decisions.

Deciding is always the hardest part. The wrong choice could ruin everything.

I turn to look at him and even though I just saw him

seconds ago, the sight of his face is once again a punch in the gut. That will never change.

"Okay," I hear myself say. "Let's talk."

It's hard to retrain yourself from the thoughts you spent years solidifying. My heart won't dislodge itself from the base of my throat. My pulse refuses to ease at my ears.

It's hard to look at Cole. It's hard to have him look at me. It's harder to look away.

We sit across from each other, food between us, and the weight of eight years overhead. I can't relax my body, every part of me tense as I lift a forkful of pasta to my lips. I chew, trying to taste it, but it's just rubber in my mouth.

There's so much I want to say, but I don't want this to escalate into a fight. It could, without a doubt. He could trigger my anger in a flash and I could unload years of pent up frustration in the middle of a restaurant for all of the people around us to witness. Not that there are many people around, anyway.

"This is awkward, isn't it?" he asks.

I swallow and nod.

He lowers his gaze, but I continue to stare at him. Even when I hated him and hated thinking of him, I realize now there was a part of me keeping him fresh in my mind for a reason. I've missed his face. There was a time it brought me comfort, there was a time it felt like home. It does strange things to me now. It makes me want to reach out to see if he's real. Because this? Us sitting across from each other like the past eight years didn't happen is like a nightmare disguised as a dream.

"Why do you stay with Grant? I saw a bed in your studio," I say.

"I only use that when I can't make it back. But I'd rather not sleep in the studio."

"Why?"

I'm not sure why it's important to me, but somehow it is. Somehow every explanation, every word, is significant after so long of being in the dark.

"Because the studio is the inside of my head."

"Where you paint the inside of mine," I add.

I glance away just as he looks up. But the intensity of his stare spreads like a warmth across my face. I am untethered. I don't know how to be around him if I'm not being angry at him. But I'm done being angry. That anger kept me bitter and it kept me trapped. I'm ready to understand. I'm ready to move away from him, from us, from what we were and what he did.

"It's what I saw in your eyes," he says, quietly.

"You saw all that? In my eyes?"

He tilts his head at my incredulous tone, the smallest hint of a smile forming on his face. I almost glance away because it's too much for me, but I don't. I hold steady, more to prove to myself that I can.

"You've always been easy to read, Mila."

The way he says my name is no different from how he says any other word, but it still hits me from a new angle. I don't know how, it's the same intangible gut feeling I got from the painting at his studio. It's like remembering something you didn't know you'd forgotten.

He makes my head spin without even trying.

I stare down at my plate again, willing myself to stop overthinking things.

"I've always heard the opposite."

"That's shocking to me. You're literally the only person I've ever met who was an open book." Cole lifts his water to his lips, but before taking a sip, he adds, "Back then."

And the words catch my interest.

"Back then?"

"Well, yeah," he says, setting his glass down. "It's harder now. Not impossible, but you're muddled by all the things I don't know about you anymore."

Intrigue flickers in his eyes as he rubs a hand over his chin. For some reason, the phantom smell of his aftershave comes over me even though he's clearly unshaven.

"Oh?" I drink from my glass, trying and failing to control my reactions to him.

"Yeah, like that tattoo on your arm."

My eyes almost widen, but I catch myself in time.

"Will you show it to me?" he asks.

"No."

"Why not?"

"I don't need a reason," I say. "I just don't want to."

"Okay. Fair enough."

He shifts, seeming to regret his question. But I'm relieved he dropped the subject so easily.

"And you know what? I think I should be the one asking the questions here."

"I can't argue with that. Ask away."

He sets down his fork and sits back, watching me. I look down at his chest, just for a break from his eyes. But it turns out to be a mistake, because the shirt he's wearing? It's one I gave him when we first started dating. Seeing it stings. I had to wipe my life clean of every bit of him just to survive. Had he been able to live amongst memories of me without issue?

The question that has plagued me since the day he left comes rushing from my lips so fast, it's like my heart vetoed my mind.

"Where have you been, Cole?"

I hate the sound of my voice when I ask it. I hate the traces of desperation, and the specks of hope that somehow he could erase all the pain he's dealt me.

"Do you want the truth?"

"Of course I want the truth. Why else would I ask?"

He shakes his head, the corner of his lips twitching down. "People say they want the truth, but then they don't like the way it sounds. Or the way it makes them feel."

"Where have you been?" I ask again, this time there's no

desperation, only resolve. I'm going to get my answers even if I have to pry them out of him.

He looks down then shakes his head, mouth opening then closing.

"I wish I could say I was out there, living my life. But I wasn't. I was out there, wasting it. I couldn't stay sober after I left you, Mila. I tried so hard, but it all kept coming down to one simple fact. I fell back into it even when I had everything to lose, and when I had nothing to lose? There was no reason not to use, no real purpose to anything."

He's right. I hate the truth—the way it sounds, the way it makes me feel. It hurts so bad to know everything I went through was pointless. To know he drifted around for years, aimlessly, while I tried to forget him. I mourned him like he'd died. Except, unlike with my mother, I found no solace in memories of him. Every day when I woke up, I had to pry him from around my heart before I could get out of bed. All that torture, for what?

I stare at my hand, which rests on the table beside my fork. I want to pick it up and go on eating, just to do something with the silence, but I don't.

He lays a hand over mine, and I let him.

His touch is tentative, but all my attention draws toward it.

I keep my eyes cast downward.

"That's where I was," he says. "I was nowhere. I was in and out of rehab. I was arrested. I was in purgatory, and I felt like I deserved to be there so that's where I stayed. I gave up on myself, I gave up on us. I was trying to forget you because I thought you'd already forgotten me. I'm sorry, Mila. I know that's not what you wanted to hear."

I swallow. "A part of me wished you'd started a new life and were happy. That you forgot me the moment you left. I don't know. It would make it easier to hate you."

"Why do you want it to be easier to hate me?"

"Because, Cole, it's so fucking hard to love you."

I look up just after I say it and his expression falls a fraction. To what? I don't know.

I can barely think.

He sits back again, removing his hand from mine. Cold air sweeps over my skin and I miss his touch, but I'd never admit it.

Cole stares past me.

"Three years ago," he says, "I met this guy who did these insane underground art shows in Chicago. The kind that just fucks with your mind and makes you feel the kinds of things I got high to avoid. But I realized I wanted that. I went so long numbing everything and suddenly, I just couldn't take the emptiness anymore. I craved to feel, I craved to hurt." He shakes his head, as though understanding how strange the statement sounds. "I started creating art. And I started feeling again. I started wanting to make other people feel, too. The very thing I avoided became my outlet. And I realized what I'd been doing wrong. Even when I was sober, every day was like a countdown to my relapse. Because I knew, I knew I wasn't strong enough. But I just couldn't figure out how to be stronger. I thought being with you could make the cravings go away. I wanted so badly for you to be my cure. The way I felt with you…" He pauses, looking at me, then he frowns and glances away again. "I never felt like that before, about anyone or anything. You made me want to be better. So damn much, I thought it was all I needed. I didn't go to meetings, I didn't get help. I just avoided temptation by wrapping myself up in you. But in the end that wasn't enough. If I'd gone to meetings, if I'd had a sponsor, I would've known one of the biggest paradoxes of addiction. An addict is just as vulnerable at the highest points of his life as he is at the lowest. That day, I'd felt like nothing could touch me. Everything I'd been pushing back, all the bullshit that drove me to drugs in the first place, was exactly what got me caught up in Tobias's web."

"The spiderweb," I whisper.

He nods. "In a way, I can't blame him. I'd set myself up for failure thinking I could make it all go away with just happy thoughts and by putting my attention on you. I was wrong."

"He was wrong, too," I say. "What he did…it wasn't right."

"It wasn't. But, neither was what I did. Two wrongs, but does it matter? We hurt the one person we both wanted to protect."

THIRTY-FOUR

COLE

THE TRUTH IS SUPPOSED to set you free, yet mine has become a cage I sit behind, waiting for Mila to process it all.

Maybe it was for the best I was unprepared. I never could have told her the things I did, in the way I did, had she not caught me off guard. Had I planned this, I would've resorted to communicating through my art, the way I always do. And that didn't go over well the first time around.

Somehow, having her in front of me, intent to hear my explanation, propelled it out of me. I don't live under any delusion my words can fix what happened between us. But I can see the shift in her eyes in the way she'd been viewing the situation. The way she's looking at me now is different from the day I tried to talk to her at the coffee shop. She didn't want to hear my voice then. She wanted me gone. But now, she looks as if she could listen to me talk all day, even if my words twist away behind her eyes. They aren't easy to hear, even for myself.

"You're different," she says. "You're more...I don't know. Emotionally mature."

"You're different. You're more guarded. You used to wear your heart on your sleeve."

"Yeah, and look where that got me."

"Do you see it?" I ask. "Tell me you see it?"

She tilts her head, staring at me.

I motion between us. "We've become so much like each other."

I glance down at her inked arm, just visible under the sleeve of her blouse. Her tattoo is a sentence written in a messy script. The way the words are slanted, it makes it difficult to read from where I'm sitting.

"You think so?" she asks.

She sits back, crossing her arms, perhaps in an attempt to keep me from eyeing her ink.

"I know you don't want to show it to me, but there's the tattoo," I gesture to her arm.

"Okay, but people get tattoos for lots of reasons."

"Yes," I agree. "But they were always my thing, not yours. As for me, I never thought I'd start a business. That was your dream, not mine. Now I've started two. And you were never into art before, but Camille tells me you collect paintings now."

The casual amusement on her face slowly drains to surprise.

"Coincidences," she says.

"I don't think so. I think we did it on purpose. We sought each other out, even when we didn't admit it to ourselves…" I pause, remembering what I'd realized a few days ago. "I think we missed each other so much we began to mirror the people we were back then. Maybe it was subconscious, a way to ensure we would never forget each other."

She goes still, her gaze moving across my face like she's waiting for me to tell her I'm kidding.

"Don't you think so?" I ask.

"I don't know. I don't know…"

She shuts her eyes long enough to take a breath, and then tucks her hair behind her ears. I stare at her through a slow blink, lost for a moment in the memory of her underneath me, mouth parted, eyebrows furrowed, the start of a moan on her lips. I miss her body. I miss the sounds she used to make. I miss the way her eyes would open in surprise right before she came.

"Will you come back to my studio with me?"

The question is greedy and selfish. Her coming to see me, sitting in front of me and wanting to listen to me is more than I could've ever imagined would happen. It should be enough. I should let her walk away. But I'm not ready for that. I want everything and anything she will give me. I want to have her to myself, away from the sounds of strangers eating and talking. Away from big tables that separate our bodies. But I know what I'm asking for is too much, and I see the struggle in her eyes as her lips part to speak. I wait for what seems like the longest second of my life before the answer leaves her lips.

"I can't," she says.

"You can't because you're with someone else?"

"No, Cole. I can't…the only reason you're asking me to is because you've ran out of words to say. You've said everything you needed to. This isn't easy for either of us, and I see no reason to draw it out longer than it needs to be."

She gets to her feet and I stand as well.

I want to tell her she's wrong, that there's one thing left for me to say. The most important words I could ever speak aloud. But in my struggle to find them, my mouth opens and closes several times until my last chance to change her mind evaporates into thin air. I'm stunned by the difference between what I dared hope would happen and the reality playing out in front of me. I was an idiot to think there was a chance we could brush off the dust on all we went through and find something new. Instead, I've given her the closure she needed to let me go. And now, the only woman I've ever loved—the woman I *still* love—turns from me and walks away.

THIRTY-FIVE

ANDREW

I WENT OUT LOOKING for Cole this afternoon to get into his head, but he got inside mine instead. Where else would I end up but at a bar to drink all night? I sit, surrounded by drunken strangers, trying to figure out why the hell the things he said won't quit eating away at my skin.

How is it some people have the power to make you regress? One moment you know exactly who you are, the next you're a teenager again, looking to solve problems with your fists.

Cole doesn't know me anymore, but it doesn't matter. He'll always remember me as the poorer half of his entourage, the sidekick who grew jealous and bitter, and ultimately betrayed him. I was all those things.

And standing there in front of him earlier, I was transported back.

I was that kid again. The kid who took the petty route, because the petty route was all I'd ever known. The kid who agreed to go on a skiing trip he could barely afford just to be around a girl who was into his rich friend.

The last night of the trip, our group of friends insisted on going to a trendy restaurant and I pretended I had a weigh-in for the wrestling team the next day, because I couldn't afford a damn thing on the menu. Cole knew and he ordered me a plate without asking. When it came, I grew defensive and made a scene, demanding to know why he'd done it. He didn't say, but he didn't have to. Everyone knew.

I know now, too. Hindsight, it gives a hell of a lot of perspective. I realize now he probably thought no one would notice he'd bought me the meal. But that night I seethed. In my immaturity, I was sure he'd done it on purpose to embarrass me. Before I knew it, I was trying to make him look bad in return, telling the girl about Cole dealing drugs at school, even when I knew it was a lie. It was easy to believe because he'd had a reputation for partying, skipping school, and doing what he wanted. But he wasn't into drugs. Not then.

I didn't know the girl would tell all her friends. I didn't expect for Cole's locker to be searched on the very same day he'd been stashing drugs he was keeping from Camille.

It was a horrible coincidence, but it didn't matter. No one believed Cole when he swore he wasn't dealing drugs, not the headmaster, not even his own parents. He was expelled from Milton. When he started a new school, I heard he ended up falling into the very things he'd been falsely accused of doing before.

A part of that is my fault, all because of my damn ego. I know I was just a kid, but thinking about it now makes me feel like a piece of shit.

So I drink, and I wonder what the hell he meant when he suggested I wasn't worked up about Mila. *What is this really about? You can't overlook someone like her for eight years.* It's about Mila for me. Of course it's about her. It's about not wanting him to hurt her again. It's about wanting to make her find the happiness she deserves after all the shit she's been through.

What the hell else would this be about?

I drain one drink after another until the bartender cuts me off. Next thing I know, I'm riding in a cab, tapping on the glass divider to get the driver's attention.

"You can leave me right here," I say.

The man eyes me in his rearview mirror with suspicion. When I pay him, he counts the fare money twice as though I'd switched the bills between now and the first time he counted them.

After I get out of the car, I stand on the sidewalk and offer the cab a salute as it disappears down the road.

The walk up to Mila's door is longer than the last time I was here. She answers the door on the fourth ring of the bell, her face full of alarm before realizing it's only me.

"Mila, hey. *Hey*, it's me, Andrew," I say, pointing to myself.

"*You scared the shit out of me.* What are you doing here?" she asks in a groggy voice. "And why the hell are you attacking my doorbell?"

She's wearing a white robe and squinting up at me, half asleep.

Rubbing her eyes, she waves me inside. When I pass her,

she shuts the door behind us.

"I needed to talk to you about something important because I just—wait. Hang on…" I struggle to remove my shoes at her entryway, needing to hold on to the wall for support.

"Andrew, it's fine." She sounds annoyed. "You don't have to take off your shoes."

"No, no. You have nice floors," I mutter.

She follows me into her living room. I resist the urge to plop down on her couch. I need to remain alert. Vigilant. Aware of all the things. I turn to look at Mila but she's not where I left her. She's standing on the other side of me now. My mouth hangs half open, but I've forgotten what I was going to say.

Her eyes narrow as she assesses me for the first time.

"Are you drunk?"

My eyes grow wide at her question, which I realize too late might serve to prove her point. I compensate by narrowing them and shaking my head nice and slow. She won't take me seriously if she knows I've been drinking.

Mila throws her head back and lets out a breath, muttering something like, *you've got to be fucking kidding me.*

"I promise I'll make this quick," I say. "I know you'll be pissed when I tell you what I did, but I want you to know we didn't do anything stupid in front of the kids. We, we were classy about it. For the most part."

Mila's eyes are no longer squinting, but mine still are, for some reason.

"Andrew, either tell me why the hell you're here in the

middle of the night, or I'm shoving you in a cab and sending you to your ex-girlfriend so she can strangle you for me."

I don't like it when she mentions my ex. I almost say this, but decide not to. It seems I'm not answering quickly enough because Mila's mouth snaps open again, impatient, and so I blurt out what I came to say.

"I went to see Cole today—"

"You did *what?!*"

"—to tell him to stay the fuck away from you."

Mila lifts a hand to her face and rubs the area between her eyes.

"I can't believe this," she says. "You've been acting so possessive ever since we kissed. I knew we shouldn't have crossed that line."

"I've been acting possessive?" The accusation sobers me up, sharpening my focus like a fixed lens. My words are still heavy on my tongue, but the intent behind them clearer. "Why, because I care about you? No, Mila, I'm not acting possessive. I'm acting like a man who you've been leading on."

The moment I say that, I know it's a mistake.

She raises her brows and her mouth snaps open in response, then closes again.

"You know what? No. I'm not having this conversation with you when you're drunk." She points down the hall. "You can sleep it off in the guest room. We'll talk in the morning when you're reasonable."

"Am I just the sideshow, Mila, or do we really have a shot?"

She turns from me, but my question whips her back around.

"We had a shot, Andrew. Then you started acting like this."

"Bullshit," I spit out. "This isn't about tonight. Or the night of the gala. It's about the fact that you're not over Cole."

She stares at me, shaking her head slowly.

"I'm never going to be what you want, am I?" I ask, swallowing back the burn that accompanies that truth.

"Like I'll ever be what *you* really want?" she shoots back, losing her temper for the first time. "Like *you're* over Amber? Because you're not, Andrew. It's so fucking obvious."

The words are a brick to my face. I take a step back and end up staggering for a few more. She shuts her eyes and presses her lips together before she speaks again.

"I'm not doing this right now. It's been one of the longest days of my life and I just can't take any more…you need to go sleep this off," she says, her voice low and sad, "Because I can't stand to be around you right now…"

She walks away, leaving me standing in her living room feeling like I've just been skinned by a dull blade.

THIRTY-SIX

MILA

I HAD NO CHOICE but to push away every single person who reminded me of Cole. Those relationships were tainted. They knew it, I knew it. It was one thing to know people didn't approve of the wedding, it was another to face them when their eyes taunted me with a silent *I told you so.*

Andrew never looked at me like that. He'd only had a detached sort of disapproval in his eyes about my ex. But now that Cole is back, the detached disapproval has become a familiar and punishing *I can't believe you fell for that guy* expression.

He feels sorry for me, like I'm this pathetic teenage girl trapped in an unhealthy cycle. I'm not. I'm just a woman who's finally pulled her big girl panties on and realized she's done scraping the bottom of the pot. I've gotten to the truth.

Every damn year, these weeks are hell on earth for me. But this year? This year takes the cake, and not just because Cole is back. Or because of what Tobias and Grant revealed. No. Last night I was hit by the worst realization I've had in a long time. It's no coincidence Andrew and I crossed a line when we did. When the ghosts of our pasts became too hard to ignore, we did what we always do—lean on each other. Only this time, we leaned too far and stumbled into a confusing space.

All these years I've had Andrew by my side, enjoying his company, secretly craving his touch, he's been the biggest part of the problem. And lately? I've been the biggest part of *his*.

Comfort.

We give each other a level of comfort that stagnates us both. It's robbed us of the urgency to deal with all the things we will never be able to outrun. All the things that have already caught up with me.

My heart is heavy when I come to a stop in front of the guest room. The door is ajar and Andrew's passed out on top of the blanket, his work suit still on.

Shaking my head, I move to the window and pull the blinds open. Light streams down onto his handsome features. He stirs, eyes opening up a sliver before shutting tighter. He lifts a hand over his face and groans.

"*Stop it*, what is this?"

"This is called reality. It's time we became acquainted."

I set a glass of water on the table and cross my arms. Andrew squints at me a few times before pulling himself up and sitting on the edge of the bed in front of me.

"Here," I say, lifting his hand to the glass as though he were a lifeless body. "Drink some water."

He takes the glass and drains it in a couple of noisy gulps. He shuts his eyes again.

"Does it have to be so bright in here?" he asks.

"Yes. Because we need to talk."

He looks at me, then at his surroundings as though realizing for the first time where he is. I can see the moment the memory of last night hits him.

"Damn," he says. "I fucked up."

"No, I fucked up. I've been fucking up for a long time."

"What are you talking about?" he asks, blinking a few times and rubbing his temple.

"Drew, we've been using each other."

His hand drops and his posture changes. He gets to his feet and takes a step toward me.

"What? How could you say that?"

"You know it's true. Think about it."

He shakes his head, lifting a hand to the side of my face. I shut my eyes. I don't realize how empty I am until Andrew puts his hands on me. His touch lights up a yearning in my chest, one that aches in familiar ways.

"It's not true," he says.

He comes closer, slipping his arms around me in an intimate hug. His breath washes over my neck as he lowers his face there. He inhales me. My insides lift, tugged by how much he wants me. It's all there, in his touch. But the things we want aren't always the things we need.

I shut my eyes and let him hold me, but the truth can't be dissuaded.

"We've been using each other," I say again. "Like crutches. That's why we can't move on. That's why we're both stuck."

His body tenses, but his shoulders sink when he exhales

and I know he understands.

"We're so good together, Mila," he says, somewhere over my head. "We make so much sense. How can't you see that?"

"We do, but only if we ignore the circumstances that brought us together in the first place. The feelings, they might be real. But the intentions...they aren't. Because nothing real can grow from the wish to suppress another truth. We could give this a try, but all the while we would know that the other person's heart isn't in it all the way. We'd know we aren't what the other person really wants." I swallow. "You were right last night, the things you said."

"No. I was drunk."

"You're a wise drunk."

His chest rumbles with a soft laugh. I know because my face is pressed against it as he hugs me.

"That, I can't disagree with."

I sigh.

"I don't want to lose you," I say, for the second time in just a few days. I can't repeat the phrase enough.

"Does it look like I'm going anywhere?"

"I'm scared to look."

He pulls back and takes my chin in his hand. I open my eyes. His face hovers over mine, his body pressed to mine. And I can't pretend I don't think, for a brief second, how blissful it would be to just give in to our attraction and forget our troubles. But we've always known the truth. The reason we've never crossed that line. We could only cross it once, and we'd never be the same.

We stare at each other for a few seconds, then I blink away and look at the floor.

"We never had a chance," he says in a low voice.

His tone scrapes at my insides, because I can hear how badly he wishes we did. And honest to God, I wish we did, too. He and I? We could be great together. In another life. But the truth is neither one of us had a chance with anyone, or anything, anywhere at anytime until we dealt with our own mess.

"We need to stop hugging like this," I say.

"Right." He steps back, his hands falling to his sides. "Don't want to tempt you into dry humping me again."

My mouth falls open. "You're such an ass."

He chuckles. When the sound fades, his expression turns somber.

"Does this mean I've lost you to Cole?"

"I can't believe you just asked me that. I'm not a piece of property you can land on top of and stick your flag into."

He smiles, amused.

"Yeah, yeah," I say, rubbing the space between my eyes. "I get how that sounded. But I'm serious. I don't like that you went looking for him, banging on your chest and warning him away from me."

"Just tell me he doesn't have a chance with you. Please, Mila. It would give me peace of mind."

"Your peace of mind isn't my responsibility, Andrew. I'm sorry," I say. "But, to be honest, I just don't see how Cole and I could ever go back."

It's the truth. I mean it with all my soul. But what I don't say is that I wish we could go back. With the exception of meeting Andrew, I wish the last eight years hadn't happened. I also don't say how I stayed up all night thinking about Cole. Or how I tossed and turned, trying to understand why, no matter how hard I try — no matter how much logic screams at me — I just can't shake him off my heart.

And I can't shake the pull to go looking for him again.

Andrew and I go still and quiet, with only the sounds of the morning trickling in from behind the windowpane. The words I spoke leave an opening. I only realize this when Andrew stares down at my mouth, like he's a thought away from kissing me. And for a wild second, I'm a thought away from letting him.

But my heart sinks, because Andrew still doesn't get it.

We've been pretending to move away from our past, but instead have only been limping in huge circles around it. Together, using each other to avoid facing the things that brought us pain. I wound up back in the place I started, hurting for answers, starving for the truth.

And Andrew?

Sooner or later he'll end up back in the place he's been dreading, too.

THIRTY-SEVEN

COLE

TELLING HER WHAT I feel would've been easier than facing the rattling in my chest as I watched her walk away last night. There's still fight left in me. There's still a furious need to win her over. I just don't know how much of that is greed. I've always been greedy when it came to her. I've never stopped to consider what I want might not be what's best for her.

And so I fight back the impulse to go after her, at least for a night.

Because impulsivity has always been part of my problem. The man I try to be, the man I've crawled through hell to become, knows how to sit in discomfort. Even if it means tying my own hands behind my back long enough to see the bigger picture.

Last night, I resisted the immediate gratification that showing up at her doorstep would have brought me. Instead, I headed back to my studio and painted until the sky behind the windows was light again. Then I slept for a few hours, waking up when Grant called my phone, though I didn't answer.

This morning, I'm still overcome by the need to create, to exorcise the demons that won't ever stop chasing me. And for hours on end, I turn myself inside out and splatter everything I am onto canvases. It's like I'm looking for answers in the abstract shapes to quell the need inside me to see her again. Looking for definitive words to spell it out for me once and for all.

It's over, man. Let her go.

But I don't find those words. All I find is her, in everything I make. And after countless hours and a dozen paintings, I start to wonder if she'll ever leave my head. My heart. My soul.

I look for reasons why I shouldn't try to talk to her again and all I find is confirmation that I'm not ready to let her go. And by the time the sun sets, I decide I should at least tell her how I feel. She should know I'm still in love with her. I don't know if it will change anything, it probably won't. But if I tell her, then at least I'll know I did everything I could.

I'm going to go try to talk her again, tonight.

With the decision made, I relax for the first time, tired from the marathon of thoughts and colors my brain has created. When a knock comes from the studio doors, I freeze. Somehow, I know exactly who it is. And when I open the door, I find the breath of air I've been struggling for from the moment she walked away.

It's as if my decision whispered out into the night and lured her right to my doorstep.

"You're here," I blurt out.

She seems nervous.

"Hi," she says. "Can I come in?"

"Of course, yeah, come in."

I run a hand over my hair as she walks inside and turns to

face me.

"I was at work today and couldn't stop thinking of an idea I have for a painting," she says. "I couldn't think of where else to go."

My mouth opens long before sound comes out. "You came to paint?"

I don't know why the suggestion squeezes my chest, flooding me with pure contentment.

"If that's okay." She fiddles with her hands in front of her, as though expecting me to say no.

"Absolutely," I rush to say. "I'll get everything set up for you."

She nods, then moves past me to stroll around my studio. There are canvases scattered throughout. Some are as big as a wall, others small enough to hold at arm's length. Aside from the pieces I've been working on over the past few days, there are canvases scattered throughout the studio, among other art projects.

She walks around the wooden table littered with pieces of multicolored glass, which were glued to a column to make a mosaic. She runs her fingers over the clay mold of a woman with her hands covering her face. On another table a few feet away, there are floor plans to another exhibit that I've been teasing away at for the past year.

Seeing my studio through her eyes makes me realize what chaos it is. Most artists have a preferred medium to express themselves and once they find it, they hone it. My head works in a million directions. Sometimes, I need color spread on a canvas. Other times, I need clay between my fingers. Most days, my ideas are intangible, concepts I could not make myself but need the help of technology to bring to life.

As I watch her, I soak in her curiosity and fascination in the pieces. It's far from what I remember. She had been only mildly interested in my art before, but now she seems lost in it. Granted, I didn't do much of it when we were together. Rare were the days inspiration struck. It had been dulled much in the way I'd dulled a lot of things. In running from my demons, I ran away from the only thing that could help me tame them.

I tear my eyes away from Mila and head to a nearby shelf to grab a canvas. I manage to set it up a few feet away from one I've been working on before she notices.

She walks over, her thumb between her teeth the way it is when her thoughts are loud.

"Full disclosure," she says, "I don't know anything about painting."

"Lucky for you, there's no experience required."

She opens her mouth to disagree, the doubt in her eyes as loud as her thoughts.

I raise a finger to stop her.

"I'll be right beside you, finishing up this painting. What is it you want to make?"

"I see it in my head, but I don't even know where to start."

I busy myself setting up a workstation for her on a side table with brushes and paints, a rag to wipe the brush on. She surveys the items I've laid out.

"I'd need water."

I smile. "I thought you knew nothing about painting."

"Well," she says, squinting up at me, "I'd guess water is part of it. Don't I need it to thin the colors? How will I clean the brushes?"

"You don't. Just wipe the excess paint off. Don't clean the brush, don't use water to dilute the colors. Let the colors mix, let them be raw. These are premixed with a slow-dry medium. It will help give you time to blend without any water."

"You're bossy," she says, amusement stirring her expression. "I think you were right the other day, you really are more like me."

Her playful retort takes me off guard. I think it takes her by surprise, too. Her eyes dart away to the empty canvas. It's as though, for a minute, she slipped into the Mila I used to know. The smartass who kept me on my toes.

I take her hand. She draws in a breath at my touch. I place the handle of a brush in her palm and close her fingers around it.

"Just don't overthink it," I say. "Art can't be wrong."

I pull my hand away from hers, my fingertips still prickling the way they do whenever I touch her. She lowers her gaze to my lips, and I swear she's going to throw the brush aside and jump on top of me the way she used to, wrapping her legs around my waist and bringing her arms around my neck. I know her so well I can see the thought of movements flash before her eyes. But that's all it was, a flash. She turns and heads to the door. The question of where she's going lodges in my throat, as I'm plunged into disappointment.

She stops at the door and removes her jacket to reveal a light blue blouse, then rolls up her sleeves. My eyes are drawn to her tattoo. Words along her forearm, disappearing under her sleeve again. I was right, it wraps all the way around. I could see it in my head even before I knew what it looked like. I'm dying to know what it says, but I'm hanging on to hope she'll stay longer.

She walks back over to her canvas and her chest rises as she takes in a deep breath.

"Okay," she says. "I think I can do this."

Sensing fragile deliberation, and fearing it could break, I remain silent. I move past her, closer than I need to, to my own canvas to recommence my painting without a word.

I work in silence with her standing mere feet away. She glances at me a few times before she pours out globs of colors to use. I pretend to focus on my task but really, my body is tuned to her every move. Even to the small sigh of uncertainty she lets out as she dips a brush in paint and lifts it to the canvas.

Her movements are stiff at first, just a single stroke of the brush before pausing. I risk a glimpse at the deep gray she's smeared against the center of the canvas. She lifts the brush once more, hesitates, then dips it back into paint. Black this time. She layers the color over the gray then goes still again.

The first mark is always the hardest. It ruins the canvas and solidifies your intent.

"You're doing great," I say.

"You're a liar," she shoots back, but I catch the twitch of her lips.

Minutes pass where she makes several short and indecisive strokes on the canvas. I take a step back from my own, lifting the brush and flicking paint across it. She watches me do it then imitates the same thing, only there's too much paint on her brush and specks of it fly across to me, landing on my shirt.

"Shit," she mutters.

"It's fine," I say, not looking at her directly.

She nods, before continuing to layer on paint, sticking to a scheme of black, white, and gray. She stops a few times, and shifts her footing. I've never seen her as unsure of anything as she is painting. The Mila I remember would never try anything she wasn't certain she'd be good at. Succeeding had been more important to her than anything. Art could not be measured in terms she craved, in numbers and certainty.

Her brush strokes grow more confident, moving outward on the canvas. She experiments with setting down a thick layer of white paint and letting it drip down onto the gray and black. I can tell when her enjoyment kicks in, the moment she allows herself to stop thinking and just go with what feels right.

I've stopped working to watch her, but she doesn't seem to notice. It's like she's forgotten where she is or who she's with. She paints like she's taken over by the vision that drove her here in the first place, until the canvas is saturated and her face an emotive reflection of it.

Over the years, I've gotten good at not letting a single drop of paint go to waste, but it's taken me a long time to get there. Mila on the other hand, lets paint fly everywhere.

When she sets down the brush, her hands are covered in specks of black and white. Not just her hands, her face, her clothes. Even my painting has specks of black where I didn't intend for there to be. But I'm pleased.

She seems to freeze as she stares at her canvas, her head tilting. A frown forms on her face.

"It's hideous," she says.

"It's not —"

"No, I wasn't fishing for a compliment, I mean, it's very obviously hideous." She wipes the back of her hand over her forehead, not realizing it only smears paint from over her eyebrows to her temples.

I stare at her, the smears and specks of paint on her skin leave me twisted up in a strange combination of need and regret.

She catches me staring and blinks a few times, thrown off guard. "What?"

"Do you realize how beautiful you are?"

Her lips part, but she swallows instead of speaking.

I take a step toward her and the air shifts around us, growing tense and warm all at once. Her pupils dilate as she stares up at me. One step, two steps, three steps before she takes in a sudden breath. I stop, then take her hand again and guide her about a dozen feet from the canvas.

"Look at it now," I say, though my eyes remain on her face.

She fixes her attention on her painting and nods slowly. I leave her there and head off to the bathroom to grab a washcloth. I'm over the sink, soaking down the washcloth when she says something.

"Yeah, I guess it looks better from here."

Coming back out, I go stand beside her. I take her hand in mine and turn the palm to face upward. Her brows pull in, but she doesn't resist. She watches as I use the tip of the washcloth to wipe the paint from her fingers. The colors smear further on her skin before dissolving away.

She grows more tense as I work the wet cloth down her palm over her wrist, where the first few words of her tattoo form an ink bracelet. The font is a thin messy script and parts of the words are hidden under specks of paint.

With my head bowed toward her, I begin to make out some of the words. I wipe away at them, paint drops breaking up and diluting to reveal the crispness of the deep black ink.

The words twist around her wrist and I can only read the end of them.

…because it felt like home.

A second sentence wraps around her forearm, but that one disappears behind where her sleeve is rolled up just above her elbow. Again, I can only make out the last part of the sentence.

…ruins that she found herself.

We're standing closer than we have in a long time. My head is bowed low over hers, and my breathing slows as her scent works to dull my thoughts. I lower her hand to her side and move the cloth up to her face.

Her eyes connect with mine, growing a fraction when I wipe away the paint on her temple. Her gaze softens and I can tell her inhibitions are dulling away at our proximity. And for the first time, it seems she also realizes there's still something left between us. Like thin threads of what we used to have, tethering us to each other.

It's there in her eyes.

"Your painting," I say. "What do you see when you look at it?"

"What?" She tenses up as though I asked her how she felt about me.

"It's okay, you don't have to say it out loud, just acknowledge what you see."

My eyes follow the washcloth as it glides over more flecks of paint on her skin.

"I see…clouds of gray and darkness," she says. "I see wayward thoughts and seething remorse…"

Her words are low, settling over the tightness in my chest. When she trails off, silence creeps into the moment and nuzzles the space between us.

She painted what she saw in me.

Regret balls up in my chest, my voice lowering as I wipe away her other cheek.

"You see it, then. You know I would take everything back if I could, but I don't know how."

"You can't," she says. "You can't undo any of it. What we

had is gone, Cole."

"Maybe it is," I say, swallowing back the burn the words bring. "Maybe what we had is gone, but maybe there's just enough left for something new."

Silence.

She gives a soft shake of the head, but her lips remain pressed together and her breathing slows down to match mine.

My fingers brush against specks of black on her blouse, just over her collarbone. The fabric is smooth under my fingertips, and I swear she stirs right before dropping her gaze.

"Mila, I didn't come to get you back. Honest to God, I never thought I could."

"So why did you come back, Cole? Why now?"

If there's any hope in her voice, it's smeared with fear. It's as though she's still terrified I'm going to ask for her heart again. She's afraid of all the things she sees in my eyes. And I realize the words I intended to say will fall short.

I have a long way to go to even think of earning her heart back.

"I came back because everything I've done, every single piece of art I've made…it always comes back around to you. Everything, Mila. Everything leads me back here. For years I've been circling around this, too afraid to face it. I've tried to move on. I've tried to leave you alone. But I can't, Mila. I just can't."

THIRTY-EIGHT

MILA

MY SKIN TINGLES FROM all the places his fingers grazed as he dabbed at me with the washcloth. He's cleaning me up and I didn't realize until I was already frozen under his touch.

Now my heart is lodged in my throat, right where it went the moment he took my hand and stared at the words written along my arm. His expression pensive as he eyed one of my tattoos. I hadn't thought of it when I rolled up my sleeves, but I'm thankful he can only see half of the words and that the context is safely hidden behind the material of my blouse.

He lifts the washcloth and wipes away at my temples with a tenderness that steals my breath. It's simple and enticing, but makes me ache in ways I'm not sure I like. I want to stop him, but I can't because there's still a part of me that doesn't *want* him to stop.

It's always been like this with him.

He has a way of turning me around and making me forget which way is up. It's a frightening sort of bewilderment because even as I begin to drown, I cannot move and I don't even want to try.

"*I miss you,*" he breathes out.

I stare up at him, not knowing how or when he came this close. My attempt to keep a safe distance between us failed, gravity luring us inward, millimeter by millimeter, and now it's too late.

"God, Mila, *I've missed you so much*."

I shut my eyes tight, shaking my head.

"You can't say these things to me," I tell him.

He drops the washcloth and brings his fingers under my chin, lifting my face to his. My jaw tenses in resistance, but my gaze locks onto his.

"Why not?" he asks. "Why shouldn't I tell you how I've missed you like crazy?"

"Because, Cole, it's not fair. It doesn't change anything. It doesn't *fix* anything. You…" I shut my lips to stop the words, but they burst through anyway. *"You broke my fucking heart."*

He blinks then swallows.

His eyes swim with all the intensity I painted on the canvas. All of the clouds, all of the remorse. It churns up like a storm. He cups my cheek and caresses my face with his thumb while struggling to speak.

"I'm sorry," he says. "God, *I'm so sorry*. I see what I did in your eyes, in the way you look at me, and I hate it. I don't know how to make it better, I don't know how to heal you, but all I want is to just…make you forget. To take away your pain, even for just a little while."

I swallow, delightful goosebumps running up my arms.

"What do you mean?" I ask.

"I want you, Mila. I want to…make you feel good."

He watches me, his expression cautious despite warming a few degrees. He tucks my hair behind my ear. I shut my eyes again, my mind shifting to imagine an eagle's eye view of us. His hands are on my face, our bodies inches apart, and I still don't understand why I'm letting this happen. Without anger to anchor me, I'm afraid I might float off.

If there's a time to walk away, it's now.

I glance down, half a breath from pulling back.

Walk away. Walk away.

My mind shouts for reason, my heart whispers a wish. I've been fighting my body's reaction to his, fighting my greedy eyes craving to take him in. I've resisted my way through an evening suspended in time. And now my willpower has dried up to reveal the bare bones of the truth.

It's the truth I keep even from myself, even now when it threatens to spill out.

Instead, a warped version leaves my lips.

"I don't know how to stop hating you, Cole. I've been doing it so long, I just don't know how to stop."

He looks down at my lips, which even now are angled toward his.

"Then don't."

His face moves in and I draw out a shaky exhale just as he slams his mouth onto mine. He owns my mouth the way he always did, determined and fierce, sending my inhibitions scattering away from an urgent instinct. My entire body reels and stirs, toes curling right where I stand. I do what I thought I'd never do again. I kiss him back, just as hard. My tongue strokes his, my desperation acute and like nothing I thought I'd feel again.

The kiss brings on a surge of ghost sensations trailing over my entire body. It's both familiar and daunting, the passion in his kiss reminding me of the type of lover he is. He tastes of wild, wild memories wrapped in mindless pleasure. I'm dazed off him, reason and pride slip through my fingers, which cling to his shirt.

"You can hate me, Mila, but I remember. I remember all the things you like and all the ways you like it. I can make you feel good. *Please*, let me make you feel good."

My body's response is involuntary, the smallest of sighs lifting from my lips. He hooks his hands around my hips and tugs me toward him, making my eyes grow wide as he holds me against his erection. My knees weaken, my head gets foggier.

"You are…everything I don't deserve," he mutters, warmth brushing over my lips. "But I still want you…so damn much."

My lips have not closed since he pulled away from our kiss, and I've yet to find the ability to form words. My mind spins around and around. The only thing that steadies me is his touch. He moves a hand down to undo the first button of my blouse. My heart picks up speed and my chest presses into him on a shaky breath. His fingers slide between the part of my blouse to brush just over my collarbone, sending nerve endings exploding across my skin.

Cole's face moves over mine without making contact, as

though he's savoring the moment. The air between us gets warmer by the second, and there's something primal about the almost kiss, something illicit in the way his mouth hovers millimeters away.

"I remember," he goes on, "the ways you moved, the sounds you'd make. The things you'd beg for. Mila, do you remember?"

A delectable shiver runs down my spine, the memory of him pushing inside of me so visceral my back arches. The smallest traces of a moan rise from my throat.

"Yeah," he says, a slow smile building on his face. "You do remember."

He kisses me again, just as desperate as before, sucking and biting and making demands without words until I melt into his arms. All hints of hesitation evaporate as my mind switches onto a primal frequency where the only thing that matters is his body against me, his mouth on mine. My clothes are suffocating me and I want to rip them away, to slip into a skin from years before, when my body was his to touch, his to take. I give in to the delirious hope he could take me in the same way he did the last time we made love and make me forget the time in between.

THIRTY-NINE

COLE

I CAN TASTE THE moment she decides to give me her body. The second desire overtakes her and her muscles relax under my touch. My fingers move to undo the buttons of her blouse. And when the material parts, I bite at her lower lip then pull back to glimpse the smooth curves of her breasts peeking out of her white bra.

I still can't believe she came back.

I lower my mouth to her neck, tasting her, breathing her in. I kiss her as I unclasp her bra. It loosens over her chest and my hand slips right underneath to cover one of her breasts. Her nipple is a hard pebble under my touch. My other hand smooths across her collarbone and up to her shoulder to urge her blouse down her arm, so low, all it takes is a soft shake of her shoulders for both her bra and blouse to slip off and fall to the ground at our feet.

When I break our kiss again, her head tips forward as her mouth searches blindly for mine. And when her hazel eyes flutter open, need quivers in them.

For the first time, I get a full view of her tattoo. Except there's more than one. There's multiple sentences running up her arm like vines all the way to her shoulder. I don't try to read them. I run kisses up and down from her shoulder to her neck. Then I kiss her shoulder again, this time giving it a soft, tender bite. She moans and I shut my eyes at the sound, wanting to hear it on a loop over and over again. It's the best thing I've heard in years. Since the last time she'd melted under my touch.

I unbutton her pants and pull down the zipper to reveal her panties. I take in the gorgeous skin they frame, and my mouth waters. My hand disappears under the waistband, my fingers slipping lower until the smooth skin yields to silky warmth. She tenses, her mouth rounding as I glide my middle finger inside of her. The move sends a jolt to my cock. Her eyes become hooded as I pump my finger into her. I kiss her between words that come stumbling out of my mouth.

"*Fuck*," I mutter.

I take her hand and place it over my pants. She swallows, and for what seems like an eternity, she just stares up at me. A deep shadow of desire crosses her eyes and eclipses her entire face.

"Do you have a condom?"

Shit. Do I?

I hide the twinge of fear at her words. I kiss her again, my mind rushing to think of where I could find condoms. I've never even thought of the possibility of having a woman in this studio. This has always been a sanctuary for my art. And my art has always been about Mila.

Mila watches me, her head tilting in realization. She must

think I'm trying to convince her otherwise because of my lack of an answer. She pulls back, her eyes narrowing in seriousness. We stopped using condoms when we got engaged. She's the only woman I've ever been with that way, but I know better than to suggest we don't use one now.

"I'll go get one." I step away, grinning to hide my concern, and point to her. "Lose the pants."

"You lose the pants," she shoots back, setting her hands on her hips.

She's topless and standing there unabashed, proud to show off her perfect breasts. Fuck. She's so goddamn sexy. I keep my eyes on her as I walk backward toward the counter just outside of the bathroom door.

There's a bag on top of it, one of Grant's overnight bags I'd borrowed to haul over some supplies. If there's any hope of a condom, it would be in there.

She pushes her pants over her thighs, nice and slow. I stare, never understanding how this woman's legs look so long when she's so damn short.

I reach the bag, struggling to take my eyes off of Mila as she bends over to peel her panties down. When she straightens again and I catch sight of the creamy skin between her thighs, I nearly lose my composure.

She's never been shy, but for fuck's sake, what is she trying to do to me?

I search inside the bag, checking the main compartments, but find nothing except the crap I put in it. I turn the damn thing upside down and shake it. Items tumble out onto the counter, but not a single one I need.

Goddamn it.

I almost slam the bag back down in frustration but catch sight of an inner zipper. My fingers fly to it, pulling it open.

"*Thank fuck*," I mutter as I pull out a long string of condoms.

Grant, bro, I fucking owe you.

I head right back to Mila, undressing in a hurry as I walk. She's killing me the way she stands there completely naked and daring me to eat her up. I've never met anyone as sensual as her, not before and not since.

Her gaze drags over my chest and finally down to my hands as I roll a condom over myself without halting my stride. My center of gravity is off when I reach her. I come in too fast, grabbing her by the waist to pull her in for a kiss. We stumble. A stool topples over and we shift to avoid tripping over it and end up colliding with my painting. The easel goes crashing to the side and I tug her to avoid falling on top of it. Instead, we fall on top of the canvas. It happens so fast, I barely have time to brace for the fall. My hand goes through the canvas and onto the floor where I manage to keep my weight from Mila. She bounces against the canvas, her entire backside falling flat against the wet paint. For a moment, we both freeze, our eyes going wide at the chaos around us. We're breathing hard, our faces a mixture of shock and excitement.

"Fuck it," she says.

She grabs my face and yanks me down for a kiss. My hand slips over wet paint and when I bring a palm to her breast, I accidentally color it white and yellow. I stare down at her body, which arches and writhes in impatience, not giving a damn about anything else. I flash her a grin and position myself over her entrance.

"Fuck it," I repeat before shifting my hips and pushing inside of her.

FORTY

MILA

His movement is sharp and punishing. I gasp when he slams into me, my body arching off the canvas to let him all the way in. Cole's face blurs for a fraction of a second as I bite my lip hard. He's so thick, filling me to the point of agony. It's an ache I crave, an ache I've missed like a delicious habit I thought I quit.

"*Fuck,*" he groans.

He shuts his eyes, lowering his face to mine. Our lips graze but we forget to kiss. He pulls out of me, slow and sinful, and the feel of his length makes my toes curl. And when he drives back into me, he does it with the same urgency, settling into an ardent pace that leaves me breathless.

He fucks me just the way he used to. Passionate, powerful, vicious. I lose my mind underneath him, just the way I always did. Forgetting the world, forgetting my hate. Squirming with desperation, overwhelmed by the pleasure he serves me.

My back slips against the wet paint and when I touch his face, my fingers leave purple marks on his cheeks. I don't fucking care. What do we look like now? Our bodies a colorful mess. Paint everywhere, me sliding up and down his painting as he fucks me hard and fast.

This feels so good, even the smell of the paint is turning me on more.

I'd beg for this anywhere.

He kisses me, tongue caressing mine in dizzying contrast to his thrusts. My legs wrap tightly around his waist, slipping on paint now smeared there.

"Did you miss this?" he asks, not slowing his pace.

He looks down at me through half-closed eyes.

My brain is still formulating an answer when he slams into me even harder, and I scream aloud at the jolt of exhilarating delight.

"*Yes*."

"No one fucks you like I do, isn't that right?"

I delay on purpose, moaning out at the delicious agony of his brutal thrust.

"Answer me," he demands. "Tell me no one fucks you like me."

"No one," I breathe out, staring up at the tantalizing look in his eyes. "No one but you."

He smiles, pleased with my answer, then pulls up on his knees mid-thrust and brings my legs up in front of him. He picks up his pace, abs flexing with every jerk of his hips. I stare, my legs are covered in paint, and so is his chest and the side of his face.

Even painted in bright colors he looks wild. I thirst for the way his lean body moves as it renders me delirious. His voice grows lower and lower, wilder and wilder with each word he speaks.

"You know why?" he asks, his hands running up my legs as he weaves his cock in and out of me. "Because every inch of you wants me, and only me. You know that."

I do. I do.

"*Oh God,*" I scream, when he deals another ruthless stroke.

I'd forgotten the kind of sex I craved, the kind only he could give me. The pleasure is so intense it feels wrong. Like I might unravel and lose myself completely beneath him.

And yet I beg for more.

"*Don't stop. Don't stop.*"

"Why not?"

My head hovers at the end of an enraptured state, my thoughts slow and useless.

"*Because I want to come,*" I blurt out.

"No, Mila. Tell me what you really want."

The admission comes out clouded between moans.

"*You…I want you…I want you.*"

He leans in, bringing my legs over either side of my head. Then he bears down and picks up his speed.

No one. No one could ever set me on fire the way Cole does. No one could leave me gasping for air and muttering pleas. I edge closer and closer and even if I could brace myself, nothing could prepare me for the way the orgasm slams into me. It's an obliterating euphoria, making my hips jerk as I moan out.

"*Yeah,*" he groans. He's watching me through hooded eyes, biting his lip before he speaks again. "*Let go, beautiful. Just give in.*"

"*Cole*," I breathe out, shaking as the aftershocks of my climax shudder through me. "*Oh my God.*"

I shut my eyes and let out a satisfied sigh. He's still inside of me, hard as ever.

"Did you come?"

"Oh no, beautiful," he says, brushing away a hair from my forehead. "I'm not done with you. I'm only just getting started."

FORTY-ONE

COLE

I'M NOWHERE NEAR DONE with her. But this paint is going to start setting soon, despite the slow-dry medium, and it's going to be hell to get off.

I get to my feet and look down at her. I've never seen anything like this. Her beautiful body lying on top of my painting, streaked by the colors, twisted up in pleasure.

I have to say, she's the single most compelling piece of art this studio has ever seen. It's like all this time I've been trying to recreate her in my paintings, and now I've created my paintings *on* her.

"Come on," I say, giving her my hand. "Let's assess the damage."

I help her to her feet, and when she turns to look down at the mess we've made, my mouth drops open.

"*Holy shit,*" I mutter, gripping her arms as I stare down her body.

She peers over her shoulder.

"What is it?"

For a moment I can't speak, caught up in the most exquisite sight I've ever laid eyes on. Her back is completely covered in paint, every inch smeared in a thick layer of acrylic. The colors have blended together, forming swirls that move down her back and over the curves of her ass and down her thighs.

"Is it bad?" she asks, realizing what I'm gawking at.

"It's...incredible," I say.

I set a hand at her waist and the other between her shoulder blades, urging her to bend over. She does, her back arching and her ass perking up in front of me. The skin between her thighs is clear of paint, which brings all my attention to it like the focal point of a painting.

"*Fuck*," I groan.

I glance over my shoulder in the direction of the bathroom. We could make it to the shower, we could start washing off this paint. *But, fuck...*

I spread her ass with my hands and she stirs, coiling in anticipation. No. No, we can't make it to the bathroom.

I usher her to the nearest table and bend her over it so her hips are level to mine. Shifting into place, I bring the tip of my cock to her and push inside, slow and steady, watching my length disappear between her gorgeous canvas. I throw my head back, not believing how badly the sight of her ass covered in paint turns me on. But I can't fucking help it.

"*Oh*," she sighs, and I think she can feel I'm harder than ever.

"*Fuck, Mila. You squeeze me so goddamn tight*," I say under my breath.

I find a steady rhythm and she lets out moans that drive me crazy. Gliding in and out of her again lunges me into an insatiable state of mind. Her searing heat wrapped around me, the tiny spasms when an orgasm grazes her but flutters away. I've never wanted a woman as much as I want her. I've never enjoyed a woman as much as I enjoy her.

"*Yeah*," she moans out. "*Oh God, yeah.*"

I can't control my grin, loving the way she's unraveling in pleasure around me. I pick up my speed, working my hips to make each thrust count, and soaking in the incredible sight of her body. With her, it's not about me, or simple mindless escape. When I'm with Mila, I'm fully present and wanting to be nowhere else. The only thoughts in my mind are how I can bring her more pleasure.

"*Just like that. Oh, just like that.*"

The delicious sounds of surprise she makes drive my moves. My instincts zero in on her breathing and moans for the sole purpose of giving her more of what she likes. It's not hard to do, it's exactly what I like, too. We're so well matched, her impending orgasm drives up my own ache to finish.

And the sight of my cock pounding into her, the way she grinds back against me in rhythm with my thrusts…it's too fucking much for me. I'm going to explode inside of her or lose my mind trying to keep it together.

"*Make me come*, Cole," she begs. "*Please.*"

The plea in the way she says my name nearly does me in. I bite hard on my lip as I fuck her just the way she wants, my fingers sinking into the skin of her hips as I pick up my pace again until she bucks and screams out.

"Fuck, Cole...yes...yes!"

She tenses and her body spasms around my cock. I'm thrown over the edge of control, my hips twitching without my consent.

"Oh, fuck," I say, trying and failing to hold off. *"I'm coming."*

She's still grinding out her own orgasm when mine bursts out of me, driving one last, long push. I hold deep inside of her, a deep groan rumbling from my throat, my heart hammering.

She goes limp against the table. Picking her up, I take her in my arms and throw her over my shoulder. She lets out a little yelp of surprise.

"Where are you taking me?" she asks, laughing.

Her laughter hits me square in the chest. I haven't heard it in years and it sounds too much like a dream. For a split-second, I fear none of this is real. Except it is real. She's naked, in my arms, covered in paint.

"We need to wash this paint off before it sets."

"I don't care," she groans. "Just fuck me some more."

My lips pull up into a grin. There's another sound I didn't think I'd ever hear again. I carry her over to the small bathroom, thankful for the standup shower I use on the rare occasions I crash at the studio. I set her down on the sink, and she clasps one of her hands on either side, her feet dangling far from the ground.

I shake my head.

She might be tiny, but this woman is something fierce.

She watches me, biting at her thumb, her eyes glazed over. She looks drunk off me, and she probably is. She came pretty fucking hard, for longer than I've ever seen from her. She's always insatiable with respect to sex, wanting more and more. There were days all we did was fuck. We'd spend sunrise to sunset tangled up in each other. There's something about being wanted by this woman that makes me feel worthy in a way nothing else can. It's always been my favorite part of being with her.

I ditch the condom, and grab more from the counter outside. When I come back into the bathroom, I lift Mila up from the sink and set her down in the shower. We kiss under the stream, water splattering paint from our skin onto the tile walls and floors.

She groans when I pull away.

I grab another washcloth and soap it up. Behind her, I get to my knees and run the washcloth slowly down her body to wipe away all the paint. I don't mind this view at all. Neither does my dick. It's going to need some time to recover, but I'm already hurting to be inside of her again.

"Did I make you forget?" I ask her.

"Forget what? I'm still trying to remember…"

Her voice is a soft echo of contentment in the shower.

I take my time washing away the paint, enjoying reacquainting myself with every inch of her body. I press my lips to parts of her skin as I rid them of paint, kissing her over and over again through the trickle of water running down her skin.

When her back and legs are clear of paint, I get up and turn her to face me. She tilts her head back under the water, eyes closed, and a look of serene satisfaction on her face. My hand glides up to the side of her beautiful neck.

I eye the tiny formation of freckles there. Three dots in the shape of a triangle.

"I don't think I fucked you well enough," I say.

"Are you kidding?"

"You shouldn't be able to stand right now."

"Oh." She glances down. "I thought I was still sitting."

I chuckle and a playful smile builds on her face. I can't get enough of her and I have no idea how I will ever be able to tear myself away from her side again.

There's still paint along the front of her body, but the shower has worked to dilute most of it and it comes off easily when I drag the washcloth across her chest and stomach. Then I get to her arms and falter. I run a hand over the ink on her arms, my fingers tracing the words. For the first time, I can read the full sentences.

She loved him in the shadows because it felt like home.

When all else was lost, it was in the ruins that she found herself.

There's a third one farther up her arm I hadn't noticed before.

Love is so short, forgetting is so long.

The last line is the only one I recognize. It's from a poetry book I gave her for her birthday once. I had tracked down a first edition version by her favorite poet, Pablo Neruda. I go still staring at it, a huge knot forming in my chest. I know I hurt her, but seeing it marked on her skin forever hurts more than I can stand.

Her eyes open and she blinks at me a few times before realizing what I've been staring at. I swallow and pull myself together.

"These are beautiful," I say.

Her gaze lowers to her arm and her shoulders hunch inward. She seems self-conscious for the first time, as though she hadn't been truly naked in front of me until now. I grip her hips and tug her toward me, letting the water wash over us both and hoping foolishly it would carry away more than just paint.

"God, Mila, please, *please* forgive me."

I didn't realize until this moment how badly I needed to say the words. I don't know if I'll ever be able to forgive myself. She tries to speak, but her lips come together again without making a sound. Her brows tilt up over her eyes and her expression mirrors the ache in my chest.

FORTY-TWO

MILA

HE'S GOT MY THOUGHTS scattered in pieces until I can't tell one from the other. Pleasure and pain, they come hand-in-hand with Cole now and I don't know if I can get used to that. Remnants of ecstasy still course through my veins, yet my heart throbs with a dull ache.

There's a reason I once fell so deep for Cole. Even when I hated him, I could not deny what hooked me in the first place. I've never found it in anyone else. He's stunning, yes, with his sharp, masculine face and bottomless gaze. But it's a way about him. He wraps me up in him, all consuming and intense.

Cole escaped reality often enough to know how to hold on to it when he could. He taught me how to do the same by hooking me into moments with plain sincerity, and a deep genuineness that seemed at odds with his tumultuous childhood. He's not in any way a perfect man, but there's no doubt in my heart he's real. Honest. Pure in the ways people who sometimes make the worst decisions are.

Even now, he's a beautiful man with a tormented soul.

"God, Mila, please, *please* forgive me."

His words sharpen my senses in an unwelcoming way. The

last eight years have compounded inside of me, a massive tumor of emotions I don't know how to hack. Even knowing the truth, even understanding the nature of addiction and the entrapment orchestrated by Tobias, I can't say I forgive Cole. He wasn't fully in control when he disappeared, but he deliberately stayed away from me all these years.

Being here with him now, as good as it feels, is also gut-wrenching. Because what was the point? Why did I have to go through so much in trying to forget him only to end up right back where I started?

Life is cruel sometimes.

My lips move, but I can't speak. My heart races and while I agonize over what to say, the silence speaks the truth so eloquently on my behalf. If I were Cole, my pride would urge me to turn away. Having a plea greeted by silence is a tough pill to swallow. But he's stronger than me. He lets out a rueful sigh and brings me in for an embrace. Relieved, I lay my head on his chest.

The shower washes over us both. Cole holds me in silence and we don't move for a long while, simply breathing and aching together. Finding unexpected comfort in allowing ourselves to acknowledge the giant fault running between us.

We end up on a mattress in the corner of his studio. I lie on my back staring at the vaulted industrial ceilings. Moonlight streams through the frosted panes of glass overhead. Seeing it's still nighttime outside is disorienting. It's as if I've lived three lives since walking into this studio. I first came for closure, I returned for the sake of nostalgia, and now? I've slept with my past. Twice.

I lift a hand to the side of my face, shaking my head.

"What is it?" Cole asks.

He rolls on top of me, hooking his arms under my shoulders and somehow keeping his weight off me even as his body presses into mine. He's watching me as I unsuccessfully try to decide where my head is at, where my heart is at. I've failed to keep track of them from the moment I learned he was back.

I stare up at his face. His handsome face that makes my heart ache with memories and hope. It's like looking at something you used to adore with all your being and having to resist the impulse to want it back.

"I don't know where we go from here, Cole. Half of me thinks I should walk out that door and never come back. I've got my answers. I've got my closure. But I can't stop my head from spinning around you."

"Let it spin. If it means you'll stay, just let it spin."

His gaze moves across my face, up and around my hairline and back down to my lips.

"Don't leave," he whispers. "Stay with me. Please, don't leave."

How could I leave? I can't tear myself away when his body

stirs awake over mine. When the memory of the blissful state he induces is as fresh as it is.

"At some point we have to face reality," I say. "And it's not in here. It's out there. You and me, we always worked when it was just us, but when we factored in the outside world? The cracks would start to show."

"That's not true."

"You know it is."

"That was then. This time is different."

This time?

"What are you saying, Cole?"

"I'm saying give this another chance. We're not over. I don't think we ever were."

I shut my eyes and when I open them again, he's as breathtaking as ever. He looks at me like I'm all there is, and as much as I wish I didn't need to see that, it sweeps me away.

"We can't go back," I say. "Too much has changed."

"Maybe we can't go back. Maybe we start over. Something new. We're new, we're different. It's like looking in a mirror, Mila. We reflect each other now."

"Cole, I just…"

He takes my mouth and my hesitation disappears between his lips as he kisses me with tenderness and warmth. It's like a goodbye kiss, the type that leaves you dazed in its passionate grief. And feeling on the cusp of saying no, I'm tugged by the sharp pain of even thinking of detaching myself from him.

I can be alone, I know that.

I'm not afraid of the ache, of yearning for things I can't or won't allow myself to have. I'm not afraid of nights where it might overtake me and seep into my pillow through tears. Loneliness hurts, but it doesn't kill you. If Cole broke my heart again? I'm honestly not sure I could go through that a second time.

Walking away is safer, so much safer. And yet I don't want to. I'm tired of surviving just to prove to myself I'm strong enough. My strength doesn't have to come from suffering. It can come from happiness.

Why couldn't it?

I open my mouth again, but Cole sets his finger over my lips, worry etched in his eyes.

"Don't answer me now. Just think about it and in the meantime, let me prove to you how things are different." He lays kisses along my neck. "You always said I was too closed off. Do you still think that?"

"No, I don't. I told you, you seem more emotionally available."

"It's you, you know that? You made me like this. Go ahead, ask me anything."

His mouth moves lower onto my collarbone.

"How many women have you been with since me?"

He turns to stone at my question, then pulls up to look at me. I know what he's thinking, but I'm not asking out of insecurity. I'm asking because I have a decision I want to make.

A ringing sound cuts into the mood. It's not my phone, but

Cole's somewhere in the studio. He ignores it.

"The question you should ask is, how many women stood a chance. The answer is none, Mila. Not one."

"I'm asking because I want to feel you inside of me," I say quite bluntly.

He blinks before recovering.

"You're the only woman I've ever been with skin to skin. You were going to be my wife."

The words run down my spine, a shiver from the past that almost was.

"What about you?" he asks.

The phone continues to ring.

"Are you going to get that?"

"No. Now answer my question."

"Same. I've always been safe."

His eyes narrow.

"How many?"

I tilt my head in response. "As many as it took to forget you."

He looks away. The sound of ringing finally cuts off, the call sent to voicemail.

"You could've spared me the response."

"Yeah? Well you could've spared me the question. No one's ever accused me of being a saint."

"Tell me this," he says, defiance flashing in his eyes. "How many knew how to handle you right? How many knew just how to fuck you?"

I peer up, as though thinking.

"*Mila,*" he warns, sensing I'm messing with him.

"None, you cocky bastard. Other men were too gentle with me, like they were afraid I'd break. You know I won't. You've tried."

His lips threaten to turn up, but he remains serious faced.

"I'm going to need you to stop talking about other men now," he says.

"Or what?"

The head of his erection presses to my entrance. I shudder at the delight of his skin on mine.

"*Or* I'm going to have to remind you whose name it is you scream when you come."

"See, that warning makes me want to be bad."

He laughs, and teases more of himself inside of me. I drag out a sigh. He's so delicious.

The phone starts ringing once more, jarring the moment.

Again, Cole tries to ignore it, sliding a little more into me.

"You need to get that," I say. "Someone's obviously trying to get ahold of you."

"I don't care," he groans, eyes closed as he pushes all the way inside. "*Fuck.* You're on fire."

The ringing cuts off, then comes back a few seconds later.

"*Cole!*" I slap his shoulder. "Get your damn phone."

He sighs, bowing his head, and when he pulls out, the suddenness leaves me empty and regretting my insistence immediately. He gets off the mattress and walks across the room to one of the tables. His ass is the most incredible thing I've freaking seen in my life.

"Yeah?" he snaps, answering his phone. His tone changes when he realizes who's on the other line. "Mom? Whose number are you calling me from? Wait—*what*?"

His posture changes, he clutches the phone tight to his ear and turns in a slow circle to face me. He stares at me, eyes widening as he listens. He sits back on the edge of the table, clutching the side for stability.

My heart jumps into my throat as I rush to his side. Even before I reach him, I hear his mother's voice trailing through the receiver, twisted up in agony.

"She's gone, Cole. She's gone."

FORTY-THREE

MILA

THERE'S SOMETHING UNNATURAL ABOUT the murmuring of a crowd at a wake. So many people gathered in a quiet room weaves tension into the air, making people's movements stiff. And anytime someone clears their throat, it spreads into the sounds of one person after another clearing their own.

As people enter, they stop to stare at the large photograph of a smiling Camille propped up on a stand. It's the Camille I remember, with a healthy, heart-shaped face and vibrant eyes. She was the first of her family to accept me when Cole and I started dating. She introduced me to all her friends and treated me like a sister.

The plastic cup of iced water cradled in my hands keeps me alert, seeping coolness across my palms and fingers. I scan my surroundings, past the countless visitors dressed in black, heads bowed together as they catch up in hushed tones.

I walk through the room alone, seeing both strange and familiar faces. More than a few times someone stops me, setting a hand on my arm to get my attention. Members of Cole's extended family who swear I look familiar but can't decide from where. Of course, when they realize I am the woman their nephew or cousin or whoever-Cole-is-to-them left at the altar, they grow quiet and awkward.

Other times, people stop me for the opposite reason. They don't recognize me and are curious how I knew Camille. I say we were close friends, and the words leave an ache in my throat. Because the more people I speak to, the more I realize how little Camille and I had spoken over the past few years. Regret throbs in my chest, all the times I pushed her away because I didn't want to think of Cole. And the very last time I spoke to her…I knew, I knew she was in trouble, and I silenced myself for fear of overstepping boundaries. Boundaries that now, just days later, no longer matter.

When I catch sight of Grant, I rush over to him. He's speaking with an elderly woman, a hand on her shoulder and his head bowed to hear what she's saying. I wait patiently nearby for him to finish.

His gaze darts to me as if he feels me looking at him. He nods at whatever the woman says, his lips tilting down, then excuses himself and comes toward me.

"Hey, Mila," he says, holding out an arm.

I lean in to offer him a quick, light hug.

Silence falls between us. He lifts a drink to his downturned mouth and glances past me. I never realized how playful Grant's typical expression is until I witness him somber. The lack of amusement in his features is jarring.

"Have you seen Cole?" I ask, trying to disguise how badly I need the answer.

"Yes. He's here with his parents. I think they're out in the hall. They're in shock, I think." He lowers his voice even further and leans in. "Elizabeth needed a double dose of Xanax just to make it out of the house."

I peer over my shoulder toward the entrance and sure enough, I catch sight of David and Elizabeth Van Buren, Cole's parents. They stand side-by-side, speaking to a couple by the door. I can make out the back of Cole's head just behind them, as he speaks to someone out in the hall. The weight that's been sitting on my chest shifts a fraction, knowing he's here.

"Tell me the truth, Grant. Is he okay?"

"Cole? Yeah, he's fine. He's just wound a little tight, thinks he needs to do everything by himself."

I've been unable to see Cole for two days as he helped with the preparations for the funeral tomorrow. I asked to help, but Cole made it clear he needed to handle things with his family, their way.

Grant tilts his head toward me. "You're worried he'll relapse," he mutters.

"*Aren't you?*" I ask, dropping my voice to a whisper. "His sister just died of a drug overdose."

I set my hand to my stomach as queasiness washes over me. Hearing the words out loud, however quietly, rattles me to my bones. His sister. Camille. My friend. I raise my water for a sip, the ice clinking against the cup in my shaky hands.

"I'm looking out for him, Mila. You don't have to worry about that. I won't let anything happen to him."

Grant looks past me and straightens.

David Van Buren steps up beside me with his wife at his side, holding onto his arm. Elizabeth's face is puffy and weighed down by a thick layer of makeup.

"Mila," David says with a thread of surprise as he observes my face. "Wow. Thank you for coming."

He holds out a hand as though I am an old business acquaintance and not someone he'd once welcomed into his family as his future daughter-in-law.

It's disconcerting, staring into a pair of eyes identical to Cole's and seeing layers of calculation behind them. I was never able to read David Van Buren, never really gauged what kind of man he really was.

"I'm sorry for your loss," I say, as we shake hands.

He nods and glances down at his wife. Elizabeth stares at me for a moment. Her face goes eerily blank, her eyes unfocused.

"Sweetheart, you remember Mila. Mila Zelenko," David offers, but when his soft nudge doesn't yield recognition, he whispers something in her ear.

She's slow to react, but her brows gradually lift in understanding.

"Mila, yes. Of course, I remember," she says, rubbing at the base of her neck.

"*Elizabeth*, I'm so sorry for your loss."

My mouth goes dry because I hate those damn words. I hated them when people said them to me after my mother died, and I hate them even more now. It feels like standing over someone who's bleeding to death and telling them you hope they feel better in the morning. There are no other words. I know this. But still, I hate the ones tradition has left at my disposal.

"Thank you," she mumbles, and her cheeks tremble as though she's attempting a smile. "Forgive me for not recognizing you, my head is…I'm just so…"

"It's fine," I say.

"It's been a long time," David says. "I wasn't aware you and Camille kept in touch after…everything."

I'm spared a response as a hand rests on the small of my back. I nearly sag in relief as Cole's face appears at my side. I wrap my arms around his middle for a quick but tender embrace. He lifts a hand to my side, but his posture remains stiff.

"Cole, I was just catching up with Mila. I hadn't realized…" He trails off, eyeing how close Cole stands beside me. "Are you here for Cole?"

"I'm here because Camille was my friend," I say, tempering back the streak of defensiveness coming over me. "But yes, of course, I am also here for Cole—"

"Oh," Elizabeth cuts in, glassy eyes rounding. "Are you two back together?"

Cole and I answer at the same time.

"Yes," I say.

"We're not."

Cole's answer hits me like a brick.

Grant's brows lift in surprise before he rushes to hide his expression behind his drink again. David looks unfazed,

Elizabeth lost. My lips remain parted from the word I spoke without hesitation as I catch a glimpse of Cole swallowing hard.

I turn to stone as quiet falls over the five of us. Hadn't I been the one who didn't answer *him* when he asked me for a second chance? Hadn't we agreed I'd take time to think about it? And now I've blurted out an answer in front of Grant and his parents without even discussing it with him first. I'm sure he didn't want to assume, but the unwavering way he answered doesn't sit right with me.

"Excuse us," David says, putting an arm around his wife again. "Good seeing you, Mila. Thank you again for coming."

I nod and attempt a small smile as Cole's parents walk off to greet new visitors, a large group entering and upping the volume of the hushed murmurs.

"Excuse me, too," Grant says, shifting his footing. He points his glass toward the food table across the room. "I've got to go...stand somewhere else." He clasps Cole's shoulder as he passes by, giving him a heavy pat. "Let me know if you need anything."

Cole nods, but remains unsmiling. For the first time tonight, we turn to face each other. His hair is combed back and his face is pale. The slow churn of pain and guilt in his eyes makes my stomach hurt.

"*Hey*," I say. "Have you eaten today? Are you okay?"

I hate those words, too. It was a question I was asked over and over after I lost my mother. Regardless of the truth, there's only one way people can answer it.

"I'm okay, Mila. Really. I'm okay."

"Cole. Talk to me," I say, setting a hand on his chest and searching his eyes.

It's hard, him being so distant, even though he's standing right in front of me. I'm trying to remind myself it's not about me. He's hurting, and as much as I wish he'd let me in right now, he has to do it in his own way.

"We'll talk later," he says. "I promise."

He leans in and presses his lips to my forehead. The move almost soothes my worries, but his posture is still stiff. And when he straightens, his thoughts remain jagged behind his gaze. A nagging sensation grows in the pit of my stomach.

No, stop. It's not about me. It's not about us.

He drags a hand across his lips and I spy dried paint on the beds of his nails. Dark colors, different from the ones he used the last time we were together. I take his hand in mine before he can lower it to his side.

"You've been painting?"

"Yeah. Went into the studio last night for a few hours."

"Oh," I say, trying to hide my sinking disappointment.

I've reached out to him over the past two days, even though I accepted he'd be too busy with family for us to speak much. But knowing he chose to be alone at the studio painting last night, rather than be around me hurts pretty damn badly. Am I being selfish?

He's grieving and I know that, but all I'm trying to do is be here for him. Why won't he let me?

FORTY-FOUR

COLE

I PLACE MY HANDS on either side of the podium and lift my eyes to the endless rows of somber faces and black fabric. There's static in the air, the sensation of standing outside just before a storm hits and knowing you're too small to stop it.

An eerie calmness settles over me. There's little I'm afraid of these days.

Everyone's eyes are on me, their faces indistinguishable because I don't have the energy to focus on a single one. Except for her. I'm numb until our gazes lock. Mila might as well be the only person in the room.

Hers is the only face I see. She sits to the right of the center aisle, several rows from the front. She's stunning in a long-sleeved black dress, her hands folded on her lap and sadness hanging off her shoulders.

The sight of her tears my insides up.

I've barely had the courage to look at her for the past few days. I keep having a vision of her standing up here, wedding ring on her finger, aching all over and wondering how the hell she didn't see it coming. Even with all the signs, we never truly believe the people around us can just cease to exist.

She would stand here, preparing to deliver a eulogy about me, and she would be thinking what I'm thinking now. That I wish I could go back in time and change the things I've done, but most of all, do the things I didn't do.

I've replayed my last encounter with Camille again and again. Each time, I alter the memory frame by frame. This time, I refuse to leave. This time, I demand she get help. This time, she survives.

I adjust the microphone and the sound echoes throughout the church. I'm reminded of the night I finally laid eyes on Mila again. She'd stood on a stage, unprepared for me to come crashing back into her life.

"Good afternoon," I say, my voice hollow. "My sister would be so humbled to know you all came out to honor her memory. It's comforting to look out at this crowd and witness how many people Camille touched in her short life. If you could stand where I stand now, it would...it would take your breath away." I nod and glance down at the podium, a knot forming in my throat. "As you all know, Camille had a unique way about her, a set of traits that were marvelously at odds but came together to make her unforgettable. She was honest but knew to lie when her little brother needed to be bailed out. She was loyal, sometimes to a fault, but would not hesitate to call you out on your bullshit—" A low rumble of stifled chuckles rolls through. "She was mild-mannered but strong-tempered. She hated attention but lit up every room. Growing up, she was competitive and smart. She rebelled without ever getting caught—something

I still don't know how to do—and came to my rescue without me ever having to ask. To be honest, I never stopped to think about how important she was to me until I realized she was gone. She leaves us all with an important reminder, to cherish each day, to look around and pay attention, because life is fragile and... and..." I drag in a breath, trying and failing to think of the words. "She left a gaping hole in me, which I will fill by planting something to grow in it. In her memory. In her honor. Because she left us much too soon, and I know all she wanted was to leave her mark on the people she loved."

Silence falls over the church and for a moment, no one seems to breathe, let alone move. Slowly, sounds of rustling fabric lift from the crowd, disjointed sniffling and quiet weeping. My father sets a hand on my shoulder and I turn from the podium and walk down with him and my mother, back to our seats. My gaze connects with Mila's again, her eyes glassy as she drags her knuckles over her cheeks.

She'd been doing so well before I came back. She'd found success and was content with her life. She was on the brink of starting something new, something safe. Then I came in with my selfish heart, wanting her for myself again and telling myself whatever lies I could muster to convince myself I was better. Yes, I have felt strong for the past three years, but I've felt strong before and faltered. How many times have I tried to stay sober? How many times have I relapsed? The day of our wedding, I didn't think anything could come between us. Yet I failed her then, and it's only a matter of time until I fail her again.

I made a mistake coming back and now shame floods me, saturating my bones.

My addiction will follow me to the grave. Whether you succumb to it or spend your life fighting it, addiction follows everyone to the very end. No amount of time, no amount of well-meaning intent can prevent the devil from seducing you in a moment of weakness.

FORTY-FIVE

MILA

THE AIR SMELLS OF newly turned earth and fresh flowers. And I hate both. I don't move, standing with my arms crossed, staring at the spot where Camille's casket was lowered into the ground. Grant is beside me. Moments ago, he'd squeezed my hand, his head bowed, as though he'd heard me think, *This is it, Camille. This is goodbye.*

My heart is lodged in my throat. It doesn't seem real that Camille could be in that wooden box. Cole stands on the other side of the grave with his parents. I watch him like I'm watching a dream, wondering what changed when I wasn't looking. Because something is different.

There's a hum of murmurs around me, several people I don't even know pat my back as they pass. The crowd begins to disperse amidst sniffling and stifled sobs. People head back down the hill to the long, paved driveway winding through the cemetery.

I want to be in Cole's arms. I want it so badly my skin aches. When he finishes speaking to a few people, he walks over to me. His hands are in his pockets and he glances at the ground often. When he reaches me, he takes my hand and leads me back behind a mausoleum. We pass a headstone with stone angels perched on top, their little arms outstretched.

Cole appears exhausted and sad, his shoulders sagging as I touch the side of his face. He looks down, blinking a few times.

"Hey," I say.

I rise up on my tiptoes to plant a kiss on his lips. It's a sweet, tender kiss, and it scares me because I realize how much I need him. Because my heart hurts, too, and the only person I want to hurt with is him.

He lets out a tired breath, running a hand through his hair.

"We'll be heading out soon," he says. "I'll see you later, okay? We'll talk."

I nod then swallow back the burn rising up my face and collecting in my eyes. I don't want to cry, not here. Not in front of his family.

"Come stay with me?" I ask, unable to control the plea in my tone.

I want to be there for him, but also, I realize I need him just as much. I need him because it's real now. Camille is gone and everything is going to shit.

I inch closer and set a hand on his chest, and I'm surprised to find his heart pulsing quickly through his suit jacket. He automatically grips my waist, but he's holding me with a hesitancy he didn't have just a few days ago.

I can feel him pulling away, breaking away at the tethers. I'm standing right in front of him and yet he seems a million miles away.

"I can't stay with you," he says.

"Grant travels a lot. You shouldn't be alone. If you want, we can stay at your stu—"

"Mila, I can't be with you."

My hand drops to my sides. I tilt my head, brows furrowing, mouth opening and closing. Now my heart's picked up speed as well, and I think I'm going to be sick.

"Seriously?"

"I made a mistake coming back, Mila. I can't risk dragging you into my mess."

He's grieving, he doesn't mean it. He's not making any sense.

"What mess? Cole, don't do this. What are you saying?"

"I'm an addict, Mila," he snaps.

I blink, my voice lowering. "I know that."

"Don't you get what that means? Even if I don't touch a drug ever again, I'm always going to be an addict, until the day I die."

"I know, Cole, and I don't care. I'm here, aren't I?"

He takes a step back.

"You should care. I could ruin your life."

My throat is burning now, too. I shut my eyes and suck in a shaky breath. But when I open them again, the deliberation in his eyes makes it even harder to breathe.

"Stop. Stop saying these things."

"It's the truth, Mila. I'm no good for you. I don't deserve you and I never did."

He turns and walks back around the mausoleum, toward

his sister's grave.

"*Cole,*" I call out, hurrying after him.

My heels sink into the grass and my pride bubbles to the surface. I stop in front of him and stare up into his eyes. I'm trying, but he's making it damn hard to be collected. I feel untethered. Ready to slip away as I fight against the warning threatening to burst from my lips. A warning that has no place being expressed on a day like today. I don't think I can stand to spend another minute with this awful nagging in the pit of my stomach, seeing him with a foot already out of the door.

Just say the damn words, Cole.

Don't say you can't be with me, say you don't want to be with me.

Be a man and say it, and I swear you'll never see me again.

He reads it all in my eyes because he goes still, fierce pain flashing through his expression.

His jaw clicks, his lips part.

"I think we…" He trails off, eyes darting past me and narrowing. "*What the hell?*"

I turn and my stomach does a somersault, crashing against my heart. Andrew heads toward us, serious faced in a black suit and blue tie.

No.

No, no, no.

I rush over to Andrew, grabbing his arm and spinning him around to face me.

"Andrew, what is wrong with you? You can't be here right now, starting trouble. Cole just put his sister in the ground."

He tilts his head before realization dawns on his face.

"I know," he says, "I'm here to pay respects."

My hand flies to my chest.

"*Fuck*," I whisper.

"I'm not here for you, Mila." Andrew shakes his head, a small smile tugging his lips. "God, you're so damn conceited."

I cover my face and let out an automatic half-laugh, despite my mood.

"Give us a minute, okay?" he asks.

I nod, and he passes me to reach Cole, who looks on edge right up to when Andrew says something then extends his hand. Cole relaxes, muttering what sounds like, *thanks*. Andrew claps a hand on Cole's back then the two walk off a little farther away to speak privately.

They leave me alone, with the dirt from Camille's grave scattered on the ground and Cole's words still wrapped around my throat.

FORTY-SIX

COLE

IT'S SURREAL HOW MUCH someone can change yet still have the same face you remember from childhood. I can't remember the last time I saw Andrew Pearson approach me without hostility in his eyes. My reaction to him is to brace for impact, but he comes to a slow stop in front of me and looks down at the ground. He extends a hand for me to shake and the words he speaks are of condolences and regret.

I think of what I said during the eulogy about Camille's life rippling out to touch so many others. I'd forgotten Andrew was one of them. He wasn't close to Camille, but he was around to witness her bailing me out of trouble more than a few times. She bailed him out, too.

And the one time I had to take the fall for her turned out to be all Andrew's fault. Everything that happened between him and me started and ended with my sister. He knows this. Him coming all this way today speaks volumes to how he feels about it.

"I appreciate you dropping by," I say. "Camille liked you."
"Did she?"
"Yeah, she thought you were a good influence."

He shakes his head. "Then I guess she never figured out you getting expelled was all my fault."

"I shouldn't have kept drugs in my locker, even just for a few hours, it was stupid."

"You stole them from her so she wouldn't take them. You were trying to be a good brother."

"If I'd been a good brother, I would've told someone who could help her."

He opens his mouth to speak, then closes it again. But I can see in his eyes what he almost said. *If Camille had been a good sister, she wouldn't have let you take the fall.*

I didn't give her a choice.

She was a senior, already accepted into college. If the school knew the drugs were hers, she'd have been the one expelled. I had less to lose. My grades were terrible. The teachers already hated me, anyway. No one expected much from me and when they had the opportunity to believe the worst, they did it without question.

Camille tried to tell my parents the drugs were hers, but they didn't believe her. Why would they? She wasn't the troubled kid. I was. It was always me.

Andrew and I stand in front of each other, neither able to think of what else to say.

"Alright, man," he says, straightening. "I won't take up anymore of your time, I just—"

My gaze darts past him to the spot where Mila had been standing just a few minutes ago.

Andrew follows my line of sight. "Where'd Mila go? Parking lot?"

I frown, looking around. Seems as though everyone else has cleared the area and Mila's gone, too.

"Yeah," I say, distracted. "Probably."

He nods toward the paved road. "Let's go down there. She should know we made it through a conversation without threatening each other, though the night *is* young."

We walk toward the paved road, which winds a path through the cemetery and down to the parking lot. The silence between us is heavy with a rift years in the making.

"You know, Cole, I never..." He pauses. "I never apologized for what I did. You were right, I was trying to bring you down just to look better in front of...uh...*shit*."

"Karen."

"Right, right. I was insecure, man. Plain and simple. I thought you were the one trying to bring me down, but all you ever did was try to be a good friend. I have a really bad habit of believing the worst in people."

"It was a dick move, I won't lie. But Karen didn't help by telling everyone she knew."

"What ever happened to her?"

"She lives in Long Island now with her wife and their two adopted kids."

"No shit."

"Yeah, man." I crack a small smile. "There was no future there for either of us."

"I saw your dad's convertible in the parking lot when I came in," he says as we walk. "I can't believe he still has that thing. Remember when you let me take it out for a drive without his permission?"

I nod. "You took a turn too fast, sideswiped a parked car, and lost the side mirror."

"You know, sometimes I wake up in the dead of night panicked, just thinking about the owner of that parked car."

"Being an adult will do that to you, man."

"Fucking hate it."

"Camille took the blame," I remind him.

He snaps his fingers.

"*That's right*. Your dad came barging into the house, ready to kill us, but Camille talked him down and convinced him she was the one driving and that she went through the gate too fast." He walks a few steps in silences then adds, "She really loved you, man."

I swallow, staring straight ahead. "Yeah…I know."

We reach the parking lot, but I don't recognize the few cars left. Mila's isn't among them.

"Where's your ride?" he asks.

"I came with Grant. He probably thought I was leaving with Mila."

Andrew starts to ask me something then hesitates.

"You want to know if Mila and I are back together," I say, without looking at him.

"I should probably ask her."

"Probably, but the answer is the same. We're not."

He watches me for a moment, his hands in his pockets as he settles into a wide stance. Then he nods toward a black Acura.

"Come on, man. I'll take you home."

I stare out at the sea of headstones and sloping hills for a few moments then nod.

"Yeah, I'd appreciate it."

We get in his car and for the first few minutes of the drive, my head is buzzing so loud I don't realize neither of us has spoken a word until Andrew taps a finger on the steering wheel.

"I don't know what's going on with you and Mila," he says, "but I need to hear that your intentions are in the right place. I want your word you won't hurt her again."

"You don't have to worry about that, you have my word."

My promise weighs heavy in my chest, but Andrew doesn't gauge their true meaning.

"Nothing happened between us," he says. "Not sure if she told you."

I don't answer him.

"But, it turns out you were right," he says.

"About what?"

"I care about Mila and I wanted to protect her. And…I mean, you already know, she's gorgeous. But you were right. This was never about her. I was just trying to forget someone, just like she was trying to forget you. But I'll be honest, all those old insecurities came right back. I never felt like I could compete with you. Not with Karen, not with Mila. It got into my head."

"The fucked up part is you're the better man, Andrew." I stare out the car window, watching the passing road. "Even when we were kids. You were always the better man."

Silence falls over us until sirens blare in the distance.

"Who is she?" I ask.

He glances at me, confused.

"The one you're trying to forget, who is she?"

He shakes his head. "Someone I hurt. Really, really bad."

"Can't be worse than what I did."

He flashes me a look, stone cold and filled with a self-loathing I've never seen in another person.

"Trust me, it is," he says, jaw flexing at the admission. "It's worse."

I shake my head, refusing to believe it.

"You know, Cole, you're not the monster you think you are."

FORTY-SEVEN

MILA

I NEVER WOULD'VE IMAGINED a day when Cole would be back and Camille would be gone. But the constant in my life remains the same. When my doorbell rang, my heart did a backflip because I thought for sure it would be Cole. But it was Andrew. I hid my disappointment and invited him in.

I nodded along, distracted, as he told me how he and Cole talked things out earlier, after I left them both at the cemetery. And while I'm glad they did, I also can't bring myself to care beyond a superficial level because my body aches and my head hurts.

I came home to cry in private but couldn't figure out how.

Andrew could see it all on my face. He stayed, even when I told him he didn't have to. And now he lounges on the other side of my couch, his arms crossed over his chest, eyes trained on the television where a heated argument plays out between two women in Spanish.

He peers over at me, brows pulling together.

"What are they saying?" he asks.

"I don't know. I don't speak Spanish."

"Then why are you watching telenovelas?"

I shrug then pull the throw blanket tighter around my shoulders.

"They can make you feel better about your life, if you can figure out what's going on."

"Please, enlighten me. Why is that woman now sobbing hysterically?"

"I think she just found out the blonde lady is her identical twin sister."

"But they look nothing alike."

"Well, yeah, because her twin had reconstructive surgery after faking her own death. But see that guy standing behind them—"

"You know what?" Andrew puts his hands up. "I'm cool. I just realized I don't care."

"Suit yourself," I say, snuggling against the armrest on my end of the couch.

We don't talk for a long time, but Andrew watches me when he thinks I'm not paying attention. His lips pull in. A few times he drags a hand through his hair. Finally, the question gnawing at him comes out.

"How are you handling everything?"

I chew on my lip, not looking at him.

"It just hit me, you know? Everything just hit me all at once today."

"And Cole? What's going on with you two?"

"I don't...even know anymore," I say, rubbing my tired eyes.

When I glance in Andrew's direction, I catch the thoughts floating through his mind.

"I know, Drew. I know I said he didn't have a chance. I'm *that* girl, apparently."

"I'm not judging you. I'm just trying to understand what changed."

"Whatever it was, it didn't hold. He's pulling away from me again. Can you believe it? After everything he put me through, after jamming his way back into my life, he's looking to just burst back out again."

"He's grieving, Mila."

I shut my eyes. "I know that."

"You're grieving, too. You should be grieving together."

"So, what am I supposed to do?"

"I don't know," he says. "Get me drunk. I'm much wiser when I'm drunk."

I roll my eyes and smooth out the blanket around me. I sneak glances at Andrew, whose attention is back on the television screen.

"Are we okay?" I ask.

He looks down before turning his attention to me.

"Come here," he says, nodding me over.

"Why?"

"God, you're so stubborn, just bring your ass over here."

I clutch the blanket with one hand then scoot over next to him. He throws an arm around me in a half hug and pulls me closer to his side. My head falls into the crook of his arm.

"I love you, Mila," he says. "Of course we're okay. We'll always be okay."

My eyes burn, but I press them together. I can feel Andrew nodding overhead.

"You're going to cry now, aren't you?" he asks.

"*No*," I say, sniffling. "Shut up, I hate you."

He chuckles, his chest vibrating beneath my face.

"Why do you always do this to me?" I demand.

He gives me a gentle squeeze.

"This is just what we do, you and me. It's all we were ever meant to do."

FORTY-EIGHT

MILA

I'VE ALWAYS SEEN CRYING as an unfortunate moment of weakness. Something that slips past your armor despite your best efforts. You wipe at your eyes, you sniffle a few times then you pull yourself together. Tonight is different. Tonight, there is no trace of armor, no deep breaths to compose myself, not a single attempt to contain the outpouring of pain.

For the first time in my life, I cry fully. I cry even when my chest hurts and breathing becomes difficult. I cry for Camille. I cry for Cole. I cry for myself and the pain I can't understand. Noises I've never allowed myself to make escape my lips and I gasp for breaths.

Andrew holds me, not saying a word the entire time. He doesn't tell me it's going to be okay, he doesn't try to shush my cries. He sits in silence as I sob into his chest. And somehow, it's everything I need.

It all stops on its own, without me deciding to let it.

I go silent, blinking at the ceiling lights of my living room. The pain finished carving its path through me and now that it's done, I feel lighter. Stronger. This episode is the single most cathartic experience I've ever had. And when I look up at

Andrew's pale face, and I think of what he said about Cole grieving too, I know exactly what I need to do. When I tell Andrew, he agrees and offers to give me a ride.

It's late when I get to the building.

I'd much rather Cole not know I was coming, but the front desk has to announce my arrival to Grant. I'm allowed access to the elevator that goes straight to the top floor.

When the doors open, Grant is out in the hall waiting for me.

"You didn't have to wait out here," I say, sensing there's a reason I won't like.

"No, I wanted to talk to you first."

I look to the closed doors behind him, my stomach clenching.

"Is he not here?"

"He's here."

My hand rises to my chest, but there's still Grant's expression to deal with.

"What is it, then?"

Grant rubs his chin, struggling with the words.

"I don't think you should talk to him. He's not in a good place right now, I'm worried."

"You think I came here to argue with him?"

He tilts his head pointedly. "I caught the tension between you two. I don't know what's going on, but I think you should give him space."

"No," I say. "No, I won't give him space. He needs me.

Look, I'm not here to fight with him. I'm not here to give him ultimatums. I just want to be here for him. That's all."

Grant stares at me, a deliberation working its way through his expression.

"Fine. Just promise me you understand he's not himself right now. He's in pain."

"I get it. Trust me."

He exhales and motions toward the door.

"Go ahead. I'm going out."

He walks past me and hits the elevator button. The doors open right away. Grant steps inside and turns to look at me.

"I won't be back tonight, if you plan on staying."

"I'm not going anywhere."

The elevator doors close.

I take a deep breath, my lungs filling in a different way than before the big cry, and head down the hall.

Grant left the door parted, not closed. I pull it open and step into the dark living space. It's a little bit eerie, everything covered in shadows from the mosaic of lights trickling in from the large windows.

The silence is what bothers me most. I walk down the hall, toward the guest room, where Cole and I crashed in the past when Grant had parties. There's light shining from around the sides of the half-open door.

I should knock, and yet I don't think of it until I've already pushed the door open and catch sight of Cole sitting on the king-sized mattress. His back is up against the headboard and his hands are moving across a sketchpad on his lap. The scratching sounds of pencil on paper grow louder as I step inside.

"Hey."

He startles, then sees it's me. Surprise flashes across his face, then concern. He sets the sketchpad aside and starts toward me, but I rush forward before he can get off the bed.

He sits on the edge, staring up at me. It's a sight I'm not used to.

"You've been crying," he says.

"I have."

I come closer to him, standing between his parted knees, and set my hands on his shoulders. He tenses but doesn't move.

"Mila, we need to talk."

"Not today," I say.

"Might as well be today. I'm just trying to protect you, you don't want — "

I press a finger to his lips.

"No talking. Just be here."

I run a hand over his forehead and smooth back his hair. He closes his eyes at my touch and lets out a breath. His chest rises and falls as silence presses in on us from all directions.

Cole stares into my eyes for several long seconds before looking away. His eyes are unfocused as his thoughts carry him far off. Seconds stretch out into hours, and it seems like he's considering the best way to convince me I'm better off without him.

I get his arguments, I can hear them buzzing all around his

head. His sister died of an overdose and now he's putting himself in her shoes. He thinks he could end up just like her, but I think he's wrong. Camille never thought she had a problem. No one else did either until it was too late. It seemed she knew how to keep herself from falling into the type of crippling addiction that destroyed her brother's life. But her addiction turned out to be much more insidious. It creeped up on her, teased her to play with the line until it toppled her over to the point of no return. And now she's gone.

I can't believe she's gone.

"I can't believe she's gone," Cole whispers.

I blink at him speaking my thought aloud almost the moment it occurred.

"I know," I say, dragging my fingers absently through the back of his hair. "I know."

More silence. I don't know how long he'll sit here, but Cole seems lost in thought. It occurs to me I should offer to get him some food or some —

Cole rakes in a shaky breath. I go still, but before I can speak a single syllable, he shatters in my arms like a semi-truck hit him. My eyes go wide as he sobs, his shoulders shaking and his hands clutching my sides. My mouth opens, words of comfort just on the tip of my tongue, but I press my lips together again, remembering where I was just a few hours ago and how loud the pain pounded in my head. So loud I could barely hear myself crying. Cole is making similar noises now. Except his are low, guttural sounds that rip my heart in two. I shut my eyes and hold his face to my chest, his tears soaking through to my skin.

My own tears begin to form as he cries. But I blink toward the ceiling, not allowing them to fall. I had my turn. This is his. But witnessing this moment makes my heart ache thinking of what Andrew went through, as well.

It's not easy, resisting the urge to say everything is going to be okay. It's physically painful to bite your tongue and resist the instinct to quiet someone's pained whimpers. It's difficult and uncomfortable and goes against every instinct to witness another human suffering and do nothing at all to stop it.

FORTY-NINE

MILA

I WAKE UP FULLY clothed on Cole's bed. Dehydrated and disoriented. I blink a few times until his face comes into focus. He's lying on the pillow beside me, watching me. His blinks are slow, too, like he only woke up a few seconds ago.

I rub my face then check my watch.

"Crap. I have to get ready for work," I say, looking down my body to confirm I'm in no shape to head to the office.

"Thank you for staying," he says.

"Thank you for letting me."

He wipes away an eyelash from my cheek. My heart stirs at the gesture, but the sadness in his expression tells me he's still in a place of doubt and fear. He gets up and helps me out of his bed. He walks me down to the elevator and even gets inside with me.

"I'll take you down," he says.

I don't say anything. I'm tired and sad, and I'm not sure I've got fight left in me. The elevator reaches the main floor. When the doors open, Grant stands there ready to come up.

"Oh," he says, surprised to see us. "Hey, guys."

His energy is light as he steps to the side to let us out.

"Hold the doors," Cole says to Grant. "I just need a

minute."

Cole gives me another hug, then brings his lips to my ear, and says. "We'll talk. Tonight?"

"Sure." I swallow, unsure I could wait an entire day for him to end us for good.

Cole walks backward onto the elevator. I stare. Will he and I ever be able to find the right place in time to be together? It seems we can't ever get it right, chance and circumstance intent on keeping us apart. Intent on proving what we might feel for each other pales in comparison to situations that hamper our growth. As though all we're ever meant to do is miss each other.

A cycle we can't break. A story without an end.

The doors start to close, but I jam an arm between them and they bounce open again. I step onto the elevator and look straight at Cole.

"Take me to the exhibit," I say.

He blinks. "I thought you had to work."

"I did. I just gave myself the day off. So take me to see the last room."

Cole glances down at the ground then back at me, just as the doors close behind me.

"I'm not sure it's a good idea," he says.

Grant groans and backs into a corner. I ignore him.

"I want to see it, Cole. And I want to see it with you."

"It doesn't change anything. Even if it did, it shouldn't. Trust me, you don't want to be with an addict."

"You know what?" I snap. "I'm just about sick of everyone

with a penis thinking they have the authority to decide what's best for me. Tobias decided you weren't right for me at our wedding, you're deciding for me now. *It's bullshit.*"

Grant pinches the space between his eyes, and mutters, *"Dear lord, please get me out of here."*

My gaze snaps over to him in warning. When he sees this, he presses his lips together and shuts up. I turn my attention back to Cole.

"*I* decide what I want. *I* decide what I can handle. *Take me to the exhibit.*"

Cole takes in my expression, trying to decide how stubborn I am. As if he doesn't already know. Grant taps a foot, staring over my head at the floor numbers ticking past, but he extends a hand to give Cole the keys to his car.

"Alright," Cole says. "I'll take you."

The elevator reaches the top floor again and Grant walks through the doors the second they open wide enough. He doesn't look back but lifts a hand in farewell.

"Good luck, you two," he calls out over his shoulder. "Next time, I'd appreciate not being trapped in your little purgatory of emotions."

FIFTY

MILA

MY HANDS ARE IN front of me, fingers twisting as I wait for Cole to unlock the front doors of his exhibit. When we walk into the reception area, I'm surprised to see it's in the exact same state as the last time I was here. The folded invitation I had carried that day is still sitting on the small side table where I set it as I viewed the sketches along the wall.

I look at Cole.

"No one's been to the exhibit since the night I was here?"

He scratches at his brow. "I didn't want anyone seeing it before you. You never went into the last room, so I told Jeff to keep the exhibit closed to the public until you did."

Cole leads me to the door in the far left corner of the room, stops and gestures for me to open it. My heart picks up, as I think of the night I came to the exhibit on my own. This had been the door Jeffrey said I would exit out of when I finished walking through the whole thing.

The last room.

I set my hand over the handle and push it open. Cole enters behind me so he can't see the way my eyes widen at the sight.

This room has dark floors and walls that were once gray

before ink scribbles covered them in an uneven layer. My eyes are drawn to the center of the room. At first, I think it's a giant chandelier, but as I walk closer I realize what I'm looking at. Thousands of pieces of paper suspended from the ceiling by thin wires and tiny lights. The pieces of paper form a swarm that tapers down closer to the floor like an upside down triangle.

It's beautiful yet haunting.

Disorderly and yet purposeful.

"What is this?" I ask.

I turn to Cole, my eyes still wide, but he only nods back to the piece, encouraging me to take a closer look. I wrap my arms around myself and take slow steps forward.

As I stare through the center of the swarm, the pages reveal themselves to be wrinkled and full of crease marks. Seems each one I focus on has torn corners or stains. But every single one of them is covered in a messy black handwriting.

A chill runs up my arms and I rub them in silence.

"After I left the hospital," Cole says, "I checked into a rehab program. They took our phones, and we weren't allowed any form of communication aside from handwritten letters. I had a lot of time on my hands. I tried and tried to figure out what to tell you, how to apologize. Words were all I had, but I couldn't get them right. I wrote dozens of drafts a day for ninety days."

My gaze darts from one piece of paper to another, only registering a line from each.

It hurts to know I hurt you.

I don't know how to say I'm sorry.

I'm dying here without you.

Maybe it's better if you hate me.

Cole stops beside me.

"How did you keep all of these?" I ask, my voice a croak.

"I sent them to Grant."

"He…he never gave them to me."

"I asked him not to. He kept them safe for me because I knew I would need them eventually, I just wasn't sure for what. I needed to make things right, I knew that. But I couldn't let you see me in recovery. And the more time passed, the harder the thought of facing you became. And after ninety days and a thousand failed attempts at *I'm sorry*, I accepted that—"

He points to the piece of paper closest to the floor forming the tip of the triangle. It's a tiny piece, with only three lines scribbled on it.

You were always too good for me.

Maybe one day I'll be stronger than my demons.

Until then, I'll just be missing you.

My mouth parts as I try to take a breath. My heart throbs, thinking of how badly I needed to hear from him, how much it killed me to be in the dark. Not knowing what happened or where he was.

My legs carry me right under the piece and I get down on my knees, then on my hands, then lie down on my back. I stare up at the pieces of paper, which look like they are floating from this angle. I shut my eyes, regretting seeing this.

Cole lies down beside me, turning his head to look at me.

We lie on the floor with his gut-wrenching letters hovering over us as though they could fall at any moment. I reach up to that last note and touch it with the tip of my fingers.

"Is this how you feel now?" I ask him.

"It is, except it's worse now because back then, I couldn't see the end of the tunnel. But over the last three years I've spent building this exhibit, I'd grown more confident in my recovery. I'd grown to believe I'd finally beat addiction."

"And now?"

I turn my face to his, which is right next to mine. His eyes are puffy from last night. His lashes lower as he stares at my chest.

"And now I realize there is no beating it, just fighting it. I won't stop, because I don't want to be that man ever again. But there's not a day I will ever be good enough for you. You deserve better than what I could give you," he says. "So much better than me."

"You keep saying that. Yet here I am. Eight years, I could've moved on but I didn't. And here you are, too. Do you know why?"

He waits, brows rising up to form lines on his forehead.

"Because, Cole, this is where we were going all along."

He searches my eyes, not understanding me.

"You said we grew to mirror each other," I go on. "You said we've changed. I agree with you on that. I can see how much you've grown, Cole. Back then, you were just hiding from it all, just waiting for the day it would catch you. And it did. Doesn't look to me like you're hiding from it anymore." I gesture around us. "You made a shrine for it. You spent three years facing it head on. Do you realize how proud I am of you for that?"

"You're saying we had to go through everything we went through to end up right here, back together."

"You treat me like I'm scared of your addiction, but I've never been the one afraid of it. I knew there would be challenges and I was prepared to deal with them together. I never needed you to be perfect. I just needed you to stay."

"*I'm sorry,*" he says on an exhale, blinking a few times. "I thought coming here would be the end of everything. But the truth is, I don't want to lose you again. Because I can't. I can't let you go, no matter how hard I try. I think I'll die missing you, might as well die loving you. Because, Mila, I am still in love with you."

He lifts his fingers to my mouth.

His face moves closer as he gently lays a hand on my cheek.

"I love you, too," I say, before pressing my mouth to his.

We kiss underneath the letters he never sent me and it's the saddest kiss I've ever experienced. It tastes like tears and feels like heartache. But it's a kiss we need, a kiss we surrender to in the vulnerable moment of laying everything out.

Our kissing deepens as the minutes pass, and my heart pushes aside its ache at the awareness it finally has what it craves. My senses awaken at the realization. Cole's tongue caresses mine and reminds me of all of the incredible things it can do.

Cole reaches up to the neckline of his shirt and tugs it over his head. The shirt catches on a piece of wire and when he pulls it, a few pieces of paper fall from somewhere overhead.

I gasp, but Cole says, "It's okay. The piece more than served its purpose."

He slams his mouth to mine again, kissing me with dizzying intensity. His fingers curl over the end of my shirt and drag it up my sides. His touch leaves a trail of sensations in its wake. With each breath, I grow more desperate. Until I'm fumbling at the hook of my bra and helping Cole pull my shirt up over my head.

More pieces of paper fall around us as Cole lifts up on his knees to hover on top of me. He doesn't seem to notice because his gaze trails down my bare skin instead. His hands work to unbutton and unzip my pants as he kisses along my neck. He moves down, drawing small circles with his tongue on my skin.

He works his way past my collarbone, over my breasts, and stops to take each of my hard nipples in his mouth. I let out a little whimper of pleasure as he gives them a small suck.

I arch my back off the floor to help his large hands tug down my pants. His lips are on my stomach, and when I kick off the pants and underwear he peeled off of me, he runs a hand up my thighs and urges my legs apart. He hovers there, too. Kissing my inner thighs and working his way up.

"You spread your legs and I'm drunk," he mutters before lowering his face to taste me.

"*Oh,*" I say, my eyes fluttering to a close.

His mouth moves slow, licking and sucking until I'm squirming and sinking my fingers into the hair on the back of his head. Oh, the incredible things his tongue can do. I twist and moan and whimper as he fucks me with his glorious mouth. He brings me right to the edge and stops abruptly to peer up at me.

My eyes are half closed but open enough to realize he's still wearing pants. He flashes me a grin then makes quick work of kicking off his shoes and pants before propping himself over me again.

This time, he kisses me on the mouth and I taste myself on his tongue.

His erection brushes against my thigh, sending a thrill through me. He finds my entrance and pushes inside of me to the hilt.

He buries his face in my neck and exhales.

"Goddamn it," he groans. *"I can't get enough of you."*

He holds there a moment and I wrap my legs around him, not in any hurry. I love feeling him inside of me, he fills me in more ways than one. We stare at each other for several seconds, then glance up at the pieces of paper that continue to rain down on us.

"Yes," I whisper, as he begins his deep strokes, watching as my face succumbs to the stimulation.

This is different from when we were at his studio. It's not wild and mindless, it's deliberate and raw. He's not trying to make me forget, he's owning up to everything. Our past quite literally hangs above us, and there's something about his movements that tugs at the sad chords in my heart. When our eyes lock, there's a heaviness in his gaze I can't place. All the while, he moves over me. Making me feel so many things at once I think I might explode.

A tear rolls down my cheek, and he kisses it away. When another falls, he kisses that one away, too. I don't know why I'm crying, but when he tries to pull away, I grip his arms.

"*Please*," I say. "I need you."

When his hips start moving again, I shut my eyes tight. He reaches me deep inside and his pulses deliver a fresh wave of pleasure that eases the tightness in my chest.

He brings his lips to my ear and chokes out words between a heavy breath.

"*I need you more.*"

I run my hands across his bare shoulders and down his arms as he takes me with a passion compounded by nostalgia and threaded with grief. It's intensity like nothing I've ever experienced, pleasure raking through my body as my heart throbs in rhythm to his. It's not sadness, exactly, it's an overwhelming, heart-bursting hope we've finally fallen into place. It's free falling through all my emotions without fear or hesitation. Because he's with me, and I'm with him. And neither of us will let the other crash to the ground.

My fingers sometimes knock against pieces of paper falling onto us. I look up to where his work of art comes undone just as I do. The pieces of paper slide across Cole's flexing back as he tenses and lets out a low groan. More of the pages fall over my head, and all around.

All the words he couldn't say before rain down on us, impossible to ignore.

But we don't care.

We aren't running from the past anymore.

FIFTY-ONE

MILA

Two and a half weeks later...

SOMETHING BRUSHES AGAINST MY cheek, causing me to stir. But I keep my eyes closed, even as I stretch across the mattress. The sheets are tangled around my body and the sound that woke me in the first place comes over me again.

"Time to wake up, beautiful."

My eyes flutter open to the brightness of the studio. Cole's standing beside the bed, a satisfied glint in his eyes.

"Do I have to?" I ask.

"Yes, you do. There's something I want to show you."

My gaze travels down to his bare chest, over the grooves of his abs, and down to where his jeans hang low on his hips. I'm tired and sore all over, but I would still climb this man like a tree.

A grin tugs on my lips at the thought.

I get to my feet on the mattress and allow the sheets to fall away as I step over to the edge of the bed. When I wrap my arms around Cole's neck, his hands smooth over my skin and settle on my lower back.

"And what could you possibly show me that I haven't

already seen?" I ask.

"*Oh really?*" He lowers his voice. "Are you so sure you've seen all my tricks?"

"Haven't I?"

We stare each other down for a few seconds until the palm of his hand snaps over my bare ass, the sound echoing across the studio. I let out a short cry of surprise at the burn, then narrow my eyes at his grinning face.

"Get dressed," he says. "We're going to be late."

"For what?"

"You'll see."

"Have you forgotten how much I hate surprises?"

He chuckles then plants a soft kiss on my lips before answering. "You'll love this one, I promise."

I let out a playful groan before prying my body away from his.

When we finish getting dressed, we step out into the cloudless spring day, where the sun beats down from the highest point in the sky. And as we ride in the back of a cab, Cole weaves his fingers through mine, the innocent gesture sending emotions fluttering in my chest. I stare down at our hands, not believing there would be a day where this would seem natural again. My arms are exposed in a floral sundress, and all I can think of is how good my ink looks beside his. I don't worry about who can read the words anymore. They are part of me and always will be. Anyone that sees them might guess we are a couple who went through hell and walked out the other side, hand in hand.

We ride in a direction I don't expect, across East Harlem and over the Madison Avenue Bridge. Seeing as his art exhibit and studio are both in Brooklyn, I'm curious what it is Cole wants to show me in the Bronx.

Reading the question in my eyes, Cole says, "You know how I've been telling you about my kids? The ones I mentor through my non-profit?"

I nod. Cole founded an organization that brings art and mentorship programs to poorly funded inner-city schools. He started it in Chicago two years ago, and now the Rise Above Foundation has locations in three states.

"You want me to meet them?"

"Of course I do. But honestly, they're the ones that keep asking to meet you."

I tilt my head and the question of *why* dies on my lips as the cab rolls to a stop in front of an empty parking lot. Six kids hang around, leaning against the side of a building and talking amongst themselves.

I'm confused when Cole asks the cab driver to wait for us, before rushing to my side to help me out of the car. The kids fall silent as they notice our approach. My eyes are on the massive mural painted on the side of the building. At first, the vibrancy of the beautiful colors is all I can see. They have a huge impact on their surroundings, bringing energy and life to a muted and depressing neighborhood.

I tear my gaze from the mural to look at the kids. One of them, a tall boy with dark brows pulled low over his eyes, steps up to Cole and they greet each other with a fist bump.

"This your girl, Mr. Cole?" the boy asks.

"*Yes*, Aidan," Cole says, with intonation. "So, let's watch our language."

"I'm Mila," I say, extending a hand to the boy.

"Aidan." He shakes my hand before gesturing to the others behind him. "These are my assistants. They helped some, but I'm the one with the talent here."

A low grumble of playful argument breaks out between the kids. They push past Aidan and take turns introducing themselves before stepping aside to let me glimpse the full mural. My mouth opens in an automatic intent to praise it, but when the details hit me, the words get lodged in my throat.

I'm speechless, staring at the intricate details painted before me.

The focal point of the mural is a woman, small but defiant, walking through a gnarly jungle of buildings and cement with her chin held high and her hair whipping through the air. She heads straight toward a menacing sight of tangled metal and precarious looking buildings. But behind her, she leaves a trail of color and life that transforms everything in her wake.

"It's you. And the city's, like, Mr. Cole's soul or some shit." Aidan glances over at his mentor.

"That's one interpretation," Cole says, a playful glint in his eyes.

"Whatever," Aidan cuts in. "You're trying to act like you ain't obsessed, Mr. Cole, but she already knows. You got it bad."

"That, I do," Cole says, offering me a wink.

Aidan addresses me again. "What do you think? It's pretty sick, right?"

I blink at his words, thinking for a second he's referring to Cole's soul. Then realize what he's trying to say.

"Yes, it's…amazing," I say. "You all did a great job. Really, this is incredible."

A smile breaks out on Aidan's face. He and the other kids start telling me about which parts of the mural they worked on and how much time it took. Before long, they start describing other murals around the Bronx.

"There's more of them?" I ask, my eyes widening as I look over to Cole.

He's watching me closely, relishing my reaction.

"We've been doing this for a while. There are three murals, total," he says, but at Aidan's frown of disagreement, adds, "Of you, anyway."

"Can I…see the others?"

"Of course." Cole sets a hand on my back and nods over to the cab, still idling at the curb. "Our chariot awaits."

We say goodbye to the kids, who seem in no hurry to leave the parking lot and return to their lives. Instead, they continue to hang out even as Cole and I ride off in the cab again. I'm quiet, staring out of the window until the mural's obscured by the surrounding buildings.

"What's on your mind, beautiful?" Cole asks, his voice low.

I bite my lip. As we rode over here this afternoon, I

realized what today is. I've been so caught up in Cole I nearly forgot. Now I'm battling shame along with the other emotions making my chest hurt. I don't want to tell him why today is an emotional day for me. Admitting it might taint the romantic gesture he seems to have planned.

Today is the anniversary of my mother's death.

When I stood in front of the mural, all I could think of is how much my mother would've loved seeing it. If anyone should be on a mural, it should be her. She had a presence that was larger than life and loved nothing more than to manifest it in bold colors that drew attention. Her hair, her clothes, her energy. Everything about my mother shone as bright as a beacon. She wanted to see me shine, but I struggled to allow myself to. It was only after she passed that I realized I didn't have the luxury not to shine. It was only then, when I gave myself permission—to draw attention, to be the point of focus—that I finally found the success I'd always dreamed of. In a world that teaches women they have to be beautiful, but not know it, and smart, but never show it, I had to believe in who I wanted to be then I had to become it.

But my mother never got to witness any of it.

Cole watches me patiently as I stare down at my hands. He's waiting for my answer.

"I guess I'm just...trying to take it all in. Trying to wrap my head around the meaning."

"You could always ask the artist," he offers.

I nod, but swallow instead of asking, afraid my emotions

will unravel if I do.

He holds my hand again and goes quiet. The mood grows somber, and I peer up at him, wondering if he knows what today is. I don't ask, and he doesn't mention it. Instead, he takes me to two other murals in two other neighborhoods. The art transcends their locations, giving the impression a person could escape, if only they stared for long enough. The murals are all about transformation, resilience and empowerment. And they all feature a small young woman, who treks on, regardless of what lay before her.

My heart aches with love and pain, and the idea Cole thinks so much of me.

I stand in front of the third mural, staring at the beautiful colors and the fierce expression of the woman, who looks as though she will fight her way through the bricks to come right at me.

And just when I'm sure I can't handle a drop of anything more, Cole takes me to one last mural.

We reach the intersection of East 162nd Street and Jerome Avenue, just across from Yankee Stadium. There, nestled at the foot of apartment buildings and facing busy traffic, stands a small, dingy strip of abandoned storefronts with their metal gates pulled down over their doors.

The sounds of the city fall away as though time itself came to a stop.

The image painted across the storefronts isn't of me.

It isn't about me, or even for me, but looking up at it makes me go weak at the knees.

It's of a woman with wise hazel eyes and black hair teased high. Her beauty is breathtaking, but it's her aura, which expands in waves of color all around, that gives her an otherworldly appearance. She holds out a single Tarot card, which is as large as a window.

On the card, at the center of an oval twisted from decorative vines, is the image of a young, naked child riding a horse and carrying an orange banner across a field of flowers. A figure of the sun shines down on him and the castle visible just beyond.

It's the sun card.

It's the symbol of optimism and fulfillment, of the dawn following the darkest of nights.

Staring up at the woman again, the full meaning of the mural hits me and tears well up in my eyes.

"*Mama*," I whisper, raking in a breath that can't get past my throat.

Cole wraps an arm around me, sensing my knees threatening to give out. Pedestrians stroll past undeterred as we stand in the middle of the sidewalk for several long minutes. Cole holds me while I wipe away at my cheeks, the pain in my chest slowly loosening to an acute sense of gratitude. All I can do is shake my head, unable to find the words.

"You did this?" I ask.

Of course he did, who else would've made my mother's image come to life like this?

"I let her down," he says. "I let you down. And I'm sorry I wasn't there, I was in no condition to come back when I heard about your mom. And to this day, I still hate that I wasn't there for you."

I sniff back a fresh wave of emotions, barely trusting myself to speak.

Cole stares up at the mural of my mother alongside me. We go still, as though the city isn't pulsing around us, busy as ever. Loud and erratic, oblivious to us and our moment. A strange lightness comes over me, until I forget the sadness and find the growing sensation of peace. Of everything settling into its place.

"My mom hated you."

As soon as I say it, I clasp a hand over my mouth and snort, embarrassed.

"No, she really did," he agrees.

I touch his chest and stare up at him.

"She would've loved this, though. Really, Cole. She would've loved this so much. *Thank you.*"

His expression grows serious as he shifts to stand straight in front of me. My heart rate picks up, even before I know why.

"Being with you, Mila, it changed my life. It was the first time I realized I could be more than what I'd been led to think all my life. It's why I started working with kids. I realized so many of them don't have someone who believes they could be better. And it's also why you're in the murals. You were my catalyst. Losing you was pain like I'd never known. I was reborn in that pain, forced to become the man I needed to be just to find these words..."

I'm overwhelmed and not ready for what I think he's about to do when he reaches into his pockets. I start shaking my head, eyes wide.

"Don't worry," he says, holding up a thin, rose-gold band that catches the sunlight. "This isn't an engagement ring. It's a promise. A promise to you. A promise to your mother," he nods over to the mural, "to be a better man, the man you deserve. To be as vulnerable as I need to be to fight my demons. I promise to make up for every single day I was gone. And one day, the scars will fade and there will only be trust left. One day, our slates will finally be clean. And on that day, I will make you my wife."

My hands shake but I smile through tears as he slips the ring on my finger. When he leans in to kiss me, I can taste my own tears. And it's crazy, so crazy how much my heart expands in my chest.

"I love you," I say against his lips.

He pulls back, as if to see the aftermath of the words in my expression. The way he looks at me sends a surge of life and hope through my entire being.

"I was hoping you still did..."

He brings my hand up to his lips and kisses the ring. I hold his gaze for several seconds before lowering my sights to the thin and fragile looking band. It's so simple and unassuming, you'd never guess it holds a promise of the future we're hovering on the edge of, the edge of us.

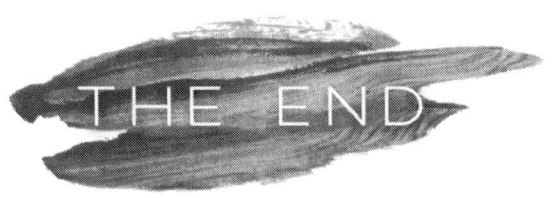

Wait…there's more!

UP AHEAD:

Get answers! Early reader Q&A

A free preview of Enamor, a friends to lovers romance —

just in case The Edge of Us left you in the mood for one.

Early Reader Q&A

What was the inspiration for The Edge of Us? *–Courtney Houston*

The idea for The Edge of Us first came to me when discovered a poem by R.M Drake over two years ago, right around the time I was working on my second romance novel, Entice. I felt the familiar spark of a plot bunny and jotted down notes for the story. The idea went on to stay buried in a folder on my computer until I came across it again earlier this year. Once again, I felt that spark. This time, though, the idea wouldn't stay buried. Mila, Cole, and Andrew began to tease away at my brain until I gave in and wrote their story.

I really did LOVE Andrew. Tell me, will we get to learn more about him? *–Ginelle Blanch*

Yes! I love Andrew so much and want to see him get his happily ever after. His story needs more time to simmer in my head, though. I just don't have all the pieces yet, and I need to make sure it's the epic romance he deserves.

I did like how Mila explained how she doesn't see Drew as Amber sees him. In one's eyes he's the villain while in the other's eyes he's a hero. I found it both beautiful and disturbing because even though Mila knows what happened in her eyes he's good. Also knowing they both were hurt by their [exes] I'm just surprised Mila didn't show any anger towards Andrew for what he did to [Amber].
–Annette Laird

That's a great observation. Mila does know what Andrew did to Amber, but I think when you witness someone's remorse as a friend, you are much more forgiving than when you were the person wronged. Andrew did do something awful, and that's a big part of why his story isn't ready to be written. I just don't know if he could have a second chance romance of if his relationship with Amber is dead forever.

We never know what became of Tobias and Grant. Do we get more of them later? *–Annette Laird*
Yes. There are a lot of nuggets in this book about Grant and Tobias that served to set up a future book about the Kreislers. I have a story for Grant that's been simmering in my head for a while. And let me tell you, I'm so looking forward to bringing that cocky bastard to his knees.

How were you able to dig into the mind of an addict? Personal experience/familial or just went with where the character took you? *– Becky Rendon*
I've never struggled with addiction myself, but I certainly know of people who have. I think we all know someone currently struggling with addiction—whether we realize it or not. Addiction is an insidious thing, and comes in many forms. Also, I have a Psychology degree, which definitely influenced my understanding of Cole. I've studied the nature of addiction along with many other taboo subjects and I'm deeply interested in exploring all facets of human nature through my writing. It's one of the reasons I love romance. I can't think of anything more vulnerable than falling in love, and only when we are completely open can we exorcise our demons.

Being that Cole overcame his own addictions, why did Camille never open up to him about hers? *–Candice Marie*

Camille never acknowledged she had a problem. Not to herself, or anyone else. She was always a high functioning addict, as Cole described it. Sometimes, those are the people in greatest peril because they can fall into the deep end of the pool before anyone ever realizes they are in trouble. A lot of early readers took Camille's death hard. Her death was not meant to serve as a shock factor to the reader, but rather a catalyst for the three main characters—who were all impacted by her death in different ways. For Andrew and Cole, it helped them put their feud aside. For Cole, it helped him exorcize the final fear that had been lingering in his head. And for Mila, it gave her the courage to step up and face an ugly truth.

Cole's parents.....do they feel any guilt about Camille's death? Do they just think it was a drug problem she had that led to her dying. Are there any feelings of guilt, like how they treated her possibly is why she took drugs in the first place? – *Annette Laird*

Oh, the Van Burens…That family is as messed up as they come. Without going into a long rant about those two, Elizabeth (the mother) uses avoidance as a defense mechanism, and so she feels blindsided by her daughter's death. David (the father) is a bit more nuanced in his exemption from guilt, he is a narcissist through and through.

During Mila's walk through of the exhibit, I felt a bit like I was drowning...which I'm quite sure was the intent. While writing it, did you feel the same? Did you have to take a moment to just breathe? – *Ginelle Blanch*

I did feel that way while writing. My intent was to make the reader feel what Cole felt the whole time he was away from Mila, even if they didn't understand that was what they were reading. It was one of those scenes I pictured like a movie in my head and one of the scenes that I looked forward to writing the most.

That sex scene between Mila and Cole in the last room at the art exhibit, the one underneath the hanging pieces of paper. Where did you get the inspiration from? That is probably one of the most unforgettable scenes I've read in a long time. *–Anna Green*

The detail of the papers falling on top of them was one of those unexpected things that happen during writing. I didn't know it was going to go that way until it did. But once the pages started to fall on top of them, I started to envision them as falling snow. The inspiration really goes back to Mila and Cole's first kiss, which was under falling snow on New Years Eve. And that kiss was inspired by one of my favorite fictional kisses I've ever seen, which was in an episode of the TV show Jane The Virgin. It's hard to explain if you're not familiar with the show, but the backstory behind the kiss left my stomach with the craziest butterflies. I never forgot it.

Mila was a great character. She seemed so vibrant yet, very very vulnerable. I'm wondering…is there much of yourself in her? I think authors write a bit of themselves into all their characters…maybe? What of her is you? *–Ginelle Blanch*

I love that you recognize Mila's vulnerability, as that's a huge part of her strength. If you read my other books, you'll find the heroines tend to be headstrong. I pull inspiration from all of the incredible women in my life, their strengths as well as their weaknesses. As a Hispanic woman, I've been raised in a culture where women are encouraged to be outspoken and passionate about their opinions. In that sense, I do think there's a lot of me in Mila's resolve and the way she's not afraid to tackle problems head on. Passive aggressiveness is just not in my nature.

While writing this book, was it always Cole who Mila was going to end up with when it was all said and done? Did you ever feel maybe Andrew was a better choice for a Mila? – *Annette Laird*

Andrew is the easy choice. He has nothing to atone for as far as Mila is concerned. It would certainly be easier for her to move on with him instead of revisiting the pain of her relationship with Cole. But while a clean slate is tempting, I think it's obvious from the first scene we meet Andrew that his slate is anything but clean. If Mila and Andrew would've chosen to pursue a relationship, they would've had to face the reality that their hearts were never fully in. They both had wounds they would never help each other heal, simply because they were too comfortable with each other to ever face ugly truths. Just because two people *could* be together, doesn't mean they *should*. And now I will duck out as the #teamAndrew people throw tomatoes at my head. ;)

Now, a sneak peek of…

Synopsis:

A hundred miles from my problems, I've found a new one just down the hall.

My gorgeous and conceited new roommate is exactly the type of guy who ruined my life.

Hating him should be easy.

Except it's not.

We fight and tease, playing a game we can't win. And when all pretenses fall away, he shows me a side to him I can't ignore.

He's guarded for a reason and he's never let anyone in...until now.

With this reckless game we play, there's one truth we can't escape: we're treading the edge of an attraction so intense it might as well be a grenade.

Julia

I take in the details of my surroundings in silence as Giles sets up the pool table. The only sounds in the room are the distant noises of the pool party happening above us. There are some people inside the house as well, their footsteps sounding from down the hall. Somewhere nearby a door closes, but the one to this room remains open.

I walk over to the rack of cue sticks and grab one, testing it out in my hand. It's been a while since I've played pool. After grabbing a second stick, I turn to hand it to Giles and the sight of him sitting on the edge of the pool table, watching me, catches me off guard.

He's still shirtless, wearing a pair of red swim trunks that fit him too well. I'm used to seeing him this way. He's always shirtless around the house. I've pretty much memorized every inch of his upper body. It's hard not to, when he's all compact and lean muscles under smooth skin.

I know he can't see himself. I know he didn't plan for the room's lighting to hit him in just the right way, casting shadows in the hollows of his shoulders, biceps, and abs, accentuating his build. He's set in a spotlight of sorts, which allows glints of the copper tones in his hair to make his green eyes glow as if they're lit from within.

Damn it.

I stare for too long, but he pretends not to notice and reaches for the second cue stick in my hand.

"Ladies first." He gestures to the table behind him.

I pass him and, reaching the pool table, I rest my forearms on the edge of it. With careful aim, I lunge my cue stick forward and send the cue ball crashing through, balls scurrying in all directions, three finding their pockets.

"Impressive," he says, from somewhere behind me, though I could've sworn he was off to my left just seconds earlier. "You landed two solids. Looks like I'm stripes."

I move around to find my next target and as I lean forward to make a strike, a hand lays on the table, centimeters from my waist. The surprise makes me miss my shot, and though I hit the cue ball, it jerks forward only an inch or two.

My skin prickles with awareness as I turn to face Giles. He's standing right there, face barely six inches from mine. So close I swear he's about to kiss me. And I'm not sure if I'd stop him.

"Can I tell you something without you getting offended?" he asks, voice just loud enough to reach me.

I don't understand how he could say anything that could offend me when he's standing so close with that look in his eyes. But I swallow, and say, "Yeah."

His gaze moves down my face, to the space between us, to my body, and I hope he doesn't notice I'm breathing just a little harder than before.

"You have the most beautiful body I've ever seen."

He looks and sounds so genuine that I couldn't make a joke if I wanted to. Lost for words, I bring my lower lip in between my teeth. And now he's looking right at my mouth.

My head spins. The air is just so thick all of a sudden and my thoughts are too fast and too slow at the same time.

"Thanks," I say, looking down at the way his arm stretches out beside me, his grip closing over the edge of the table. If he set his other arm the same way, I'd be trapped between them.

And I realize I'd like that, a lot.

But he doesn't cage me in. Instead, he brings his hand up to my face and runs a finger over the edge of my forehead, collecting my hair and tucking it behind my ear. He's never touched me before. His fingertips grazing my face make my heartbeat go off rhythm.

"I came here for a reason," he says under his breath, almost to himself, "and now I can't remember what that reason was."

I feel the same way. My cue stick is still in my hand, the only reminder we came here to play pool, but suddenly the thought of that game isn't as enticing as standing here so close to him. His hand lowers from my face to my arm, caressing my skin along the way, triggering trickles of sensations that spread across me. His touch is foreign and yet strangely familiar, as though my body has imagined this moment even while my mind has refused to consider it.

"I get the weird feeling you're hiding your body," he says. "That you don't feel comfortable in your skin but…"

"But what?"

He shakes his head. "But I've seen your body, Julia. And I swear, I can't stop thinking about how it'd feel under mine."

Oh my God.

Did he just say that? The room warms ten degrees in an instant.

"Giles…" I trail off, unsure of what I want to say.

Stop talking. Keep going. Touch me.

My thoughts are turning me in a dozen directions, making it hard for me to know for sure what to say, what to do. My eyes are on his lips, despite not wanting him to spy just how badly his touch and proximity affect me.

"I keep wondering if the curiosity is mutual," he says, hopeful.

"I can't say I haven't thought about it," I hear myself respond in a voice I barely recognize.

I've never seen this look in his eyes. It's like he's been pulled under a spell, lids lowering, words slow. His hand comes up again and he brushes his thumb over my bottom lip, pulling it slightly down. I let him.

Desire, hot and thick, spreads wider across his face with each passing second.

"And this mouth? I think about it a lot, too. What it would taste like...what it would feel like..."

My lips part farther as I exhale in surprise.

Is this happening? I wait for the inkling to pull away from him, to stop this before it goes further. But no part of me wants this to stop. The heaviness between my legs makes every other thought in my mind seem so small and trivial. And Giles? I bet he's anything but.

He brings his face closer and I've resigned to let him kiss me. But instead, he leans into my neck, just behind my ear, and presses his lips there. I close my eyes, unprepared for the way my nerve endings go wild.

"Do you like this?" he asks, warm breath tickling the sensitive skin he just kissed.

I don't think. I just nod. Because I'm breathing him in and he smells like sun and salt and things that would melt on my tongue. He's never come at me this way, so direct. And I find I have no weapons in my defense. Every inch of my body surrendering in turn to the idea of letting him touch me.

He continues to lay kisses along my neck, leaving behind an ache that grows increasingly hard to ignore. His fingers play with the end of my shirt, hiking it up to reveal the top of my shorts as his hand slides under my shirt and across the skin of my back, holding me.

His other hand moves up my side, fingers grazing the lower edge of my bra before heading down again. Between his touch and his kisses on my neck, I can't take how desperately I want him. The sparks of energy shooting through make it difficult to stand.

He unbuttons my shorts and cool air brushes my lower abs as my underwear becomes visible. I should feel exposed, vulnerable, but he's holding me close to him, with just enough room for his rough, warm hand to flatten against the exposed skin of my lower stomach and slide downward, over my shorts and between my legs. His palm hooks there, holding me firmly. The delicious pressure from his hand makes me bite down hard on my lip.

"Fuck," he whispers, resting his forehead against mine. His eyes are closed but his expression is strained and tortured. "Please," he says in a tone I've never heard from him before, a feral sound that tugs between my thighs. "Tell me what gets you off and I swear to God I'll do it. I'll give it to you in ways you never knew you wanted. I'll reach you in places no one else will. You'll scream things you never knew you could."

He says these things as his palm strokes me over my shorts and I can't stop the moan that escapes my lips, can't help but tilt my hips forward in invitation. The thought of where this could lead no longer fazes me. All I know is how badly I'm aching, how strong the burn is.

Want more? Visit www.veronicalarsenbooks.com/enamor

Thank you for reading.

Please consider leaving a quick review, they help books get discovered and mean a lot to authors.

Do you like to be teased? Be the first to receive exclusive giveaways, excerpts, cover reveals, and news on my upcoming novels.
Join my mailing list and check out my other books over at my website, veronicalarsenbooks.com.

———

Check out my full-length standalone novels in the Hearts of Stone series…

ENAMOR | ENTANGLE | ENTICE

Check out my Bite-sized Romances…
YOU AND ME | HIM OR ME

———

Reaching the author:
www.facebook.com/authorveronicalarsen
www.veronicalarsenbooks.com/contact

Acknowledgements

When I first started, I had no idea how much work and how many people it would take to publish a novel. With each release, it seems as though I've got more people to thank. I'm grateful for this. It's a testament to the many incredibly talented and supportive people in this industry.

To my readers, you are the reason I keep hitting publish. I'm in awe of how you continue to embrace my stories and my evolution as a writer. You hang on through all the slow-burn and angst, and trust my vision to the end. There's so much about the stories and characters that I never explicitly say in my writing, and yet you pick up on it all. You're sharp and that makes me proud as hell. Thank you for reading.

The Lovelies in my reader group—thank you for embracing my weirdness and whims and allowing me to be myself.

All the bloggers and **early readers** who helped share and promote this novel—your dedication is inspiring. Thank you so much for all you do for books and readers. Most of all, thank you for taking a chance on my book when the options are so plentiful.

To my publicist, **Heather with L. Woods PR**—You're one of the hardest working women in this biz. I'm so grateful to be able to collaborate with you in getting eyeballs on my releases. Also, I just freaking love you!

Lea Burn—Are there any words that could describe our editing process? It's magic and chaos and in the end, my stories are better because of you. Thank you for working so hard and caring so much.

Kelli Spear — You were a lifesaver for this novel. Thank you for your proofreading, but mostly for your sharp eye on what was missing.

Andrea Lefkowitz — The dedication to this novel speaks for itself. You are amazing. I couldn't have done any of this without you. Your feedback helped shaped this story to be the best it could be. But aside from that, you've been a constant source or support and strength over the past year. Now if you could just accept pineapple pizza, we could finally be friends.

Staci Brillhart — Not only did you open my eyes to the fact that the original cover for this novel was completely wrong, you took time out of your busy schedule to help me get it right. I can't even explain how much this meant to me. I admire you so much for your tenacity and confidence. Thank you, from the bottom of my heart for lending me a helping hand.

All the author friends I've made along the way have inspired me through their own hustle and accomplishments. I love you all for being talented, progressive, intelligent, and fearless in the pursuit of what sets your soul on fire. In particular I'd like to thank my two author-wives **Courtney Houston** and **Nikki Sloane** — who put up with my daily struggles, rants, and insecurities, and who motivate me daily to be better. Thank you to **Danielle Pearl**, **Alta Hensley**, **Kandi Steiner**, and **Len Webster** — my Australian soul sister — for all your support with this novel.

To my family — my muggles…you're always in my corner. You not only cheer me on, you hold me up. I love you guys.

And last…but never least, my wonderful **husband**. It takes one hell of a man to be with a novelist. My head's always in the clouds, the deadlines never end, and the mood swings…oh, the mood swings. You're my compass, guiding me through it all. You hold my hand and my heart. You're everything. Every single word.

24305372R00223

Printed in Poland
by Amazon Fulfillment
Poland Sp. z o.o., Wrocław